Praise for Sharon Ward

Sharon Ward's IN DEEP is a stellar, pulse-pounding debut novel featuring a female underwater photographer. A heady mix of underwater adventure, mystery, and romance.

— Hallie Ephron, New York Times bestselling author

Pack your SCUBA fins for a wild trip to the Cayman Islands. *In Deep* delivers on twists and turns while introducing a phenomenal new protagonist in underwater photographer Fin Fleming, tough, perceptive and fearless.

— Edwin Hill, author of *The Secrets We Share*

How much did I love In Deep? Let me count the ways. Fin Fleming, underwater photographer, is a courageous yet vulnerable protagonist I want to sip Margaritas with. The Cayman Islands are exotic and alluring, yet tinged with danger. The underwater scenes and SCUBA diving details are rendered in stunning detail. Wrap that all into a thrilling mystery and you'll be left as breathless as - well, no spoilers here. You must read it to find out!

— C. Michele Dorsey, Author of the Sabrina Salter Mysteries: No Virgin Island, Permanent Sunset, and Tropical Depression

Breathtaking on two levels, Sharon Ward's debut novel IN DEEP will captivate experienced divers as well as those who've only dreamed of exploring the beauty beneath the sea. The underwater world off the Cayman Islands is stunningly rendered, and the complex mystery involving underwater photographer Fin Fleming, especially the electrifying dive scenes, will have readers holding their breath. Brava!

— Brenda Buchanan Author of the Joe Gale Mystery Series

In Deep is a smart and original story that sucks you in from page one. Edge-of-your-seat suspense, a hauntingly realistic villain, and a jaw-dropping twist make this pacy read unputdownable until the very last word.

— Stephanie Scott-Snyder, Author of When Women Offend: Crime and the Female Perpetrator

Ice Water

Ice Water

The Fin Fleming Scuba Diving Mystery Series
Book 9

Sharon Ward

Covers by Cover2Book.com

ISBN eBook: 978-1-958478-35-6

ISBN Trade Paper: 978-1-958478-39-4

ISBN Hard Cover: 978-1-958478-36-3 or 978-1-958478-41-7

ISBN Hard Cover Second Edition: 978-1-958478-40-0

Printed in USA

First Edition

For Scott, the bravest man I know

And Jack, still the one

Contents

Chapter 1
Bert

BERT STAYED THERE ALL DAY, hidden under Brock Moran's tiny house. All alone, waiting for his brother to give him the signal to leave as they'd agreed.

There wasn't a lot of room under the tiny house. You could barely even call it a crawl space. It was just a few inches deep, really nothing more than an indentation in the sand. He'd had to slither in on his belly while all the shooting was going on.

The day wore on, and the island seemed quiet, but you never knew. Newton Fleming and his do-gooder friends might have left someone there to keep watch. He'd keep waiting for Peter to send a text.

Hours later, he had a thought. It had been too quiet. If there was anyone else on the island, surely they'd have made some kind of noise over the last few hours, but he'd heard nothing. Not a peep.

It was hot under the tiny house. Uncomfortable lying on his stomach. He was hungry and beyond thirsty. He had to pee like mad.

And he was angry like you wouldn't believe.

Angry at that witch Honey Hynes—or Fin Fleming, which he knew was her real name. Angry at Garth, and Ken, and Arthur and the whole team at Kraken Industries for letting the plan go sideways. He was supposed to get rich out of their stupid scheme, but that wasn't likely to happen now.

He was especially angry at his brother for leaving him here all alone on this cursed island after the shootout.

"You'll be my eyes and ears on the island," Peter had said. "We can't make it work without you."

Well, the plan hadn't worked even with him.

He'd tried texting Peter for a pickup, but Peter had replied that now he couldn't come as they'd planned. He had "other things" to take care of. He'd told Bert to take the boat they'd hidden under the pile of dead fish and make his way to the *Golden Kelp* on his own. Explain what had gone down to criminal mastermind Seb Lukin, all on his own.

Everyone knew that admitting failure to Seb Lukin was practically a death sentence, but Peter didn't seem to care that he was sending his brother into danger. Again.

Peter had sent him a shrug emoji and told him to grow a pair. Some big brother he was. That was the last Bert had heard from him, and that had been hours ago.

Bert couldn't spend the rest of his life hiding in the crawl space, so at last he clawed his way out. Still lying on the sand, he turned his head carefully, looking around. He sniffed like an animal, tasting the air for any sign he wasn't alone.

Finally convinced that everyone had deserted the island, he stood up and made his way to the pile of dead fish that blocked the island's only freshwater spring. His escape boat was underneath, well hidden by the stinking, rotting fish.

The stench of the dead fish made his eyes water, but he tied a handkerchief over his nose and went to work, flinging the decaying carcasses aside as he burrowed around to free his boat. As soon as he'd uncovered the boat, he tied its line to a nearby tree and then removed the metal plate they'd used to block the flow of water from the spring.

Even after the water began flowing again, this far inland the inlet was still too shallow for him to ride in the boat, so he followed its path toward the ocean, pulling the boat along with him. As soon as the water was deep enough, he climbed into the boat and put on a life vest.

He was too afraid the engine's noise would attract someone's attention if he really wasn't alone on the island, so he used an oar to push the boat along until it reached the shore and then it slid gently into the ocean. Once the boat was cleanly riding the gentle waves, he started the engine and took a heading toward where he knew that Seb Lukin and the *Golden Kelp* waited, just over the horizon.

Chapter 2
Ice Diving

We were filming Rafe's latest movie on location outside Anchorage Alaska, and it was darn cold. Reluctantly, I removed my half-frozen hand from the pocket of my down parka and pulled off one double-layered mitten to pull back the cuff of my other mitten and look at my dive watch. Rafe had been under the ice for forty-five minutes, and I was getting worried.

I was standing on the shore of Squirrel Lake, a 100-foot-deep alpine lake located in the valley near North and South Suicide peaks in the vast Chugach State Park. The terrain around the lake is absolutely breathtaking.

In fact, the entire state is spectacular. Everywhere I looked the view was so stunning that it seemed like it had been created especially to inspire awe and wonderment in everyone who saw it. Mountains, glaciers, trees, water, and sky. The area had it all, and it was all magnificent.

The surroundings mesmerized me, and I frequently found myself lost in wordless admiration for the stunning world around me.

Chugach State Park is immense, containing approximately 495,000 acres of land. It's one of the four largest—and arguably one of the most beautiful—state parks in the United States.

The land here is rugged, alternating among tall mountain peaks, ancient glaciers, wild ocean shore, fast moving rivers, deep, impenetrable forests, and vast ice fields. All this, and it's not even that far from downtown Anchorage.

Of course, traveling across this terrain is a whole lot different than traveling ten miles in my home turf of Georgetown, Grand Cayman.

I'd always thought the Cayman Islands were the most beautiful spot on earth. The two locations couldn't be more different, yet there was no denying the beauty of my current surroundings.

Several members of the movie crew were standing around laughing, joking, and drinking cup after cup of hot coffee. Not one of them seemed concerned about my husband, superstar action hero Rafe Cummings, who was diving deep under the four-foot-thick ice that completely covered the surface of Squirrel Lake, where he was filming the last of the underwater scenes for his latest movie.

Unlike his usual starring roles, which seemed designed to show off his handsome face and ultra-fit physique to maximum advantage, in this movie Rafe played an arctic explorer. He'd spent most of his scenes in the current film bundled up in bulky parkas and heavy drysuits that hid his famous face and body.

Even so, the producer—his best friend T-8—had still found a way to introduce a few scenes where Rafe appeared shirtless or in skimpy skin-tight swim trunks. Rafe and I had laughed about it because although he really is a terrific actor, his movies rarely give him a chance to do more than look fabulous on screen.

But dang, he was good at looking marvelous on-screen. He was even better at looking utterly spectacular offscreen.

Lucky me.

"Shouldn't he be heading for the surface by now?" I asked Nathan, his long-time stunt double and the man whom I'd thought was supposed to be his safety diver on this dive.

Nathan smiled condescendingly. "Don't worry, Mrs. Cummings. Rafe will be fine. He's done this sort of thing before you know."

I sighed. "I may be Rafe's wife, but my name is Fin Fleming, as I've already told you several times. And I'm the person who certified Rafe as a diver in the first place, so I'm very familiar with his dive history."

My voice sounded so snippy that even I cringed. Snarkiness probably isn't the best way to gain Nathan's cooperation, and I was afraid that very soon I might need his help to rescue Rafe.

"Oops. I need more coffee," he said as he turned away from me.

Too late. Obviously I had already annoyed him. I bit my lip in silent frustration. I couldn't help it. I was worried about Rafe.

Another five minutes passed while everyone in the crew chatted among themselves, not even glancing at their watches. How could they be so unconcerned about Rafe?

I needed to do something. I would not let my new husband drown or freeze to death underwater while I stood around doing nothing.

I scurried over to Rafe's trailer and went inside. His spare drysuit hung from the shower rod, and I wasted no time climbing into it. It was a little big across the shoulders, but not so big that it would be unmanageable under water. I snapped a pair of ankle weights on to counteract any air that might collect in the excess shoulder space, pulled up the zipper, and grabbed a pair of heavy dive gloves.

A pile of full tanks on several identical BCDs was just outside the trailer. I quickly set up Rafe's spare regulator on a tank and lifted the entire assembly over my head so it could slide down and settle against my back. After tightening the BCD's cummerbund, I trudged over to the large triangular hole the crew had sawed in the ice to allow Rafe, the safety divers, and the camera crew to enter and exit the water. Each side of the triangle was more than five feet long. Given the thickness of the ice and the near sub-zero temperatures, I didn't even want to imagine the difficulty involved in creating and maintaining the opening.

The crew had fastened a tough rope to a heavy cart they were using as an anchor point on the surface of the ice. The safety crew had done the first few dives alone to fasten a sturdy nylon line to the underside of the ice every few feet so the actors and dive crew could use it as a guide to the exit.

I knew the crew had followed all the safety rules. I was probably worrying for nothing. Even so, I couldn't shake the eerie feeling that something was wrong. The feeling made it impossible for me to relax.

Nobody else on set seemed concerned about Rafe, and that meant it was up to me to make sure he was okay. I was going in, under the ice, alone.

The dive entry point was near the edge of the river that fed the lake, so I assumed the current would be heavy. I'm a strong swimmer, and I'd often dealt with worse currents than I expected this one to be. I wasn't too concerned about fighting through the rushing water, but I still wanted to have two guide ropes leading back to the exit point in case any unexpected problem arose. I didn't want to take any chances that an unexpected surge might push me off course.

I grabbed a spare reel of rope I saw near the cart and tied it off to the anchor point next to the original spool. If there was something wrong under the ice, I wanted to make sure Rafe and I had a backup option to guide us back to the exit point. I clipped the reel to a D-ring on my BCD, adjusted my mask and gloves, and stepped into the hole.

At almost six feet, I'm tall for a woman, and the realization that the ice here was nearly as thick as I was tall made me pause for a nanosecond.

I frequently dive on wrecks, in caves, and in other areas with overhead environments as part of my job as chief underwater photographer at the Madelyn Anderson Russo Institute of Oceanography—RIO for short. But the thick icecap here gave me the willies, especially since I was in unfamiliar surroundings and diving solo. At least, I'd be diving solo until I met up with Rafe and the rest of the film crew.

The watery world under the ice was nothing like what I usually saw in the Caymans, even accounting for the difference in the terrain and the fish. The temperature of the sea water around the Caymans typically runs in the low to mid-eighties year round.

The water here was a frigid thirty-three degrees Fahrenheit, and I felt the sting on the exposed areas of my face almost immediately. I regretted not rummaging around in Rafe's gear bag for a full-face mask before diving. Then again, if Rafe could deal with this cold, then so could I.

I clipped the reel I had selected onto a D-ring on the front of my BCD so I could let the sturdy nylon rope spool out behind me. I also kept a hand on the line attached to the ice as I moved toward the still distant filming area.

My bubbles rose and nestled up against the bottom surface of the ice, exactly the way they nestled against the ceilings on a wreck, which was somewhat reassuring. It was darker down here than I would have expected, both because of the late day slant of the sun and the filtering effect of the ice.

I found a small underwater flashlight in my BCD's front pocket and flicked it on to help light up the eerie gloom ahead of me.

I hadn't gone much farther when I saw Rafe up ahead. I recognized his bright blue drysuit, but even from a distance it was obvious that something was very wrong.

For one thing, he was alone. There should have been a film crew and several safety divers around him.

For another thing, the nearly invisible severed end of the original guide rope was ominously floating in the current far away from him. Rafe was hovering in place, not moving at all. I wondered if it was possible he'd lost track of the part of the line that led back to safety and was afraid to move forward.

Then I realized Rafe had somehow become tangled in the other end of the free-floating rope. I figured that the crew must have been trying to cut him loose and accidentally disconnected themselves from the portion of the rope still attached to the exit hole.

Since I couldn't see them anywhere nearby, they were very likely lost. There was a barely visible pile of camera and lighting equipment on the bottom forty feet below him, but no sign of the crew or the safety divers.

Strange.

And very, very disturbing.

I couldn't fault the film crew for ditching the equipment. No equipment is more valuable than a life. And rather than hold on to the cameras and lights, as long as they had sufficient air, they should have immediately dropped everything to help the tangled diver or returned to the surface for more help.

But except for Nathan, I hadn't seen anyone from the crew on the surface or while I'd been following the guide rope to this point. I had to assume the crew had lost their way under the ice.

Visibility was so poor and the current so strong that they would be traveling blind unless one of them had taken an accurate compass reading on the exit position. I thought this was unlikely, given how lax they were about so many rules for safe diving. And besides, if that were the case, I'd have passed them on my way toward Rafe.

I didn't let my anxiety slow me down. I kept swimming, speeding up when I realized that my husband wasn't moving at all. After I'd gone about ten feet closer to Rafe, my heart gave a heavy thud at the realization that there were no bubbles coming from his regulator, which was floating freely beside him in the water. He wasn't breathing.

There was no one nearby to help.

I would have to rescue him from the entanglement and resuscitate him all by myself

Chapter 3
Rescue Attempt

MY LATE STEPFATHER Ray Russo had made me practice rescue skills until the training made my reactions instinctive. As he'd taught me to do, I stopped moving, took a deep calming breath, and only then did I make a plan.

I didn't rush into action until I knew what I needed to do and the right sequence for the steps. It was hard for me to stay calm enough to take even those few seconds of delay, but it would be better and safer for both of us in the long run if I didn't give in to panic.

I clipped the flashlight to my vest and then rummaged in the pockets of the BCD to see what other tools I had at hand. I felt a rush of thankfulness when I touched a pair of dive scissors. It wouldn't be easy to snip through the heavy nylon rope, especially wearing the thick drysuit gloves, but at least with the sharp scissors I had a shot at success.

I'd reached the location of the last anchor clip that had attached the original guide rope to the ice. I let the severed end of the rope slip through the clip and drift away. I still had a tight hold and a sturdy grip on the secondary reel I'd attached to my BCD, so I knew I could find my way back to the exit point.

I thanked the universe that I'd had the foresight to bring it along. To make sure I didn't lose sight of him in the rapidly fading daylight filtering through the thick layer of ice, I swam ahead as quickly as I could to where Rafe floated motionless in the water, never taking my eyes off him.

When I reached him, I assessed his condition. His eyes were closed and he was unresponsive. I purged his regulator and put it in his mouth. An irregular stream of very tiny bubbles merged from his regulator. Their size and infrequency told me that the entanglement had badly compromised Rafe's breathing. But so far at least, he was still breathing, at least a little bit.

I swam behind him and began snipping away at the thick coils of rope behind his drysuit hood. I'd have had to be a blind idiot not to recognize the significance of the perfectly tied knots at the back of his neck. This was no accidental entanglement.

I knew I should try to preserve the knots for law enforcement as evidence of attempted murder, but my first priority was saving Rafe's life.

Someone from the team of safety divers or on the film crew had deliberately done this to Rafe. But unless they'd planned an alternative way out of the water, they probably hadn't realized they might doom themselves as well as Rafe when they trapped themselves under the ice with him.

I put the thought aside and concentrated on freeing Rafe from the cord that encircled his neck. It was hard work to snip through the many layers and strands of the heavy rope. I had to work quickly to save his life but position the shears carefully to make sure I didn't nick his air hose.

It felt like forever before the last strands fell away, leaving Rafe's airway open and unconstricted. When the rope parted, I stuck the piece I'd severed, including the remains of the tightly tied knot, into my BCD pocket.

I spun around to face Rafe. I was dismayed to realize that the thin stream of bubbles I'd noticed earlier had stopped. He was no longer breathing on his own. I took a deep breath from my own regulator, pushed his regulator mouthpiece aside, clamped my lips over his, and blew into his mouth.

Even while I was sharing my breath with him, I was carefully coiling the line back onto the reel attached to my BCD and swimming toward the exit hole. I didn't see or sense any other divers nearby. We were all alone. I knew that meant the other divers must have deliberately abandoned Rafe.

But what could be their motive? Rafe was usually well-liked. He'd always been pretty popular with the crew and other cast members on all his previous movies.

I had no clue as to who would have wanted to hurt him. I wasn't crazy about the idea of the people who had done this to Rafe swimming behind me, but I had to assume they were smart enough to recognize that I was the only one under the ice who had a clear path to the exit hole.

Since it would mean their own doom as well as Rafe's and mine, I had to hope they wouldn't try to harm either of us until we'd reached safety. I'm great at multi-tasking, especially underwater, but even I couldn't single-handedly do CPR on Rafe, swim to safety, hold the reel, and fight off bad guys all at the same time.

And no matter what went on around me, my first priority was always going to be Rafe's safety.

After giving him another mouth-to-mouth breath, I put his regulator back in his mouth, purged the valve, and watched to see if he took a breath.

He did not.

I gave him a bear hug, pushing hard on his chest to force him to expel the air I'd blown into his lungs. Several bubbles escaped from his regulator, so I knew the forced exhalation had worked.

I watched closely to see if he followed that exhalation up with a spontaneous inhale, but he didn't. I was on the edge of panic, but I forced myself to remain calm and went through the process of blowing air into Rafe's lungs again, while swimming backwards along the line heading toward the exit hole.

I breathed air into him again.

And again.

By now we were just a few kicks from the exit hole, so I swam as hard as I could. When I was directly beneath the opening in the ice, I swam up straight through the triangular hole, my arms around Rafe to push him to the open air as quickly as I could.

As soon as I broke the surface, I spit out my regulator and shouted. "Rafe needs a doctor. Stat."

Nathan, who as safety diver should have been on the dive with Rafe, dropped his coffee onto the ice, where it instantly froze. Then he used both arms to pull Rafe out of the water, laying him flat on the ice and beginning to perform CPR.

He was doing it badly, but I had to give him credit for trying.

Or did I?

By all rights—and the terms of his contract—he should have been on this dive with Rafe, not swilling coffee on the surface.

With a mighty kick of my long fins, I used my arms to push down on the ice and crawled out of the water. The water in my hair and on my drysuit turned to ice instantly.

I climbed out of the hole and staggered for a second on the slick, snow-covered ice before I pushed Nathan aside. Then I knelt beside Rafe and swept his mouth with a finger to be sure his airway was clear. Once I was sure he could breathe without obstruction, I turned him on his left side and slapped the middle of his back hard.

As I'd expected, Rafe vomited up a mix of bile, black coffee, and lake water. While he was semi-upright, I unzipped his drysuit and then rolled him onto his back to begin CPR compressions. Even as I began compressions, I was yelling out instructions to save his life.

"Get the AED from T-8. And somebody get me a knife. Where's the emergency oxygen? Get it now!"

Nathan was still standing uselessly beside me, but eventually he unfastened his dive knife from his right thigh and handed it to me before running off to T-8's trailer. I used the knife to cut Rafe's drysuit undergarment open so I'd have a clear field when the AED arrived.

"Oxygen?" I yelled, but I could see that nobody had any idea where the emergency supplies were, because they all shuffled their feet and looked blankly at each other. I gritted my teeth and fervently wished that Doc and her superbly trained team of EMTs were on site.

Finally, Nathan knelt beside me with the AED. "Do you know how to use this?" he asked. It was obvious he had no idea.

Nodding, I grabbed the device from him and attached the electrodes to Rafe's bare chest. "Clear."

Nathan rocked back on his heels as Rafe's body contracted in response to the shock. I checked his heartbeat.

No reaction.

"Will he be okay? What should I do now?" said Nathan.

"The best thing you can do right now is find him some oxygen. There should be a couple of canisters in my gear bag. It's on the bed in Rafe's trailer," I said, working hard to sound calm while my heart was screaming in fear.

Nathan ran off at top speed.

I was back to doing chest compressions while waiting for the AED to recycle. Its battery was low and it was taking forever to get back to the ready state. I wanted to scream at the universe. When T-8 strolled up at his usual leisurely pace, I screamed at him instead.

'You call yourself a producer? Your set is a danger to everyone on it. Where's the safety equipment? Where's the medical team? Why was Rafe diving alone, without his safety divers? I swear if Rafe doesn't come back from this I'll kill you myself."

T-8's face went white. "What's going on? What happened to Rafe? What can I do to help?" His voice had lost its usual California drawl and gone back to its street origins. I could hear how scared he was when he realized his long time best friend was in real danger. He dropped to his knees beside Rafe and grabbed his hand.

I glared at him. "Go help Nathan find the oxygen canisters in my gear bag. It's in Rafe's trailer, in the bedroom. Call an ambulance. Then get Doc on the phone. I need her to talk me through this."

I saw the flickering recharge light on the AED. "And pay more attention to crew safety on your sets from now on." I practically spit the last words because I was so angry.

T-8 had the grace to look chagrined. We both knew he'd been cutting costs on this project, but I hadn't realized his economizing had gone so far as to put his team in real danger.

Without another word, he rose and loped across the icy ground to Rafe's trailer. Less than a minute later, he popped out carrying two oxygen canisters.

Just before he reached me, the AED finished the recharging process, so I shouted "clear" and pushed the button. This time Rafe's heart began beating again. I grabbed the oxygen from T-8 and put the cannula in Rafe's nose. I watched him like an overanxious granny looking after her first grandbaby.

T-8 put his cellphone up to my ear. "Doc," he said.

I wasted no time on pleasantries but recited the necessary statistics as though we were doing rounds together.

Doc spoke cautiously. "You've done everything right, as usual. Is Rafe breathing on his own now?"

I fretted as I put my ear in front of his face to make sure I could feel the flow of air from his nose or mouth. "Yes. Rapid and shallow, but he's breathing on his own with supplemental oxygen. His body temperature is still too low though."

"Get someone to help you move him inside. Cover him with warm blankets, and if he's alert enough, give him hot soup or drinks. Call me back after you get him situated."

Nathan brought over a body board, and I supervised while he and T-8 positioned Rafe on it. They carried him to his trailer and placed him on the bed. I pulled a silver space blanket out of my own first aid kit and wrapped it around him.

Rafe's eyelids fluttered, but he didn't wake up.

"Go to the craft trailer. Bring back hot coffee and clear soup," I said.

Nathan took off at a run just as Rafe let out a groan. He began to shake and shiver.

I took his hand. "You're okay now. I've got you. You're in our trailer, safe and warm. Nathan's getting you some nice hot soup and that will help warm you up.

Without waiting for me to ask him, T-8 cranked up the trailer's thermostat. The sudden blast of warm air did nothing to dispel the chill I felt at the thought of how close I'd come to losing Rafe. I looked around for his heavy wool knitted beanie, which I found on the kitchen table. I brought it back to the bed and put it on his head, pulling it down low so it covered his ears. Then I rolled heavy wool socks onto his feet and pulled the blanket back up to his chin.

Nathan slammed the trailer door when he returned with a huge mug of hot soup. He rummaged through the kitchen drawers until he found a spoon, then he put both items on the nightstand. "I'll help you get him sitting up."

He and T-8 reached over to lift Rafe's shoulders while I mounded the pillows behind his back. As soon as I finished, they gently positioned Rafe so he was sitting up against them. "What else do you need?" Nathan asked.

"Will you search the set to see if there any strangers around or anyone who seems out of place. Ask if anyone recognized the safety divers that went with Rafe on the dive this morning."

He started to turn away, but then I had another thought. "After that, look for another entry hole in the ice. It would be somewhere out of sight."

Then I held a spoon to Rafe's cracked lips and tipped a few drops of soup into his mouth. "T-8, please plug in the AED so it's fully charged just in case we need it again. And if you wouldn't mind, see if you can find my phone. I need to make a call." Then I turned my attention back to my husband, begging the universe to help him pull through.

Chapter 4
Calling Newton Fleming

I WAS STILL FEEDING Rafe the hot soup, a few drops at a time, when I felt a soft, warm blanket settle over my own shoulders.

"You're freezing too. In fact, you're shivering so hard I don't know how you can hold on to that spoon. Why don't you take a minute to get out of your wet drysuit and warm yourself up," said T-8.

He put my phone and two steaming mugs of soup on the nightstand next to Rafe and touched my shoulder. "Go on. Take care of yourself. I'll keep giving Rafe his soup while you put on something warm and dry. Have a few bites of soup yourself to help warm you up. It won't do Rafe any good if you make yourself sick. In fact, it'll make him feel crazy guilty."

I'd focused on taking care of Rafe and hadn't realized I was still wearing my soggy drysuit. It wasn't until T-8 mentioned how cold I seemed that I actually started to feel the bone deep chill. Suddenly I was aware of my own violent shivering. I stood up, wrapping the blanket even tighter around my shoulders. "Thank you."

He looked me in the eye. "I'm sorry this happened on my watch, but I'll do everything I can to make sure Rafe comes through this unhurt. I've already started making doubly sure the set is in compliance with safety regs. The AED is back on the charger. I promise you I'll never again let anyone overlook that precaution on any movie set of mine. And we'll always have oxygen, and a body board—whatever you and Doc recommend. I promise."

His voice cracked just a little, and I knew T-8 was feeling the terror of almost losing his life-long best friend. I was still furious at him even though it was obvious he was miserable and feeling guilty over the horrific nightmare that had befallen Rafe.

He should have felt bad. If he hadn't been cutting corners then Rafe wouldn't have fallen prey to whomever had it in for him.

I put down the mug and the spoon I had been using to feed Rafe and grabbed a pair of heavy sweats and some thick woolen socks from a pile on the shelf over the bed. "I'll be back as soon as I've changed. Shout out if you see anything that looks worrisome."

T-8's sorrowful eyes met mine. "Take your time. Sit near the fireplace and get warm. Eat your soup. I promise to take good care of Rafe, and I'll let you know if anything changes."

I knew he was trying to reassure me, but T-8 could be such a spaceball sometimes that his words didn't provide any comfort. Who knew what, if anything, he'd find worthy of telling me about? I resolved to change into dry clothes quickly and get back to Rafe's bedside as fast as I could, just in case.

I left the bedroom and entered the main living area of Rafe's trailer. The decor was the height of opulence. It was modern, spacious, and ultra luxurious, with gleaming granite counters, an eight-burner induction stove, a three-person hot tub, a cedar lined sauna with two tiers of benches that could easily accommodate five people, and a gas fireplace. Rafe and I had laughed about it together when we'd first seen it.

"I would have given my right arm to live in a place like this back when I was a kid," he'd said. "Now it's just a place to hang out when I'm away from home. It's a waste of T-8's money, but this is the first time in his life he's ever had any money to waste, so..."

I'd known that Rafe was remembering his own childhood—growing up homeless, living in an alley with his older brother Dougie and his best-friend T-8, whose original name was Tate. Back then, nobody would have expected Rafe to amount to anything, especially not a highly sought after movie star.

But anyone who knew him would know that nobody deserved success more than Rafe Cummings. He worked unbelievably hard, and he was loving, caring, kind, smart, sweet, and funny. Everyone, especially me, adored him.

After changing my clothes, I flipped on the fireplace switch and sat at the counter to drink my soup straight from the mug. I could feel the spicy liquid warming me from the inside, and the cozy fire and thick blanket still wrapped around my shoulders were both doing their parts to warm me up on the outside.

My shivering subsided slightly, and I felt like I could talk without my teeth chattering. I picked up my phone and pushed the favorites code for Newton Fleming, my father.

As usual when I called, no matter where he was or what he was doing, Newton answered immediately. We'd had a little bit of a falling out a few months ago when he dragged me into an undercover investigation he was running. I'd been very angry when I realized what was going on, and we hadn't spent much time together since then. I wasn't quite ready to forgive him, but I missed him like crazy.

"What's up?" he said, a smile in his beloved voice.

I valued our relationship all the more because he hadn't been in my life while I was growing up. I deeply missed our former closeness, and I was happy to see that he didn't hold my anger at his actions against me.

"I need your help. It's about Rafe." I couldn't keep the sound of tears out of my voice.

There was a brief pause while he considered how to respond. "Are you both okay? You're safe?"

"No. We're out here on a movie set in Alaska and someone tried to kill him. I need your help to get him out of here before they try again. And it's freezing cold, and he's shivering so hard... I don't know what to do for him. I need Doc." A pause. "I need you."

"Then I'll be there. Always."

His words warmed my heart in a way that the hot soup never could. I was so overcome with love for my father that I couldn't speak.

He must have guessed because he said "Text me your location and then don't worry about anything. I'll fly out within the hour and I'll make all the arrangements to get to you from..." he paused a moment to look up the name of the airport...Ted Stevens Airport in Anchorage.

You just stay with Rafe and relax. We'll be there before you know it." He paused a moment. "I love you."

I could tell he'd completely focused on the logistics of getting here because he hung up without saying goodbye—his usual habit when he concentrated on any objective. The flight time between Grand Cayman and Anchorage was likely to be twelve to fifteen hours, depending on the route the pilot chose and how long and how often he had to stop for refueling. Then Newton would have to rent a car and make his way here over rugged terrain. There were time zone differences and terrible weather and too many variables for me to contend with right now. He'd get here as fast as he could, and I contented myself with that knowledge. I went back into the trailer's bedroom to rejoin my sleeping husband.

T-8 looked up when he heard my footsteps. "Did you get ahold of Newton okay?"

I nodded. "He's on his way. Has Nathan reported back yet?

He looked away. "Yes. He said he found another exit hole in the ice, around a bend, behind some trees. This was a well-planned attack on Rafe. But there are no strangers around the set now. Apparently nobody knew who the new safety divers were, but they'd checked and the new guys were definitely on the roster to dive today. Nobody's seen them since they went in the water with Rafe. Oh, and Nathan's in the clear. I confirmed he never went in the water at all today. He showed me his schedule and it said he was off the dive rotation, although I'm sure that's not right…"

I sighed. "We'll get to the bottom of this. We just have to keep Rafe warm and safe for now."

He patted my hand. "Yes, and that goes for you too. Why don't you lay down and rest for a while. I'll stay here and keep watch over you both. You'll be safe. I promise."

At first when he said those words I couldn't imagine being able to rest at all because I was so scared for Rafe. Then I looked at my husband restlessly tossing and turning and still shivering. I succumbed to temptation.

I crawled under the blankets and snuggled up to him. He sighed deeply and immediately stopped his restless stirring. I think I might have been asleep beside him before T-8 had even shut off the lights.

Chapter 5
Arrival

THE NEXT THING I knew the sun was in my eyes. Rafe was still sleeping, but his breathing sounded easier and more normal than it had last night. I crossed my fingers that this was a good sign and not just wishful thinking on my part.

The smell of coffee drew me into the kitchen, where a steaming pot of the hot nectar awaited me. I put on a heavy sweater, pushed my messy hair back out of my eyes, and poured myself a mugful.

After a couple of big gulps, I looked around. Rafe and I were alone in the trailer. Where was T-8? I wondered if he'd started the coffee and then left us alone after promising to keep watch over us.

I walked around the counter and noticed one of the kitchen chairs wedged under the doorknob as though someone wanted to keep an intruder out. A quick glance showed me that both trailer doors were locked, so someone must have locked at least one of them with a key from outside. After another sip of coffee, I put my mug on the counter and removed the chair before pulling open the other door.

I screamed.

There was a body lying across the steps, covered in a thin layer of snow. Ice crystals dotted his eyelashes, and his lips were blue.

"Tate," I yelled, grabbing his shoulders and shaking him.

He slowly opened one eye. "What?"

So, not dead.

That was something to be thankful for.

"What are you doing out here? Have you been out all night? You're lucky you didn't freeze to death…" I was so surprised at finding him sprawled out on the steps that I rambled.

He stood up with difficulty, wobbling and holding his head. "I was watching over you and Rafe. I needed to make sure no one went after him again. It was almost dawn and way too cozy in the trailer to stay awake so I made a pot of coffee, locked both doors, and came out here for some fresh air. I must have fallen asleep."

I noticed the empty mug on the ground next to the steps, the spilled coffee staining the thin crust of newly fallen snow. "I can't believe you fell asleep still holding your coffee."

He followed my gaze to the discolored spot on the snow and his eyes widened.

When I turned my head to look back at T-8, I suddenly felt dizzy. I put my hand out to grab the rail and missed, toppling over onto T-8. We both tumbled to the icy ground.

He ended up on the bottom of the pile and bore the brunt of my weight. After recovering from the shock of the fall and the cold snow on our faces and hands, we each took a minute to catch our breath.

"I think the coffee's been drugged," I said.

"Yep," he replied. "I agree." All trace of California was gone from his voice, and I could hear the tough east coast street kid he'd once been.

We rolled over and got to our knees. "We need help," I said.

He pulled himself up using the handrail on the steps, then he reached down to lend me a hand. Once I was erect, he half walked and half dragged me behind the trailer. "Stick your finger down your throat. You've gotta get the poison out."

He immediately took his own advice, and watching his performance made it unnecessary for me to do anything to force myself to vomit. It happened all by itself.

When we were through retching, I said, "We need water, but we can't touch anything in Rafe's trailer. Can you make it to the craft trailer with me?"

We held each other up as we staggered across the open area created by the circle of luxury trailers. There were no early shoots planned for today, and it was still just after sunrise, so the craft trailer was empty except for a lone member of the catering staff.

He took one look at us and said, "You two had quite a night." He picked up a pitcher of water from the nearby table to pour us a couple of glasses.

I held up a hand. "Bottled water only, please. And we'll open the bottles ourselves."

He looked surprised, but he probably got crazy requests from movie people constantly, so he just pulled two bottles out of the refrigerator and handed one to each of us.

"Thanks, James," I said as I twisted off the cap. The first few swallows of the invigorating liquid seemed to clear my head of its lingering fog.

"Yikes. We left Rafe alone and unguarded." I dropped my water and took off at a run. It wasn't my all-time best pace, but it was the best I could do just then.

T-8 jogged along beside me, and his long legs helped him pull ahead within a few steps. He pounded up the steps of Rafe's trailer and flung the door open.

Rafe was sitting at the counter just about to take a sip from a steaming mug of coffee.

At the same time, T-8 and I both yelled, "Noooo."

T-8 was closer to Rafe and he lunged across the last two steps and the trailer's spacious kitchen to knock the hot liquid away from my husband.

I was a couple of steps behind T-8 but I rushed past him as he dealt with the flying coffee and threw my arms around Rafe.

"You're awake," I sobbed, smothering him with kisses.

Rafe laughed. "Yup. Happens every morning. What's the big deal about today?"

"What do you remember about yesterday?" I asked him.

"Nothing." He sniffed. "I might remember more if I'd had some coffee. What's going on with you two? You're acting weird."

It was only then that I realized he was completely unaware of his near-death experience.

T-8 and I looked at each other. Neither of us was really sure what was going on. "It's a long story…" I started.

I broke off when I heard Newton's voice from the doorway. "Why don't you wait for me to get settled in and then you'll only have to tell the story once."

I rushed over to hug him. "You made good time. Thank you for coming so quickly," I whispered in his ear.

He kissed my cheek. "Any chance of a coffee?" he asked. "It was a really long journey."

"That's part of the story. At least I think it is. Let's go to craft to discuss it." I stepped past him to hug Doc. "Thank you for coming." I said. Then I whispered to her. "He doesn't remember what happened. And I think someone tried to poison us all last night."

"Got it," she whispered in my ear. Then she spoke out loud. "Since I'm new to this whole movie business, I'd love to see the craft setup. They always sound so great in interviews with stars." She took my arm and we walked across the huge open circle made by the dressing room trailers toward the big food service trailer. It was still early, so very few people were out and about.

Newton, T-8, and Rafe took off toward the aroma of hot coffee that had just started to perfume the frigid air. Doc and I hung back to let them go ahead of us.

Newton was taking in every detail of the movie set without appearing to look around or gawk, and it was obvious to me that Doc was evaluating Rafe's condition.

If you didn't know her, she would have seemed completely focused on our conversation as we walked across the open space surrounded by the crew housing and equipment trailers.

Once we entered the craft trailer, Doc unzipped her brand new heavy down parka. "It's nice and warm in here," she said. "Feels heavenly."

She put a hand on Rafe's wrist and drew him aside, ostensibly to peruse the food on the breakfast buffet and get his advice on the best choices, but I knew she was surreptitiously taking his pulse.

I stopped at the main counter and asked James, the chef on duty, if he'd draw a carafe of coffee from the communal urn so I could take it over to our table.

He gave me a big smile. "Sure thing, Mrs. Cummings. But you don't have to wait for it. Go ahead and join your party and I'll bring it over to you along with cream and sugar and utensils. Maybe you'd like a tray of muffins and donuts—or I can whip something up if anyone wants an omelet or…"

"Thanks, James. But I think we're good on breakfast for now. And I'll take the tray over myself. You have enough to do getting set up for the crowd." I returned his smile, but I was wary of eating or drinking anything that didn't come from the communal supply or that I didn't see made right in front of me.

He shrugged. "It's no bother, but if that's what you want to do…" He pulled an empty carafe from the shelf above the urn, filled it, and placed it on a tray along with spoons, mugs, a bowl of single use creamers, and a dish with an assortment of sugars and artificial sweeteners. "Here you go," he said when he slid the tray across the counter.

"Thanks." Trying not to laugh at the surprised expression on his face, I hoisted the tray over my shoulder and balanced it flat on my palm the way my best friend Theresa had taught me to do when I occasionally filled in as a waitperson at Ray's Place on Grand Cayman.

Back at our table, I passed out mugs and spoons while T-8 poured coffee into each mug. Once everyone had taken their first few sips, I told the story of the attempts on our lives. "I believe someone tried to drug T-8 and me. I think someone went in the trailer while we were sleeping and put something in the coffee. T-8 passed out on the front steps, even during a snow squall, and we both vomited shortly after drinking just a few swallows of coffee. Whatever the poison is, it must be in either the coffee beans or the water…"

Newton interrupted. "It could have been anywhere. In the coffee or on the cups you drank from or the spoons you measured or stirred with."

Everyone at the table pushed their coffee aside.

"Let's get out of here," I said.

Doc and Newton started piling the cups and utensils back on the tray.

Rafe held up a hand. "I have to finish the movie. I can't leave Tate and Liam in the lurch with such a huge financial liability. It's my responsibility to finish what I started."

T-8 shrugged. "Don't worry about the movie. Yesterday was your last underwater scene. We can do the rest in front of a green screen or we'll build a set once we're back on the island. I don't need money as much as I need to know my best friend is safe, and I'd never get over it if anything happened to you."

I swiveled my gaze between the two friends, and I saw the exact moment when they'd mentally agreed leaving was the right thing to do.

I stood up. "I can pack in under ten minutes, including Rafe's stuff. T-8, just pack your personal stuff and let the crew dismantle the rest. Dad, is there room for all of us in your car?"

He waved his hand vaguely toward a huge, bright yellow Hummer hulking just outside the circle of movie crew trailers. "Three rows of seats. Adequate storage for your gear and clothes unless you over-packed." He grinned. "I'm ready to go whenever you are."

I was still concerned about Rafe's health after his ordeal, so I asked him to stay with Doc and Newton at the table while T-8 and I packed. Before we walked over to the Hummer, T-8 called Liam Lawton, who was my ex-fiancé and his current business partner, to ask him to fly out to supervise the crew as they shot some final B-reel and then disman-tled the set.

Chapter 6
Homecoming

SURPRISINGLY, despite my worries, the road trip back to the airport was kind of fun. Newton supplied us with ample quantities of very-bad-for-you snacks, and when we stopped for gas, we bought a round of hot chocolate loaded with decadent whipped cream. For once, even Rafe indulged in our junk food binging.

We played loud music on the radio and sang along to the oldies playing on KTMB out of Anchorage. Sometimes when a particular favorite song played, one of us would tell a story about what the song meant to them or where they were when they first heard it.

Other times, we just gawked at the scenery, which was magnificent. The glaciers, the mountains, the sky, the forest, the rivers, and the wildlife were all spectacular. If I hadn't been so worried about Rafe, I would have thought the trip to the airport was a total blast.

But that didn't mean I wasn't beyond thrilled to finally land at my hometown airport—Owen Roberts International. We all know there's no place like home, and even though I've traveled all over the world, Grand Cayman has always been and will always be my home. The soft ocean breeze, the delicate fragrance of the abundant flowers, and the pervasive tang of the ocean in the salty air had never been sweeter or more precious to me.

My friend Joely Wentworth was standing in the airport's lobby to meet Newton and drive him home. Standing next to Joely, Stewie Belcher was waiting to pick up Doc, and he offered to drop the rest of us off. I'd driven Tate and Rafe to the airport when they'd flown out, and Stewie had dropped me off at the airport when I'd gone out to join them a few weeks later. It was easy for him to take the three of us to my car in the parking lot at RIO, our mutual workplace, since he was going there anyway. Thanks to Stewie's kindness, we didn't have to juggle multiple cars or hire a cab.

Once at RIO, we transferred our luggage to my car, and it wasn't long before I pulled into my driveway on Rum Point. Rafe, Tate, and I wanted to brainstorm about who might have been behind the attack on Rafe, and just as importantly, why they might have wanted him dead.

My mother Maddy Russo and her fiancé Dane Scott, Deputy Superintendent of the Cayman Islands police, were just leaving my home. Ever the thoughtful dad, Newton must have texted ahead to ask her to stock my house with food. Since Rafe had been away for several weeks before I flew out to join him, it was a sure bet there wouldn't have been anything edible in the place otherwise. My miserable eating habits are legendary.

Dane had been pet-sitting for our tiny wire-haired dachshund Penny while I was gone. When Penny realized we were back, she went crazy with excitement and rushed over to greet Rafe and me. Chico and Henrietta, the free-range rooster and chicken that my next-door neighbor Liam and I shared responsibility for, scurried over right behind her. It was a very happy homecoming.

As he often does, Rafe grilled some steak tips out on the backyard patio while I chopped veggies for a salad. Maddy had stocked my freezer with some ice cream, so T-8 made a quick sauce with some fresh strawberries to pour over it for dessert, and our meal was complete. By unspoken agreement, we didn't talk about the attempt on Rafe's life until we'd finished eating and loaded the dishwasher.

Finally, Rafe pushed back his chair. "Tell me again what happened."

I went through the story again, trying hard to remember more details. One of those forgotten details was that Nathan, Rafe's stunt double and primary safety diver, hadn't been in the water with him.

Rafe furrowed his brow. "Then who was under the ice with me? At least one of the divers should have been Nathan. I remember he was there while I geared up, and he was all ready to go. In fact, he was standing beside me just before I went in the water."

"His agenda said he had a free day. He showed it to us," I said. "It must have been someone else standing near you."

T-8 frowned. "I didn't hire anybody new in the crew, and I'm sure Nathan was on the roster that day." He whipped out his phone and checked the day's film schedule from his cloud account. "Yes, it was supposed to be Rafe, Nathan—and you." He looked at me. "Why weren't you on the dive?"

I flushed, feeling guilty at his implied accusation, but I knew I hadn't done anything wrong. In fact, I'd only just arrived the day before, and I'd been looking forward to diving under the ice with Rafe.

I'd been disappointed at my exclusion from the dive. I pulled out my own phone and showed him my personal schedule, sent to me directly from his production assistant. It said 'free day' in bold red letters.

T-8 checked Nathan's individual schedule, and it said 'free day' in big red letters, just like mine had.

Rafe looked at the overall company schedule and confirmed it showed that Nathan had been the only safety diver assigned to accompany him. "Bro, you've been hacked," he said. "And it looks like the hacker has it in for me."

After a few seconds of silence while we digested this news, I pulled out my phone and called Chaun, my friend the tech genius. He and his roommate Benjamin Brooks were on their way home from dinner at Ray's Place, RIO's hugely popular restaurant and tiki bar. Since Chaun and Benjamin live just down the street from me, they agreed to stop in to see if Chaun could figure out what had happened to the movie company's network.

Barely five minutes later, I saw their headlights sweeping across the front of my house as they pulled into the driveway. The three of us went outside to greet them.

Chaun hopped down from the seat of Benjamin's car. As usual, he had on long, baggy basketball shorts, white socks pulled up high on his calves, and bright red Chucks. He usually wore a large t-shirt branded with a company logo or an iconic rock band. Today, his shirt featured the RIO logo.

He rushed halfway down the walk to greet us, his face glowing with happiness at seeing his friends again. "I missed you guys," he said, throwing his arms wide as though he meant to enfold us all in a major bear hug. "I'm so glad you're back."

I'd only been gone a few days, but Rafe and T-8 had been away for several weeks. Chaun was shy and a little eccentric, so it was hard for him to make friends quickly. Besides Benjamin, whom he'd known since college, Chaun didn't have many friends outside of our group, so he sorely missed us when we weren't around.

After he greeted us, he knelt down to rub Penny's silky ears and her furry belly. "What's going on?" he asked me while continuing to pat the blissful dog.

I explained that a malevolent person or persons had penetrated the network at T-8/Lawton Productions, and that it had nearly resulted in Rafe's death. "Luckily, I had a premonition that he needed me. I got to him just in time, but we don't know who the divers who went with him were, or why they wanted to harm him. They had already disappeared before I found him."

I looked at Rafe, blinking back tears when I remembered how close I'd come to losing him.

T-8 spoke up. "It's my job to figure out who they are, but while I'm working on that, Chaun, I need you to harden the network and make sure they can't get in again. And it will be just as important to backtrace the intrusion if you can. That will give us a good start on finding the killers."

Chaun idolized Rafe, and we could see on his face how horrified he was that he might have lost his friend. He took a deep breath and stood up to his full height of four-foot-eight and straightened his shoulders. "I'm on it. Nobody comes after my friends and gets away with it."

Back when we first met and Chaun had started consulting at RIO, he'd installed everything needed to access and manage RIO's network from my home. Chaun hadn't charged RIO for his time or the equipment, although he said he'd done it for my convenience. The most I ever did with all the cutting-edge paraphernalia was access my files in the cloud, although Chaun used it regularly to update the Institute's system when he didn't have time to go all the way to RIO from his home on Rum Point.

Tonight, his foresight and the equipment would prove invaluable.

Chaun marched toward my open front door and went inside. The rest of us fell in line behind him. He went directly to my home office and sat down at my desk, stretched out his fingers, and shook his hands like he was about to play a piano concerto at Carnegie Hall.

The thought made me smile. When it came to technology, Chaun was as much of a virtuoso in his field as anyone who'd ever graced that famous stage was in theirs.

The rest of us backed out of the office to give him some room to think, although Rafe immediately went to the kitchen and gathered a plate of cookies, a large bowl of popcorn, a family size bag of chips, and a glass of icy cold lemonade.

Rafe knew from past experience that Chaun's genius required fuel to be effective. He placed the offering on the table beside my desk next to where Chaun was sitting. "Thank you," Rafe whispered softly before he left Chaun to his work.

Then Rafe put together another tray full of snacks for the rest of us. T-8 and I were thrilled with cookies, chips, and the buttery, salty popcorn like he'd served to Chaun, but this time the tray also included several healthy options for Benjamin and Rafe to enjoy.

He flipped the switch to turn on the fairy lights in my backyard. The four of us went outside to the patio and sat on the tile coping with our feet dangling in the warm water of the pool while we waited nervously to see what unauthorized changes Chaun could uncover about the sabotage to our film schedules—changes that might easily have led to the death of my husband.

Benjamin took a grape from the bowl Rafe had placed on the tiles between them. They both knew there was very little chance that either T-8 or I would go for fruit as a snack when there were cookies and popcorn available.

We assumed whoever had tampered with T-8's carefully planned crew schedules would have been vigilant about covering their tracks. We were prepared to wait as long as it took for Chaun to crack the case, and we expected it would be hours, if not days, before that happened.

I looked over at Rafe's face, glowing happily in the fairy lights as he and Benjamin discussed freediving. But then I noticed the grey circles shadowing his eyes, and I realized that although he was trying hard to cover it, he was exhausted.

Doc had given him a clean bill of health after she examined him, but he had just come back from the dead after nearly dying in the icy cold Alaska waters. Of course he was tired.

I took his hand. "Why don't you go in and get some rest? I promise to wake you right away if Chaun finds anything."

He smiled wryly and shook his head. "I'm fine. And anyway, it was me they tried to kill, not you. The least I can do is stay awake while Chaun is trying to trace the killer." He bit back a yawn.

Benjamin's gaze met mine from Rafe's other side. "I'm up for going inside and hanging out on that nice comfy couch. It's getting chilly out here."

That was a lie. It was the usual eighty-five degrees here on Grand Cayman, and the wind was barely moving. Obviously, Benjamin was concerned about Rafe too.

"Me too," said T-8.

The three of us pretended we were freezing, so we gathered all the food and went inside. Benjamin helped me put the food away while T-8 and Rafe went into the front room to relax.

By the time we joined them, Rafe had zonked out on the couch. I covered him with the ocean blue hand knitted afghan I keep in a basket in the corner. Penny jumped up on the couch, snuggled in beside him, and went right to sleep. I dimmed the lights and then the rest of us tiptoed out to the kitchen.

T-8 and I were just about to pop another bowl of popcorn when we noticed red and blue lights flashing outside my window. We rushed to the door and flung it open. Newton was already on the doorstep just about to knock. Maddy and Dane were standing on the walk behind him.

At the same time Chaun flung open the door of my office. "Houston, we have a problem." He looked abashed. "I think they caught me."

"What's going on?" I was terrified because my whole family had shown up this late at night. I was savvy enough to realize that something terrible must have happened.

"Can we come in? And T-8, would you please make some coffee? We're gonna need it," Newton said.

Only after he spoke did I notice how disheveled Newton looked. *Human Magazine* constantly called him a 'silver fox' and had named him one of the world's sexiest bachelors. He was known for his style and perfect grooming at all times. Hair perfect; clothes perfect; pretty much everything perfect.

But right now he looked like hell.

Newton stepped inside and put his arm around my shoulder. "It's Liam. They believe his plane went down. We haven't heard from him. And there have been breaches in both the Lawton Industries network and in RIO's network."

Chaun gasped. "This could be my fault. I was probing the networks looking for intruders. I found them right about the same time they found me." He turned to me. "I'm so sorry. If Liam's plane crashed, it might be all my fault."

Maddy stepped forward. "No, it's not your fault, Chaun. We don't know what happened yet. It may not be related to whatever you were doing at all." She put her arms around his shoulders and gave him a hug. "Even if the other guys found you on their network, you had nothing to do with causing the plane to go down. We don't know anything about the accident yet. For all we know, Liam might be just fine."

Dane pushed forward. "My team is in touch with the authorities in Alaska. As soon as they know anything, we'll know it too. Until we hear from them we should all just stay calm."

Despite the warm evening, I was suddenly freezing. Liam and I had been engaged for years, and good friends and coworkers for years before that. If I hadn't met Rafe, Liam and I might still be together.

I love Rafe with all my heart, but I couldn't imagine my life without Liam's friendship.

Penny's cold wet nose pushed against my ankle mere seconds before Rafe wrapped his arms around me. I turned into him and put my head on his shoulder to hide my tears. I didn't want to hurt him by showing how badly the news of Liam's accident had shaken me. My feelings for Liam were complicated, but I should have known my wonderful husband would understand.

He smoothed my hair and whispered in my ear, "It's OK to be upset, but maybe he'll be fine. And Dane is right. We don't know anything yet. Let's just stay calm until we find out something for sure."

He walked me over to the couch where just a moment before he and Penny had been napping and helped me sit down. He took the soft blanket he'd been using and spread it across my knees. "Benjamin, please take care of Chaun, and T-8, you stay here with Newton in case any questions about T-8/Lawton productions come up. Maddy, will you help me in the kitchen please? I think we're gonna need some coffee."

Chapter 7
A Vigil

RAFE AND T-8 had grown up together living on the streets. They'd often been hungry, so Rafe's first impulse was always to feed someone whenever they had troubles. Rafe hadn't been part of my family long enough yet to know that Maddy was utterly hopeless at cooking and food prep.

Despite her lack of culinary skills, she bravely followed him into the kitchen. At the very least she could make tea and put some cookies on a plate.

Rafe, on the other hand, is a genius in the kitchen. Within a very few minutes he came back carrying a tray packed with sandwiches, cookies, chips, snacks, fruit, coffee, and sodas. It looked like it could be the entire contents of our kitchen. He set the tray down on the glass coffee table.

Maddy followed him out of the kitchen, and he led her over to sit beside me on the couch. He handed her a cup of tea and a plate with two of the lemon cookies she always turns to in a crisis.

He brought me a plate with a ham and cheese sandwich slathered with spicy mustard and a huge handful of potato chips, along with a glass of lemonade. I was sure he'd eventually eat something himself but knowing him it would probably be something like two blueberries and a sip of mineral water.

Benjamin hovered near the edge of the group consisting of Newton, Captain Peter Roberts, and Dane. None of them were eating. I could plainly read the worry on Newton's face.

T-8 got up and brought Chaun a ham sandwich and a cup of black coffee. "Let's eat outside near the pool," he said as he handed him the plate. Despite his efforts to always be perceived as the coolest guy in any group, T-8 was surprisingly fond of Chaun, who is decidedly not conventionally cool.

Chaun shook his head. "I'd rather stay here in case there's any news."

T-8 nodded and brought chairs from the kitchen for the two of them. I had to smile at the typical T-8 oblivious behavior. There were at least four other people standing, but he didn't even offer to bring them chairs.

Then again, I should probably give him the benefit of the doubt. Maybe he'd looked around and seen that if anyone wanted to sit, there were plenty of empty spots on the long couch, the matching loveseat, the easy chair, and the rocker in the corner.

Sure. Maybe that was it. Anything is possible.

Each person present cared about Liam in our own way, so for the most part we were just pretending to be sociable. Except for Chaun who wolfed down most of his sandwich, the rest of us were barely eating. We'd been going through those polite motions of sociability for about an hour when the shrill ringtone of Dane's police phone broke the stillness.

We were all startled, but Chaun jumped a mile and dropped his plate. He was so intent on hearing whatever news Dane received that he didn't even notice when Penny took over clean-up duty and ran off with the last bite of his sandwich.

Penny was so thrilled with her prize that I didn't have the heart to leave the room to chase after her. Besides, I wanted to be right here and paying full attention if Dane got any word about Liam's fate.

We were as still as statues while we waited for Dane to pass on the news to us. At first, his eyes lit up. After another minute his face fell, and we could tell the rest of the news was bad.

"Thank you," he said just before he disconnected, "Please keep me posted if you find anything else."

He closed his eyes and sighed before he slipped the phone back into his pocket. "The plane went down in a very remote area. They've tried to contact the pilot on radio and got no response. Cell coverage out there is spotty, so the fact that neither Liam nor the pilot is answering their calls may not mean anything. It will probably take the rescuers all night to search the area. They'll keep me informed."

We all groaned. While keeping our obvious worries about our friend to ourselves, we told each other everything would be okay. Eventually, both Rafe and Chaun fell asleep sitting up. Benjamin looked dead on his feet, and Newton had massive dark rings around his eyes. Maddy was trembling with exhaustion, fear, and worry.

It was too much stress to bear. We couldn't continue like this.

I stood up. "We can't all exhaust ourselves while we're waiting to hear the news because there may come a time when Liam needs our help. Here's what I propose."

"We keep one or two people awake monitoring Dane's phone." I looked at him. "I promise they will wake you right away if it rings, but you should sleep now if you can, because later you may be too busy. T-8, you take the sofa in my office. Newton, do you still have a key to Liam's place?'

He nodded.

"Good. Dane and Maddy can sleep in the guest room over there. Benjamin and Chaun, you can use the guest room and the couch here or drive home if you'd rather sleep in your own beds. Rafe will be using our bedroom, and I'll join him there later when it's my turn to sleep. Newton, you and I will take first watch. We can sleep later, but right now, we need to talk anyway so it might as well be us on watch."

Rafe started to protest, but a huge yawn interrupted his first words.

I gave him 'the look.'

I hadn't been a wife for very long, but it hadn't taken me much time to master 'the look.' I'm a quick learner.

I took my husband's arm. "You know you're not a real superhero—just a regular guy. You nearly died the other day. You need to rest."

He shrugged sheepishly and then got up and walked toward our bedroom. "Promise you'll wake me if you hear anything?"

"I promise."

He smiled his angel smile, but he looked like he was exhausted. He trudged away without another word of protest. That alone was an indication that he must be totally beat.

Newton watched him go. "I'll get Maddy and Dane settled and be right back." The three of them left through the sliding door in the back, so I guessed they planned to use the gate between Liam's and my yard.

Liam had boarded the gate up after I married Rafe, but he'd calmed down a few weeks later and now it was back to being the easy passage it had been before. He'd restored the chicken gate between our properties too.

On the far side of the room, Chaun and Benjamin held a quick whispered discussion. Benjamin announced their decision. "Since we only live a short distance away, we'll head home. But please remember to call us the instant you hear anything." They went out the front door to go to their own home, less than a half mile away.

I opened the door to the linen closet in the hall and pulled out some sheets and pillows for T-8. I was going to make the bed for him, but he surprised me by taking the pile of linens from my hands.

"I can handle it myself. You've got enough on your plate." He smiled and went into my home office, closing the door behind him.

I went to the kitchen and put on a fresh pot of coffee. Newton and I had a lot to discuss.

Chapter 8
Heart-to-Heart

The coffee had just finished its drip cycle when Newton came in through the slider. "Sit down," he said. "You look dead on your feet." He took two RIO-branded mugs from the cabinet above the coffee maker and filled them with the aromatic brew.

"We need some snacks to go along with the coffee," he said before he pulled my 'secret stash' cookie jar out of the cabinet over the refrigerator. I kept it hidden away in the highest cabinet to discourage any late-night cookie binges.

The inconvenient location wasn't helping to reduce my cookie consumption. He laughed when he opened it and looked inside. "You're gonna need a lot more cookies."

I'd already known there were exactly four cookies left in the bin. I'd been saving them for a potential cookie emergency. After a moment's reflection, I realized this qualified.

"Don't worry. I'll ask Gus to bring a bunch of cookies from RIO over in the morning," he said. Then he pulled out his phone and sent a message to Gus Simmons, his VP of international sales, who was also the husband of my best friend Theresa. Theresa ran food services at RIO, so getting his hands on a couple of batches of RIO's famous chocolate chip cookies wouldn't be an issue for Gus.

Crisis averted.

Newton can be maddening, but he always comes through for me. I smiled fondly at him, before remembering we were currently on the outs.

He took a sip of the steaming black coffee in his mug. "Okay. Let me have it," he said. "I know I deserve it."

I took a deep breath. "Let's not even discuss how unthinkable it was for you to take *Tranquility* and leave Rafe and me stranded while we were on a dive." My voice got very loud when I remembered how Newton's actions had almost ruined our last day on Little Cayman. "ON OUR HONEYMOON."

He nodded. "It was a terrible thing to do. But I knew you'd be okay. And in my defense, you weren't answering your phone, and I needed you."

I shook my head. "No, you wanted me; you didn't need me. You have any number of trained operatives you could have called on…"

Newton opened his mouth to interrupt me, but I held up my hand in the universal 'stop right there' sign.

"I don't understand all the details about this organization you and Liam are involved in. All I really know is that you're the good guys in some global fight. But it's your fight. Not mine."

"If you knew…" he started.

I gave him the stop gesture again. "I've made it clear to both you and Liam that I want no part of it. Going undercover is too stressful for me. I'm not cut out for that kind of work."

He nodded. "I agree. I miscalculated how difficult going under-cover would be for you. It's just that you were so good against Seb Lukin…"

I shook my head. "I never tried to be someone I'm not with him. All I did was stand up for what I believe in, and I only did what I had to do to help people who needed help."

I took a deep breath, fighting to stay on topic. "But whether I'm good at the job or not isn't really the issue here. You dragged me away from my new husband less than a week after our wedding. You never gave me a chance to decide on my own whether or not I wanted to do it. You railroaded me into your operation without the proper training and background. You didn't have a good plan in place, and you gave me no real backup. That slipshod approach put me in incredible danger. You even put my innocent new puppy at risk, and you very nearly got me killed. They shot both Rafe and me. They beat Liam to within an inch of his life, and he may never regain full use of his hands. The whole operation was a disaster."

Newton looked down at his own hands, and I noticed they were shaking before he stuffed them in his pockets. "I know. I'm sorry. After we realized how bad the situation was, we tried to get you to come home. We sent you the code word several times."

I frowned. "Next time, forget the code words. Just say: 'Come home. Get outta there. The mission is over.' Use whatever words you want to use, as long as it's clear what you mean."

"Next time?" he said. "You mean you're willing to take on another mission?"

"No," I said. "And whatever you've got going on with Rafe's movie, end it. Right now."

Chapter 9
A Hard Conversation

THERE WAS a moment of stunned silence before Newton said, "How did you know I had people there?"

I rolled my eyes at him. "How could I not know? My life goes along for years without touching any crime, without any bad guys coming after me, without any unexpected dangers, and then you arrive in my life and almost immediately every scumbag in the Caribbean is after us. At first, I was willing to let it go because I thought I could handle the danger—and because I was so happy to have you back in my life. But now you're getting people I care about involved in your intrigues and putting them in danger they're not equipped to handle. I draw the line when your enemies target my husband. This has to stop."

He sighed. "I know, and I agree with you. But unfortunately, the consortium is the kind of organization that once you get in, it's not that easy to get out."

I couldn't believe what I heard. "And that's why you got me involved? Your own daughter? Because you knew that after I accepted the first mission, I'd never be able to get out?"

He shook his head. "No, I got you involved because I thought you could help me get out."

His statement puzzled me "I thought you were the head guy in this top secret organization. Who's stopping you from getting out?"

He bit his lip. "I'm not *the* top guy, but I am *one of* the top guys. And that actually makes it harder to quit. Someone at your level could get out just by refusing to take on the next few missions they offer. At my level, they'd get nervous that I know too much."

I tried not to show my anger. "First of all, I never agreed to join the consortium, whatever it is, and I never agreed to take on any missions at all. So it seems to me that I shouldn't have any trouble opting out since I never opted in."

He looked sad. "They think you accepted at least a couple of missions. Like the time you and I went out to the *Golden Kelp*. Or the time you and Liam teamed up to rescue the kidnapped women..."

I interrupted him again. "First of all, you insisted on joining me on the *Golden Kelp* that time, even though I didn't want you to come along. That wasn't a mission under the control of the consortium. I decided to go on that yacht to protect RIO's reputation. And the next time, when Liam and I rescued those poor women, it was because I wanted to get my friends back before I lost them forever."

Newton defended himself. "Interfering in Seb Lukin's drug deliveries? Going after Lauren Forster? Hiring Davy Jones? You have to admit from the outside, it might look like you're part of the team."

"I didn't even know there was a team to be part of back then. Like I said, I was just doing the right thing," I shook my head in denial.

So did he.

"And then you went after Kraken Industries," he said. "And you can't deny that you knew right from the start that one was a mission."

I nodded. "But you left me no choice."

Stubbornly, we glared at each other. I couldn't see a way we would ever reach an agreement or any sort of understanding on this topic.

Suddenly Rafe was there beside me, instead of in bed sleeping where he belonged. He looked right at Newton. "You got her into this. You will get her out. Or we'll go so far away you'll never find us, and that will be the last time you ever see Fin."

Newton looked so sad it nearly broke my heart. "I wish it could work that way. I'd gladly spend the rest of my life missing my daughter if it meant she would be safe and happy. But we all know it won't work like that. You two are famous. No matter how hard you try to keep a low profile, do you honestly think nobody would recognize you? And you'd have to live a quiet life far away from here. Could you do that? No more jetting off to exotic locations for dive trips or to make movies. No more columns in popular magazines. No more global awards for either of you. Never see Maddy, Theresa, Genevra, T-8, or especially Dougie? Never again?"

Newton brushed a tear from his eye. "It's not that easy to leave the people you love behind. I tried it when Fin was little and I failed miserably. I was so happy when I turned up unannounced all those years later and you let me into your life. I've loved getting to know you."

"I'm so proud of you, and because you care so much and you have such a strong moral compass, I knew you'd be good at this stuff. I knew you'd always see any operation through to the end. I lost sight of what was best for you because I wanted to show you off. I'm sorry, but I did it, and now here we are."

My heart was breaking. I'd only known Newton for a few short years, but he is my father and I love him. I could see that even though he'd brought it on himself, he was in a hard place now. He obviously didn't know how to get out of the situation either.

I wasn't sure what to say.

Luckily, the ringing from Dane's phone broke the silence.

Newton pushed the button. "Dane Scott's phone. Please hold." He stood up and went to the sliding door that led to my back yard. "I'll be right back."

"We're coming with you," I said. Rafe went to my office door and rapped with his knuckles. "Tate, we're going next door."

Tate's only response was a loud snore.

We all shrugged, silently agreeing to let him sleep. We could easily wake him if it turned out that there was anything we needed to talk about.

Rafe and I joined hands and followed Newton across the lawn and through the gate that led to Liam's house.

Chapter 10
Missing

MADDY AND DANE hadn't gone to the big comfy bed in Liam's master bedroom, or even the slightly smaller one in his guest room. Instead, they were under a lightweight blanket, dozing on opposite ends of the couch in Liam's home office.

Maddy awakens easily, so she popped up as soon as she heard the sliding door glide open. "What is it? Have they found Liam?" She'd always been fond of Liam and she was thoroughly impressed by his many talents.

During those years when Liam and I had been engaged. she'd expected him to become a permanent part of her family. Plus she was soft-hearted—she hated to see anyone she cared about hurt or in danger.

Newton shrugged. "I haven't talked to them. It's Dane's phone. They're on hold. He'll have to get the news."

Dane bit back a yawn and took the phone from Newton's outstretched hand. "Dane Scott here," he said.

He listened intently for several seconds while the rest of us held our breath. We could tell the exact moment he heard bad news because his skin instantly turned a pale ashy grey.

Maddy and I both tried to hold back our stricken gasps. Rafe immediately put his arms around me and fighting to hold back tears, I rested my head on his shoulder.

Dane was still listening, but he reached out and grasped Maddy's hand, giving her a reassuring squeeze. Newton went pale and left the room. He and Liam had been friends for years. Newton was the person who'd originally recruited Liam into the international law enforcement consortium, so he felt the pain of loss twice over.

Dane said, "Thank you. Please keep me informed if you find anything else. Someone will always be able to track me down at this number." He disconnected the call and took a ragged breath.

"They found the wreckage. The plane definitely crashed. They've been trying to put out the fire, but the pilot must have stopped for fuel just a few minutes before the plane went down, because the fire's still raging. If Liam and the pilot had been trapped in the plane when it crashed, there's no chance they survived. The rescuers have started a search and recovery mission in the surrounding area just in case they managed to bail out before the plane went down and the fire started. If Liam's out there somewhere, they'll find him."

I remembered how cold it had been while Rafe and I were in Alaska. And I knew that Liam's hands were still healing after the Kraken team had broken all his fingers. And since it wasn't the first time the evil ones had broken his fingers, nobody was sure how much use of his hands he'd ever regain.

The thought of Liam being alone, probably injured, stranded at night in the freezing wilderness, without even being able to use his hands, nearly killed me. I felt so helpless.

Rafe knew that some part of me would always care for Liam, and he understood. He rubbed my back gently to soothe some of my sorrow and pain. When I stopped shaking, he said, "I'll call Benjamin and Chaun to let them know. Then if you want, we can charter a plane and fly out there to help in the search."

"You can take my j…" Newton started to say before remembering that Liam had been traveling on Newton's private jet. I could see on his face the exact moment when Newton's guilt over the accident doubled or even tripled. "Dane, next time they contact you, let them know I'll personally foot the bill for the search and recovery efforts."

I looked out the window where the sun was just about to rise. That was Chico's signal to herald the day and make sure everyone was awake. You couldn't blame him for his cheerful cock-a-doodle-doo. He had no idea that anything was wrong. How could he? When he finished his crowing, Chico and Henrietta came in through the open sliding door looking for their breakfast.

I left the sanctuary of Rafe's arms and we slipped out to my own house to fill a bowl with seeds for Chico and Henrietta. When we came in, T-8 was slumped at the kitchen counter.

"What's going on?" he asked. "Has there been any news?"

"Fire," I said. There was no way I could choke out more than that one word.

Rafe took T-8's arm and pulled him over to the counter. "Help me make some coffee, Bro. I think we're gonna need a lot of it this morning."

For once, T-8 didn't remind Rafe that he disliked being called Bro. His face went pale beneath his tan as he realized the implication of that one word I'd forced out.

Chapter 11
Obligations

T-8 IS EVEN MORE useless in a kitchen than I am, but he could set out a loaf of bread, some butter, a jar of jam, and boxes of cereal for those who wanted to eat. Rafe efficiently loaded up the coffeemaker and then made a cup of tea and a slice of dry toast for Maddy.

Tea and toast were her usual breakfast, but I could have told him she wouldn't be able to eat it. She might drink some of the tea, but until we took some action to find Liam, she wouldn't be able to do more than pretend to eat.

Once I'd put food and water out for Chico and Henrietta, I took Penny for a quick walk. When we returned, the room was still full of silent, weary, shell-shocked people. I put down a bowl of kibble for my dog, but even she seemed unable to eat.

I poured a cup of coffee and picked up my phone to call Benjamin and Chaun to let them know what we'd found out. Chaun answered on the first ring. I told him about the fire.

"We're on our way," he said. The tremor in his voice was plain to hear.

Rafe and I made eye contact, and he gave a slight nod. As though he'd spoken aloud, I knew we were on the same wavelength.

"Dad—Newton—if you meant it when you said you'd charter a plane, Rafe and I would like to join the search for Liam. Can you help us get there fast?" My father is a multi-billionaire, so chartering a plane is not a big expense for him, but still, I hated to ask. Especially after our frank discussion last night. It felt like I was taking advantage of him.

He nodded. "Mind if I tag along with you two? I'd like to pitch in on the search. If you want, we can probably leave this afternoon."

T-8 stepped away from the counter, where he'd been moodily staring out the window. "Rafe and Fin have an unbreakable commitment today." He looked at us. "You have that promotional tie-in shoot this morning. New soft drink, remember?"

We both groaned.

"Can't you put it off?" I asked.

He shook his head sadly. "No can do. They timed the advertising campaign to build excitement before the movie release. They've got all kinds of media commitments already in place. They planned that both the movie and the drink would hit the market on the same day. We won't have trouble with the movie making the deadline since we're ready for edits and scoring, but the beverage company doesn't have anything at all they can use, and they need all the time we can give them."

I sighed. "Can't they use some of the footage from the film?"

He shook his head. "Nope. The contract states that you and Rafe will be opening and drinking 'Ice Water' at the bar at Ray's Place. We don't have any footage like that."

Rafe said, "No way to get out of it? Postpone it?"

T-8 shook his head. "Liam negotiated the contract, so you know it was airtight. And you also know that RIO needs the fees they'll earn for the use of the RIO name and facility. Not to mention Fin's appearance in the spot."

Hands on my hips, I demanded, "Well then, how long will this shoot take?"

T-8 looked sheepish. "You're committed to stay with it for at least a week or until they are satisfied, whichever comes first." He held up his hands in a placating gesture. "But realistically, it should be no more than two or three days. After the first week, you can cancel your participation outright or if you choose to continue, they have to pay double rates. They have a big incentive to finish on time."

Newton stepped forward. "I hate to wait that long. I want someone on site right away to represent Liam's interests. I'll fly out today. But don't worry, Fin. I owe you one. I'll charter another plane for you to fly out as soon as you and Rafe finish filming the ad. Who knows? You could end up arriving just a few hours behind me."

We both knew that wasn't likely. I'd already been on enough film sets to know that filming always consumes the entire time allotted to it, if not more. But I couldn't see a way out of this so I nodded. "Thank you."

"Are we even now?" he whispered, the hope clear in his voice.

I bit my lip. I was still angry, and I knew chartering a plane wouldn't even put a dent in Newton's pocket change, so it wasn't like he'd made some huge sacrifice on my behalf.

But I love him, and I know he loves me. I wanted us to be close again. On the other hand, I didn't want him to think it was okay to keep pulling me into his missions.

"Getting there," I said. "But right now, I'm going for a dive. I need to clear my head before that commercial shoot kicks off later this morning. We'll see you all at RIO as soon as we've finished. T-8, will you bring Penny with you when you leave? That way we won't have to leave her alone or stop back here to pick her up when we're finished."

T-8 nodded. "Sure thing," he said. "I love that little rascal." Penny glowed like she knew exactly what he'd said. And she was so smart, she probably did.

I thanked him, and then Rafe and I went out the rear slider to cut across the backyard to pick up our dive bags.

We have doubles and even triples of all our dive equipment, and we always stow a set of our gear in the breezeway between my house and the garage. We went in and pulled a couple of dive skins off the hanging rack and folded them into our gear bags. We loaded the bags and a couple of empty tanks I needed to return to RIO's dive shop into the trunk of my car, and we were good to go.

As word of our relationship had leaked out into the world, we sometimes found ourselves accosted by press and fans alike at RIO. They knew if my car was in its assigned slot that I'd eventually appear, and they frequently staked it out.

Instead of using the reserved parking space with my name on it right outside the main entrance, I'd taken to parking in an anonymous spot in the far section of the RIO parking lot to possibly avoid a mob scene. It was a long way to carry our gear, but Rafe was so popular and so recognizable that I liked to ensure he had every bit of privacy we could wrest from the world.

It was still early, so other than the café and the dive shop, none of RIO's attractions were open. Most divers were either out on a day trip or inside taking a class, so there weren't a lot of people around yet.

But we never knew how the situation might have changed by the time we returned from a dive, making the parking ruse a simple precaution against a possible mob scene. I'd seen what happens when fans decide to besiege Rafe, and it's scary.

We were here so early that I thought we had a shot at beating Stewie in to work this morning, but as usual, he was already hard at work. We could hear him singing an old Neil Young song while we were still at least fifty feet away.

Rafe winked at me, and I nodded. Then we both joined in singing on the chorus. "Searching for a heart of gold…" We sang as loudly and as off-key as we could. Stewie's singing stopped abruptly, and his laughter bubbled out around ours.

He poked his head out through the top of the open Dutch door. "Good morning. You two are here early. Trying to get a jump on the film crew?"

Stewie seemed his usual cheerful self, so I assumed he hadn't heard about Liam's accident yet. I wished I didn't have to be the one to tell him. His face crumpled at the news, and although he didn't actually cry, he blinked back tears.

"That man has more lives than a cat," he said. "Just you watch. He'll come through this without a scratch. Maybe a dislocated shoulder and some more broken fingers, but not another scratch." He tried bravely to offer a smile.

I knew Stewie wasn't being flippant about the danger to Liam. He had great respect for the younger man, but his first thought was to comfort me, and he knew I'd be worried sick about Liam.

Rafe and I nodded, but there wasn't much we could say since none of us knew any details yet.

"We're going diving," I said. "Probably to Fish Tank. The film crew will be arriving a little later, and we'll be back for that. Will you please ask Noah to be sure he has plenty of snacks and refreshments ready for them? And they'll probably be here for lunch and dinner, so he should prepare for a larger than usual crowd."

Stewie laughed. "Once word gets out that Rafe is here, the crowd will get even larger. At least it'll be a profitable day at Ray's Place. Although I think they're probably already aware of it, I'll remind Noah and Theresa about what's going on."

Then Stewie helped us carry full tanks down the dock to my boat, the *Tranquility*. I almost cried when I saw her up ahead, riding proudly on the gentle waves and gleaming in the sunrise. I hadn't been away that long, but I felt like I hadn't seen my beloved boat in ages.

We stowed the tanks and our gear, then I climbed up to the flying bridge and started the engines while Stewie and Rafe took care of the lines. When Rafe raised his arm in the signal that we were good to go, I backed the boat out of her slip and we headed out to the dive site.

Fish Tank is one of the most popular dive sites on Grand Cayman because of the shallow depth, easy entry, gentle currents, and its abundant and vital sea life. Rafe tied us to the mooring ball while I idled in place. Once he signaled that *Tranquility* was secure, I shut the engines off and hurried down the ladder.

I really needed this dive. As soon as I hit the water, I took a deep breath through the regulator and felt my anxiety begin to melt away. I was home again, in my happy place, and soon, I would find the solace I needed.

We followed the mooring line down to the reef plateau and then swam into the mild current flowing along the gentle slope. The bottom was rife with sea sponges, elegant staghorn coral, and colorful sea fans, all swaying serenely in the slight surge.

We joined a school of brown chromis and stuck with them until we met up with a pair of Queen Angelfish and a couple of indigo hamlets who were far too cute for us to resist. We abandoned the school of chromis to watch the hamlets cavort.

Almost immediately, a couple of parrotfish swam directly in front of us, and as we turned to watch them pecking at the coral, we noticed a trumpetfish lurking in a nearby stand of sea grass. The abundance and variety of life at this site was so entrancing that our bottom time flew by. Luckily our dive computers vibrated in sync when it was time to head back to the *Tranquility*.

We held hands during our three minute safety stop at fifteen feet, watching the teeming life below us with joy. We saw a couple of conch moving sedately across the sand, and even a few garden eels popped their heads up, swaying in the current as though waving goodbye. I took a deep breath and felt the last vestiges of stress leave my shoulders.

Chapter 12
The Shoot

WE'D JUST FINISHED GETTING *Tranquility* settled in her slip at RIO when a stunning leggy blonde approached us. She wore hot pink short-shorts, a matching pink sun visor, and huge designer sunglasses. She carried a clipboard in her perfectly manicured hands.

"I'm Adriana," she said. "I'll escort you to hair and makeup. They're waiting for you." She glanced at her watch. "You're only a few minutes late."

I peeked at the dive watch on my wrist. "Sorry about that. We didn't mean to be late. I'm showing we're still a few minutes early."

She frowned. "And you are?"

I laughed. "Fin Fleming. And this is Rafe Cummings."

She looked me over and clearly found me totally unsatisfactory. "Of course I know Mr. Cummings," she said. "This way please."

Rafe winked and held out a hand to steady me when I stepped over the *Tranquility*'s gunwales, and then we followed Adriana.

As we passed the dive shop, I stopped and stuck my head in through the open Dutch door. "Stewie, we're back, but I have a favor to ask. Apparently, we're late, so if you get a minute, would you please dunk our gear in the rinse tank? If you don't have time, don't worry. I'll get to it myself after the shoot."

Stewie smiled. "No problem. I'll send Austin over as soon as he gets back from his break." He looked at his watch. "But I think you're right on time."

I shrugged and winked at him. "Not according to Adriana." I stepped away from the dive shop and noticed Adriana and Rafe had stopped a few paces ahead on the shell path, where it branched off to the pool house. She was tapping her foot impatiently.

She pointedly looked at her watch as I approached. "I told you you're late. And I don't want to keep Mr. Cummings out here in the sun. We don't want him to tan up too much."

"I'd be more worried about his fan base recognizing him," I said pointing over my shoulder to where a small crowd of people were staring at Rafe while trying to get up the courage to approach him. "We've been attacked by over-excited fans before."

Adriana sniffed. "I'm sure he has. But don't worry. Our security team will keep him safe. Now let's get going."

She led us to the locker room doors. "Mr. Cummings, the hair and makeup team are in there waiting for you." She handed him a card. "Here's my cellphone number if you need something or if anything's not to your liking." She smiled sweetly at him.

Then she jerked her thumb over her shoulder. "The ladies locker room is over there. They're waiting."

"Thank you, but I know my way around." I turned and went inside where a team of stylists was indeed waiting for me.

They washed my hair and then blew it dry before combing in some kind of gel so it would look wet, which it had been before they started working. When they finished with my hair, they made up my face and then held up two tiny bikinis on hangers for my inspection.

"Your contract says you get costume approval. Which one do you prefer?" said the lead stylist.

I shook my head. "I have my own wardrobe here. I'll get dressed and meet you on the set."

They packed up their bottles and brushes and wheeled the ginormous cases out of the locker room. I went to my locker, pulled out a new pair of khaki colored cargo shorts and a new blue RIO-branded T-shirt still folded neatly in its package. Blue flip-flops completed my ensemble. Now fully ready, I headed out to Ray's Place where the filming was supposed to take place.

Rafe was already sitting on one of the bar stools under the thatched roof of the tiki bar. They had turned his stool around so its back was against the edge of the bar and Rafe would be facing out toward the cameras. The lighting crew was just finishing their setup, and the makeup team was standing by in case he needed a touch up.

Which he didn't. He never did.

Several extras, including Bari, Austin, Stewie, Doc, and a few people I didn't know were on the far side of the bar, practicing miming a crowd having a great time. Oliver and Genevra were sitting at a table with Maddy and Dane, pretending to eat dinner. It was funny watching everyone acting like they were talking and laughing without making a sound. It was even funnier watching people dance with no music.

I walked over and sat on the empty stool next to Rafe. His face lit up when he saw me. I smiled back at him. I noticed Adriana scowling at me from behind him.

"You're not in costume," she said sourly.

"I have costume approval in my contract. This is the costume I've approved," I said, as pleasantly as I could. It was a struggle not to snark back at her.

She scowled but said nothing else about my apparel.

The makeup team came over and combed more of the wet-look stuff through my hair before touching up my lipstick. The lighting crew gave the director a thumbs up. The actor playing the bartender took his place behind the bar, and we began a run through.

I recited my lines. "Rafe, it's so hot. I need something cold to drink."

Maybe not the world's most intriguing opening line, but we were only filming a thirty second commercial, not Shakespeare.

Rafe looked deep into my eyes and smiled his glorious smile. "Let's order this very cool new drink I just tried. It's called Ice Water. It's like magic, because it's always cold, even without refrigeration. You're going to love it."

I nodded enthusiastically, like this was the best idea I'd ever heard, and Rafe turned to the actor behind the bar. "Two Ice Waters, please."

"Coming right up, Mr. Cummings," said the beaming bartender. He reached below the counter and pulled out two silvery white bottles.

The name of the drink, Ice Water, was printed on the label in blue letters in a vaguely runic typeface. He placed the bottles on the bar and smiled at the camera. His perfect teeth gleamed.

The idea of this new drink was that each bottle contained a small, highly pressurized capsule of compressed carbon dioxide. The sudden change in pressure when the consumer unscrews the cap releases the pressurized carbon dioxide—commonly known as dry ice. The sudden intense cold is supposed to immediately evaporate and instantly cool the bottle's contents.

Rafe and I each reached for a bottle and pretended to twist the special cap. Then we lifted the bottles to our lips and mimed taking a drink.

"Perfect," said the director. "Do it just like that. Let's roll."

Rafe was famous for making every take unique when he was starring in one of his beloved action movies. Apparently, this director wasn't looking for spontaneity.

Good luck to him.

The makeup team came over again and combed even more of the wet-look stuff through my hair and touched up my lipstick again. They looked Rafe over, and as usual, decided he looked perfect. I had to wonder why Rafe never needed a touch up, but I always did. I guess that's why he's a star.

As soon as they walked away, the lighting crew gave the director a thumbs up. "Places everyone," he called.

The actor playing the bartender resumed his place behind the bar, and we began filming.

"Rafe, it's so hot. I need something cold to drink," I said, trying not to laugh at my banal lines.

"Let's order this very cool new drink I just tried. It's called Ice Water. It's like magic, because it's always cold, even without refrigeration. You're going to love it." Rafe smiled his glorious smile and paused for my excited nodding to subside. Then he turned to the actor behind the bar. "Two Ice Waters please."

"Coming right up, Mr. Cummings," said the beaming bartender. He reached below the counter and pulled out two of the silvery white bottles with icy blue letters spelling out the name of the drink. He placed them on the bar and smiled at the camera.

Rafe and I each reached for a bottle and twisted the special cap.

There was a puff of vapor from the lightweight metal bottle in my hand. It grew almost painfully cold for an instant before its temperature quickly began to subside to a more bearable level.

The bottle in Rafe's hand also emitted its expected puff of vapor, but instead of lifting the bottle to drink as we'd done in rehearsal, he leaned over and kissed me, still holding the bottle front and center, in the perfect position so the label faced the camera.

Just as his lips touched mine, his Ice Water bottle exploded, sending shards of metal and glass flying. I flinched and ducked, avoiding the flying shrapnel by shutting my eyes and turning my head.

When I opened my eyes, Rafe's hand that had been holding the bottle was already dripping blood, and the poor actor playing the bartender was holding a hand to his cheek. Blood gushed between his fingers.

Lots of blood. Covering his face and staining his clothes.

He looked stunned. "My face," he whimpered.

Doc pushed her way through the make-believe party crowd and approached the actor. "I'm Doctor Warren, but you can call me Doc. May I take a look?"

I could tell the actor was in shock because he simply stared at her. She took his lack of response as permission and gently moved his hand away from the wound on his cheek. Stewie raced up beside her and placed her medical bag on the bar next to her.

Doc gently cleaned the wound with some gauze from her bag. "You'll need stitches. I can do them here, but I'd like to take you downtown to see a friend of mine. He's a plastic surgeon, and if we let him do the work it will help to minimize any potential for scarring. Is that okay with you?"

He whimpered at the word 'scarring,' before he drew in a deep breath and nodded.

"You okay, Rafe?" Doc asked.

He was wrapping a paper napkin around his hand to staunch the bleeding. "Just a scratch. All I need is an adhesive strip. Fin can see to it."

"Hmmm," she said. "It looks like a little more than a scratch, but I don't think you're in any real danger. If you're sure you don't need my attention right away, I'll check on you when I get back. This man's injury looks more severe, and his face is crucial to his future. I want to make sure we take care of him first, but you're welcome to come along with us if you want someone to look at your hand right away."

"I'll be fine. I'll come by the infirmary later and you can see for yourself." He smiled at her and reached out his undamaged hand to clasp mine.

Doc helped the injured actor come around to the front of the bar and walked him out to the main parking lot while Stewie called one of her team to meet them there with our ambulance. They were gone from the lot within minutes.

Noah and Austin had quickly gone to work cleaning up the blood and sweeping up the remnants of the bottles scattered around the floor and on the bar.

The whole emergency was over so quickly that the film crew and the crowd scene extras hadn't even started to chatter yet. Many of them were still wondering exactly what had happened.

"We'll be right back," I said.

I slid off my stool and Rafe and I walked across the lawn to the backdoor of RIO's main building. We went directly to the infirmary where I cleaned the gash in Rafe's hand and put pressure on it to staunch the bleeding. Once the flow of blood stopped, I put a small bandage on the wound to keep it clean and we were good to go.

But before we went back, I wanted to discuss the incident with Rafe.

"Do you think that exploding bottle was an accident?" I asked.

"Nope," he said. "Do you?"

Chapter 13
Rumination

I took his good hand and led him over to the infirmary's small waiting area. The room contained a mini fridge filled with soft drinks and a pod-style coffee maker atop a small table in one corner. A couch and two chairs faced the wall-hung television set in the opposite corner. A coffee table and two end tables rounded out the furnishings.

Rafe grabbed two cans of lemonade from the mini-fridge and joined me on the couch. We leaned back and I put my head on his shoulder. We both kicked off our flip-flops and put our feet on the coffee table, even though we knew Doc would never have allowed it if she'd been around.

Rafe gingerly pulled the tab tops on the two cans and handed one to me. "You could have been badly hurt, maybe even killed," he said. "I can't believe the bottle exploding like that was an accident."

"It wasn't," I said. "But you were the target, not me, and especially not that nice young actor. I hope he'll be okay."

"I know. Poor guy. Well, he'll always have a spot in my movies, no matter what his face ends up looking like," Rafe said.

I smiled at him. "Good. He deserves a break. But you do know that if you hadn't changed your performance from the way we rehearsed it, that shrapnel would have hit you." I reached over and caressed his neck. "Right here. Your carotid. You'd have been dead within minutes even with Doc standing only a few feet away." The thought made me shiver.

"But why do you think I was the target? It could have been Newton's enemies after you…" he said.

"I'm not the one who was floating fifty feet under the ice with a rope tied around my neck and my regulator floating free when my alleged safety divers left me there to die. The movie set had a dead defibrillator, even though you know Tate and Liam usually run a tight set when it comes to health and safety. We barely got the AED charged fast enough to bring you back. That was just a few days ago. You're lucky to be here."

He kissed my hair. "I'm lucky I had you to come to my rescue, Lady Superhero. But then someone tried to poison you and Tate. And now Liam's plane goes down…" He bit his lip. "There's something very bad going on.

"Ya think?" I asked him. "I'd assume it was the Kraken Industries team seeking revenge if they hadn't all died on the beach that day."

He rubbed the back of my hand with the long, cool fingers of his uninjured hand. "We need to talk to Newton. He's going to have to tell us what's going on. We've got to find a way to get you out of the crosshairs."

I shook my head. "Looks to me like you're the one they're aiming for, Love."

Pensively, he said, "Nope. The attempts on me are just warning shots over Newton's bow. He'd feel bad if I died, but it would kill him if anything happened to you. By coming after me, they're letting him know that they can get to you whenever they want to. At most I'm collateral damage to them. They want something from him. They want it bad, and they aren't squeamish about how they get it."

"He's right, you know," said Newton from the waiting room doorway. "Next time they strike they'll have their sights set on you. I can't allow that to happen. I'll give in and do whatever it is they want me to do if doing it can prevent anything bad happening to you."

He walked over to the coffee maker and selected a pod. "We need a plan to keep you two safe while I work this out. And we have to find Liam and bring him home." He paused briefly while he waited for the coffee machine to stop hissing. "And I think there's a mole on my team."

For the first time ever, Newton looked his age. His skin was gray and pale, his hair was ever-so-slightly disheveled, and a corner of his RIO branded polo shirt was untucked.

On anyone else, those facts wouldn't be worth a second glance. But this was Newton Fleming, making even this minor level of dishevelment worrying. Although each of those details was irrelevant on its own, together they painted a picture of distraction and fear. If we could solve the real problems he faced, he'd bounce right back to his usual confident suave self.

I spoke up. "We're safe enough right here, right now, in this room. So let's attack first things first. I think identifying and neutralizing the mole will make the other problems a lot easier to solve. Agreed?'

He lifted his shoulders and turned out his palms in an exaggerated shrug. "Yes, but my consortium is small, and I have very few confidantes. If there's a mole, I don't see where or how they're getting their insider info."

I patted his knee. "We'll figure it out. There are a finite number of ways they could be getting the details of your ops. I'm no expert, but I do read a lot of spy novels..."

He and Rafe both chuckled.

"...and from my advanced research in genre fiction, I believe these are the most likely methods. They could be using electronic surveillance. Someone you trust could be feeding them information you told them in confidence; someone could overhear you talking on your phone or in public; or someone you normally don't take notice of could be eavesdropping or examining paperwork in your home or office." I paused. "Anything I missed?"

He smiled at me with something almost like his usual verve. "I think that covers it."

"Good. Step one. We have Chaun run a complete sweep of your penthouse, the Fleming Environmental offices, your car, Maddy's place, Joely's..."

He interrupted. "Joely's not involved. She'd never..."

I held up a hand. "I agree. She'd never. But that doesn't prevent somebody from slipping a bug in her purse or cloning her phone. We have to check everyone."

He didn't look happy, but he nodded. "That includes Gus, Theresa, Oliver, and Genevra." The group consisted of family and our closest friends.

Gus Simmons is his VP of international sales, and in addition to being my best friend and the VP of food services at RIO, Theresa is Gus's wife. My brother Oliver works at Fleming Environmental, and Genevra, his new wife, is a member of Newton's international law enforcement consortium.

For years, she worked for Liam at Quokka Media as well as with me at RIO, making her ideally positioned for spying. She's also one of my closest friends—or at least she had been until I found out that secretly she'd been my "handler" for Newton's consortium.

No matter what, I'd have staked my life on the loyalty of every one of these people, so if we could quickly eliminate all of them as the mole, then we could focus faster on more likely suspects.

"I agree we need to include them," I said. "And we'll have to look at other people who might have the opportunity to overhear something you might not want them to know. Maddy. Dane. Stewie. Tate, T-8/Lawton Productions employees, and Quokka Media staff. Everyone at Fleming Environmental and RIO. It could end up being a wide circle. That's why it will help us find the leak faster if we can eliminate the people we're most comfortable with as quickly as possible."

He nodded bleakly. "I get it."

"Good," I said. "Let's each make a list of everyone we come in contact with that could have access to what should be secure information. If you've been to a restaurant, a bar, anywhere that you might have carelessly dropped a word, list the time and location.'

Rafe and Newton both nodded somberly. We all knew this was serious life and death level business.

When I was sure they were on board with the plan, I continued. "We may have to use that list to identify people outside our day-to-day circle, and I firmly believe that's where we'll most likely find the leak."

Newton opened his mouth, thought better of speaking, and closed it. A second later, he finally spoke. "I hate suspecting my family and employees."

I nodded. "Me too. I trust all my friends and everyone in our family, but between all our business interests we each have a lot of outside contacts. Couple that with people who randomly cross our paths on any given day and the list could get huge pretty fast."

I rose and went over to Doc's desk in the main room of the infirmary. In one of the desk drawers I found notebooks and pens for each of us and went back to the waiting area. "No time like the present. Let's get started."

They both bent their heads to their work.

I stood up again. "I'm going to call Chaun before I start so he can schedule an electronic sweep of all our homes and offices." I walked out and sat at Doc's desk to make the call.

Chapter 14
Take Two

I'd no sooner finished making the arrangements with Chaun when Genevra came in. "The director asked me to see if you know when you and Rafe will be back on set. He said if you're not back soon, he's going to shut down for the day and bill the costs back to RIO because of our security breach."

I sighed. "Gen, it hasn't been a great day for us so far. In fact, the last couple of days have been awful."

She nodded sympathetically. "I know. Do you want me to tell him to let everyone go home?"

I started to nod, but Rafe got to his feet and said, "No, we're on our way." He turned to Newton. "Dinner at our place tonight?"

Newton nodded and smiled. "Thank you." His voice sounded tired and old. "I'll bring dessert."

Rafe grinned at him. "Thanks. And make it a good one. My wife likes her sweets."

Knowing how true this was, we all laughed before we headed toward Ray's Place. When we approached the tiki bar, I was surprised to see Adriana sitting on "my" barstool, dressed in a teensy pink bikini. Hair and makeup people clustered around her, doing their thing.

"Hey, what's all this?" Rafe asked the director when we were near enough for conversation.

"I thought you might want to do a run through with Adriana, see if it works out better. She's a pro, and your wife…"

"Is a pro as well," said Rafe. "Fin's been in more movies than I have. And she's in my contract, Jon. You know that."

"Just try Adriana out. Nothing says we have to use her takes, and maybe watching Adriana will help Mrs. Cummings…"

"Fin," Rafe and I said at the same time.

"Fin," Jon, the director, continued smoothly. "Maybe it will help her to see how someone else would do it."

Rafe's ears turned red, which I knew was a sure sign he was annoyed at Jon's request. Rather than let him show his irritation in front of the crew, I put my hand on his arm. "Why not let her try? It can't hurt, and maybe I will learn something."

Rafe held very still for a minute before drawing in a deep breath. "Fat chance," he said to me. He turned to Jon. "If you want me to do a run through with Adriana, fine. But no filming."

Jon scowled but agreed to the stipulation. Adriana shot me a look of triumph, which luckily Rafe missed seeing or her chance at fame would have ended before it began.

The makeup people finished with Adriana and barely glanced at Rafe, who as always, looked spectacular. The lighting crew finished their adjustments and gave Jon the thumbs up.

The call came. "Places everyone."

To my surprise, Noah walked onto the set and stood behind the counter. He was a great looking guy, and he certainly knew his way around the bar. I guessed they'd pulled him in as a replacement for the injured actor. He'd covered his usual RIO branded tee with a colorful Hawaiian print shirt that brought out the blue of his eyes. The stylists had artfully mussed his hair so it curled over one eye. He grinned and winked at me as he moved into position.

Adriana wiggled onto her bar stool and Rafe leaned way back on his own, keeping as far away from her as he could. She scooted her stool closer. He scooted his away. I bit back a smile.

Jon watched this dance for a few seconds before speaking. "Rafe, I really liked the way you leaned over and kissed Fin in the last take. Think you could do that again?"

"Doubt it," he said. "I try to be more spontaneous than that. I like to do something a little different with each take."

This was Jon's first job as a director, and Rafe is the most popular action hero movie star in the world. Even if he was the director, no way was Jon going to be able to impose his methods or wishes on Rafe, and they both knew it.

Jon smiled a fake smile. "Okay then. Action."

Adriana licked her lips as though she'd been wandering in the desert for days. Leaning forward so her breasts were almost totally visible in her skimpy top, she said her line in a sultry voice. "Rafe, it's so hot. I need something cold to drink."

Rafe looked into the camera, not at his costar. "Let's order this very cool new drink I just tried. It's called Ice Water. It's like magic, because it's always cold, even without refrigeration. You're going to love it."

Adriana pursed her lips and nodded. Rafe turned to Noah. "Noah, two Ice Waters please." He smiled as though he and Noah were friends. Which they were.

"Coming right up, Rafe," said Noah. He reached below the counter and pulled out two silvery white bottles. He smiled at the camera and placed both bottles on the bar in front of Rafe. I noticed with surprise that the lettering on the label was red on these bottles. The first batch we'd used had blue labels.

Rafe and Adriana each picked up one of the bottles and twisted the cap. There was the expected puff of silvery mist. Adriana looked momentarily startled at the sudden coldness of the bottle, but she kept on with her performance.

She lifted the bottle to her lips and drank. And drank. It looked like she was trying to empty the entire bottle in a single go, and I thought she must be angling to replicate Cindy Crawford's iconic Pepsi commercial. Rafe took a few sips from his bottle and smiled.

"Good stuff," he said just as Adriana spewed her mouthful of water into his face. She was coughing and gasping.

When she put her hand to her throat in the universal symbol for choking, I sprang into action. I strode onto the set and pulled Adriana off her stool. I put my arms around her midsection and pumped hard, doing the Heimlich maneuver.

She was still gasping and clawing at her throat, so I did it again. This time, something flew out of her mouth. Rafe deftly caught whatever it was and put it in his pocket.

Noah poured a glass of regular water and put it on the counter in front of Adriana. She grabbed it and took a sip. "Thank you," she said to him.

He scowled. "Don't thank me. Fin's the one who saved your life. All I did was turn on a tap."

She turned to me. "Thank you," she said ungraciously. I could see she was annoyed that accidentally choking on the product might have ruined her big break. Somehow, she seemed to suspect it was my fault.

I waved my hand in the air. "No biggie. I'm glad you're okay."

Jon walked into the bar. "Let's try one more take before we finish for the day. Fin, still no chance we can get you into a bikini?"

I glared at him and folded my arms stubbornly. "I'm a PhD marine biologist, a prize-winning documentary film maker, and a celebrated underwater photographer. I wear clothes that allow me to do my work without having to worry about wardrobe malfunctions. Get over it."

His mouth dropped open. "Got it," he said finally. "Are you both up for another take?"

We nodded and took our places. Two of the makeup crew came over. One touched up my lipstick and the other dabbed at the water Adriana had spewed on Rafe's face. Lighting gave the thumbs up.

"Action," Jon said, sounding resigned.

I said my line. Rafe said his. Noah put two bottles with blue labels on the bar. Rafe and I picked them up and clinked them together before twisting off the caps. A silvery mist emerged, and the biting cold ebbed away quickly. We each took a sip from our bottle. He leaned over and kissed me, still holding his bottle so the label faced the camera. I shut my eyes and smiled dreamily.

"Cut and wrap," said Jon. "Beautiful job, you two."

Chapter 15
Diamond Girl

RAFE and I scurried away from Ray's Place and down the pier to the *Tranquility*. By now it was heading into cocktail hour, and we didn't want the growing crowd to mob Rafe or tie him up for hours signing autographs.

I climbed up to the flying bridge and started the engines while Rafe released the mooring lines. As soon as we were free, I backed out and piloted the boat out to Training Spot Two, a nearby dive site that RIO's dive instructors often use for open water skills demonstrations for some of our certification classes.

I pulled up to the mooring ball, and Rafe grabbed the line with the long-handled gaff. As soon as he finished tying us off, I went down and joined him on the deck.

"You were amazing," he said. "I believe you saved Adriana's life."

I shrugged. "All in a day's work." I held my fingers to my lips in a shushing gesture. I hadn't forgotten that even our most private locations might be under surveillance from Newton's enemies or even his own organization.

I handed Rafe a small pad of paper and a pen that I'd fished out of one of the drawers in the boat's galley. He nodded, immediately understanding what I had in mind and put the items in one of the pockets of his cargo shorts. We spoke aloud while deciding to sit on the bow and catch some sun before we headed home. Rafe grabbed a couple of cans of lemonade from the fridge for us to drink, and we walked along the gunwales to the bow.

As soon as we'd settled with our backs against the transom, Rafe pulled a small object out of his pocket and handed it to me. Then he wrote on his pad. "Choke thing."

Surreptitiously, I examined the item. It looked like a fancy-cut loose diamond about the same size as the enormous stone in the engagement ring Liam had given me when we were together. That meant it was about five carats in size. It caught the sunlight and refracted it into a glorious rainbow that glowed against *Tranquility*'s clean white hull.

I looked at Rafe with wide eyes. It was a sure bet that Adriana hadn't had something like this in her mouth before gulping down her drink, so I concluded that it must have been inside the bottle.

"Blue / red print," I wrote on the pad.

Rafe nodded. He'd caught that detail too.

"Red diamond. Blue explodes. ???" I wrote, while he nodded.

"Let's go out for dinner tonight instead of staying home," I said out loud. "We need to talk."

Chapter 16
Recovery Dive

BEFORE WE HEADED BACK to RIO, we decided to take the time for a dive. Although we'd gone diving early this morning, Rafe had only been diving in icy-cold fresh water for weeks while he'd been filming. He was eager to spend some quality time enjoying the vivid colors and abundant sea life in the beautiful, warm waters of the Caymans.

Before we started gearing up, I sent a text to Newton. "Early dinner? We'll pick you up. Y/N?"

By the time I'd finished setting up my regulator, he'd responded with a Y and a thumbs up emoji. I breathed a sigh of relief that I could enjoy my dive without worrying.

Rafe and I did simultaneous giant stride entries off the rear dive platform and met up at a depth of ten feet underwater. We joined hands and continued our descent along the mooring line.

At this site, the area directly beneath the mooring is flat, a mix of sand and hardpan, so other than an occasional conch passing through or the abundant garden eels that made this spot their home, there wasn't that much to see until you swam to the thriving coral that surrounded the hardpan—about twenty or thirty feet away in any direction.

As soon as we reached the coral, the world exploded with color. Large orange tube sponges, huge yellow brain corals, silvery purple sea fans, and deep brownish purple elkhorn coral proliferated, creating a haven for a myriad of reef fish.

Bright aqua parrotfish with their toothy beaks pecked at the coral. Pairs of majestic French and Queen angelfish swam slow stately circles around each other. A cute little puffer tootled along beside us as though he didn't have a care in the world. A couple of purple tangs swam nearby, and a massive school of blue chromis hung like a cloud near the edge of the nearby drop off.

A perfectly camouflaged trumpetfish lurked in the sea grass, hiding out to catch any unwary fish who happened to swim by. A black durgon placidly watched us from several feet away.

We dropped over the edge of the wall and came face-to-face with a spotted moray eel who poked his head out of his lair as though he couldn't wait to say hello to us. We smiled and then swam slowly along the wall. A few feet further on, we found two lobsters sitting side-by-side in their respective coral crevices, just watching the world go by. We dropped down a few more feet to peer under an overhang where we often spotted a large nurse shark napping. We were in luck, because she was there, snoozing away.

We swam past without disturbing her and then checked our computers. It was time to turn around. Just as we started to ascend along the wall, a spotted eagle ray swam over the rim and out into the blue, almost like he was doing a ceremonial flyby. Rafe and I grinned at each other, delighted to be back among our favorite creatures.

We stayed over the coral for our safety stop, hovering easily at the recommended fifteen feet and watching the busy world below us until it was safe to reboard the boat. Rafe climbed the ladder first, and once I was sure he was fully aboard, I went up.

We both dropped our empty tanks in an open slot in the rack and secured our gear bags under the benches that lined the gunwales. Just before I climbed the flying bridge to head back to RIO, I saw the pensive look in Rafe's eyes. We felt safe out here on the water, but we had no idea what dangers might face us once we were back on land.

As soon as we had docked at RIO, I tore a page out of a notebook I keep in the ancient canvas tote bag I use instead of a purse and wrote a note to Chaun asking him to sweep all the places Newton, Rafe, T-8, or I worked or typically hung out, including Ray's Place, the dive shop at

RIO, and Rafe's mansion in Hell. I found a roll of tape in the *Tran-quility*'s junk drawer and taped the note shut. Then I wrapped it in another page from the notebook, and then a third, liberally taping each layer to prevent anyone from seeing what was inside.

As we walked past Ray's Place, I handed the wad of tape and paper to Noah and asked him to get it to Chaun as soon as possible. Then we made a beeline for the main RIO building, hoping none of the revelers at the bar had spotted us.

Chapter 17
Dinner With Newton

RAFE and I showered and changed in the locker rooms at RIO before heading out to pick up Newton. Our plan was to try not to look like ourselves when we left the grounds, so we could potentially evade anyone who might be following us.

For my disguise, I dressed in a bright yellow dress and matching kitten heels that I kept hung on the back of my office door for emergency dress up needs. I blew dry my hair so it flowed long and straight and dabbed a little bit of makeup on my face. I donned a straw sunhat with a yellow ribbon that hung down my back and a pair of humongous designer sunglasses, both of which I'd picked up in RIO's gift shop. That was the full extent of my disguise.

When we met up, Rafe wore a pair of beige linen pleated pants and a white linen collarless shirt. He rarely dressed up except on the red carpet, so that was about the best he could do from the choices he had in his locker. To throw off anyone looking for us, he'd added a goofy looking red bucket hat with lobster claws that hung down over his ears, which he'd also purchased from the gift shop.

I think he hoped people would focus on his silly hat and miss recognizing his familiar face. It might work, even though he always looked spectacular no matter what he wore.

We called a cab, and when it arrived, we walked out RIO's front door with a crowd that had just left the aquarium show. Rafe did that thing he does where he seems to shrink, and instead of his usual lengthy strides he took short mincing steps. We asked the cabdriver to drop us off at Camana Bay, the glitzy shopping area near Newton's office.

Rafe and I strolled around the shopping area for a while, casually moving in the direction of the Fleming Environmental Investments building as we window shopped. When we were only a few steps from its main entrance, we split up.

Rafe headed toward downtown Georgetown, while I went in the front door of Fleming Environmental. I rapped on Newton's door as I walked by, then I went straight into the office he keeps for me there because I am on the board of directors and a senior VP, although I rarely do much work for the company except when Newton is out of town.

I changed into a navy-blue linen pantsuit and a white silk shirt I keep hanging on the back of the door of that office. I swapped my yellow shoes for a pair of black stilettos I pulled out of the bottom drawer of the massive cherry wood desk, wrestled my hair into an unintentionally messy bun and slung a burgundy leather messenger bag over my shoulder.

Then I walked out the building's side entrance and headed toward the cab stand. I hopped in a taxi and asked the driver to take me to Morritt's, a large time-share community on the East End.

I paid the driver in cash when we arrived and walked into the lobby of the main building. I spent a moment or two admiring the artwork and then I checked out their gift shop.

I bought an extra-large canvas tote bag with a picture of a parrot on it, a pair of flip-flops, a very large and very touristy t-shirt, and a pair of tailored Bermuda shorts before I walked out of the lobby and across the sand to the Wyndham Resort next door.

Once there, I went into the ladies' room off the lobby and changed into my new t-shirt and shorts, stuffing my suit, stilettos, and briefcase into the new tote bag. Then I strolled out to the lobby, where Rafe was waiting for me, wearing cut off jean shorts, a baggy black tee, teeny wire-rimmed glasses with purple frames and lenses, and a different silly looking hat. This one looked like a stingray had perched on his head.

A few minutes later, Newton joined us in the lobby. No power on earth can make Newton ever look anything less than perfectly polished, but the bespoke shorts and pressed polo shirt he now wore were sufficiently different from the grey pinstripe suit he'd been wearing in his office that I hoped he'd fool anyone who'd managed to follow us this far. We walked out of the Wyndham's lobby and jumped in a waiting cab. The driver let us out at Captain Herman Fish Fry, and Newton paid for the ride with cash.

Nobody was at the restaurant because it was a bit late for lunch and a tad early for dinner. We made our way to a shady table on the porch above the crashing waves, which we hoped would make it difficult for anyone to overhear us in case the restaurant became more crowded while we were there. Rafe sat facing the ocean with his back to the porch to reduce the possibility that anyone might recognize him. Newton and I sat so we could each observe a little more than half of the dining area.

We all ordered fish with rice and beans and lemonade to drink. Newton also asked for a bowl of conch chowder, one of his favorites. Once we had our food, we relaxed a little bit and began to talk.

I had been carrying the diamond all this time, moving it from my pocket to my bag to a different bag each time I changed my appearance. I rummaged through the stuff in my gigantic new tote until I found the diamond and pulled it out. It nestled in my palm while I showed it to Newton. I told him about the exploding bottle, Adriana unexpectedly taking my place for the commercial run-through, the different color printing on the bottles, and how Rafe had almost miraculously caught the diamond in mid-air when Adriana expelled it while I was performing the Heimlich. Oddly enough, nobody on set had asked Rafe to show them what caused her to choke.

Newton was trying hard not to laugh when I told him how Rafe had just casually reached up and caught the projectile. Like me, Newton knew that most people wouldn't have been alert and agile enough to catch it, and most people probably wouldn't have wanted to touch it anyway, given where it had most recently come from.

Newton praised us for recognizing that the different color print on the bottles was more than likely meant to alert the distributor to route the cases of water to the normal retail outlets or to an illicit diamond smuggling supply chain. He laughed about the drink's name. "Ice is a slang term for diamonds," he said.

"And for murder," said Rafe, who had a great ear for speech patterns, especially the ways that villains in the movies speak.

Newton was shocked that the bottle used on the first take had exploded in Rafe's hand. "It's possible it was a malfunction, but it doesn't seem likely. No manufacturer in their right mind would release the product if there was any chance of the bottles exploding like that on a normal basis. The bad guys were definitely trying to hurt one of you—or at the very least put another scare into you."

He paused to take a sip of lemonade. "But they overplayed their hand with their little stunt, and they must be unbelievably careless to lose control of a bottle with a valuable diamond like that in it. But because of their carelessness, we know for sure that the bad guys exist, and we can even take a good guess at their game plan. So now all we have to do is trace the water's distribution network and we'll find the smugglers."

Rafe took a sip of his lemonade. "Did T-8 ask you to review the contracts that Fin and I signed to appear in the commercial?"

Newton shook his head. "No, he didn't. Today was the first time I ever heard about the commercial. Why do you ask?"

Newton was a very accomplished lawyer, and he reviewed almost all the contracts any of us negotiated, regardless of which of the many companies we were involved with was party to signing them.

We discussed how surprised we were that T-8 had okayed a contract without asking Newton to check it over first. He'd gotten himself in a tight spot once before by doing that.

I wondered out loud, "Do you think he might have been aware of something in the contract's terms that would have set off a red flag for you, Newton?

I felt guilty for suspecting T-8 of nefarious doings. He and Rafe had been best friends since they were little kids, and they were intensely loyal to one another. Rafe and I were staring at each other in shock at the thought that T-8 might have been involved in the evil doings that had been going on, but Newton made a "slow down" gesture.

"It's entirely possible that T-8 had Liam review the contracts instead of me. After all, they are partners in the production company, and Liam is just as familiar as I am with the nuances of personal performance contracts."

He looked at me. "For that matter, so are you since you've been negotiating all the annual documentary contracts on RIO's behalf for years. Did you notice anything odd in your contract?"

I shook my head. "I thought they gave in pretty easily on a few points, but I chalked it up to their eagerness to get Rafe on board for their product launch."

Rafe scowled. "I wish I'd never heard of Ice Water."

Newton had a little half-smile on his face. "If it wasn't this product commercial, they'd have found another way to drag you two into this. I believe Adriana's accident was just another warning shot from the bad guys, although it probably wasn't meant for Adriana."

He looked at me. "This time they weren't fooling around. They aimed directly at the person I love most in the world. I think you were the one meant to choke."

That scared me for a minute, because with Doc no longer on the RIO premises, there might not have been anyone around to save me with the Heimlich, but then I shook my head. "I don't think so. If they wanted me to choke, they wouldn't have used a diamond to do it. I think the delivery team simply made a mistake and dropped a case of the wrong bottles at Ray's Place. I bet the bad guys are chewing their nails wondering where the bottles with all the diamonds went. And somebody is probably in big trouble for losing track of the valuable shipment."

By now the restaurant was starting to fill up with people, so we decided to leave. We went into the restrooms to change back to our usual clothes. We hoped that if anyone assigned with tailing us stumbled across our trail at this point, they'd simply think they'd screwed up earlier and lost us.

We didn't want them to know we were on to them. We hoped that if someone were tailing us and we'd managed to evade them, they'd simply have stationed themselves at one of our usual haunts hoping to pick us up again, without realizing we'd deliberately given them the slip.

Once we'd finished changing, we took a cab from the restaurant, paid cash for the ride, and had the driver drop us off a quarter mile past RIO. We walked back the way we'd come and entered the grounds through the vacant lot beyond the new mermaid grotto. Then we cut around to the pool house and entered the main RIO building from there. Once inside the main building, we walked down the hall and out the back door before we casually sauntered over to Ray's Place.

Chapter 18
Chaun's Sweep

CHAUN and his best friend and business partner Benjamin Brooks were just finishing dinner at a table at Ray's Place. The bar patrons were mostly regulars and RIO employees, so nobody even bothered to look up when I walked past the tiki bar to join them, even when Candy, the bar's resident Cayman parrot, squawked out her usual, "Look! It's Fin Fleming."

Chaun and Benjamin sat at a large round high-top table in the back, so there were plenty of seats for us to join them. Unbidden, Noah brought over a pitcher of lemonade and placed it next to the half-empty pitcher of margaritas already there.

"About time you got here," Chaun said. "I've been dying to know what's going on."

I held a finger to my lips in the gesture for silence.

Chaun lowered his voice to a whisper. "Sorry."

"Did you get my note?" I poured lemonade for Newton and Rafe while waiting for Chaun's reply.

"Yes. I'm still working on the sweep, but this place is clean, and so is most of RIO. Your office and the conference room are both okay for sure. I haven't checked the dive shop, the mermaid grotto, your homes, your cars, the locker rooms, or your boats yet. That's all on the list for tomorrow, so be careful what you say when you're home until I get to it and give you the okay. I'll do your phones before I leave tonight so we can text or call each other if need be. Now tell me what's going on? I heard there was an explosion. And a choking."

Rafe and I took turns filling Chaun and Benjamin in on what had happened. As usual, Chaun was very upset about anyone trying to hurt either Rafe or me. He was all for getting up and finishing the bug sweeps right then until we managed to convince him that it would look suspicious if he were to suddenly head off to all our houses at this time of day.

Instead, I suggested that since it was a known clean environment, we should all sleep at his house that night, which he thought was a terrific idea.

"I've never been to a pajama party before. This will be epic," he said. Then he remembered his housemate. "But only if it's okay with you, Benjamin."

Benjamin grinned affably. "Of course. Anything to keep our friends safe."

I'd mostly grown up on RIO's research vessel, the *Omega*, so I hadn't had any friends my own age. Like Chaun, I'd never been to a pajama party, and I was secretly thrilled by the idea.

I used Chaun's phone to text Rosalina that we'd all be away overnight and asked her to let Dane and Maddy know not to worry about us. We finished our drinks quickly and headed off to Chaun and Benjamin's place, which was right down the street from my house on Rum Point.

Although the décor at their place was more "busy bachelors" than my house, the layout of the two homes was nearly identical. As a result, Rafe and I felt right at home almost immediately.

Newton hadn't said a word since we'd arrived, keeping to himself in a corner, seemingly deep in thought. I watched him through the kitchen window when he stepped into the backyard and made a phone call. The cynical side of me assumed he was checking in with his consortium team, but he proved me wrong when the doorbell rang a little over a half hour later.

"Where do you want this set up, Mr. Fleming?" said the leader of a crew wearing the uniforms of workers at the Ritz. They stood in a line on the walkway carrying enough food to feed an army. They had all manner of junk food—enough to satisfy even Chaun and me—plus soups, sandwich fixings, a dessert tray, and a barrel of soft drinks. In addition, they'd brought salads, lean meats, and fruit for Benjamin and Rafe, the healthy eaters in the crowd.

Newton waved them toward the kitchen, and the procession of porters went past us and set up the food in an efficient buffet before going back outside to bring in several large hampers.

"Where would you like the breakfast things stored?" the lead person asked.

Newton deferred to Benjamin, who showed them to his pride and joy, a large walk-in pantry next to the kitchen, where there was ample shelf space to hold the baskets of food and urns of coffee. My house had a larger eat-in kitchen than theirs, but no pantry, which was fine with me. Until Rafe moved in, I'd never had anything to store in a pantry anyway.

Once they'd situated all the food, the crew from the Ritz made one more trip out to their van. This time they returned with beautifully gift wrapped parcels for each of us. Chaun quickly tore his open, revealing a pair of blue silk pajamas, a matching robe, and some sheepskin slippers.

The rest of the packages each contained a similar assortment of items, perfectly sized and suited to our individual tastes. I'd have been as awestruck as everyone else if I hadn't been the recipient of similar perfectly chosen gifts throughout my life—all of them ostensibly from Newton but usually chosen by one of his employees.

The thought made me sad, until I remembered that Newton had sworn that he'd only stayed away all those years to keep me safe, even though it hurt him at least as much as it hurt me for us to be apart.

I was also concerned that we were having a pajama party when things were so dire. Liam was missing—possibly hurt or even dead. Someone had tried to kill Rafe at least twice, and me at least once. We were under siege from who knew where, and it felt like Newton was making light of the situation by throwing a bash. It didn't seem right.

Plus the possible security breach of Newton calling the Ritz scared me, since now their staff knew where we were. Of course he'd lived at the Ritz for years, and Liam had even worked there himself for a long time. Given that history, Newton must feel confident that the staff was trustworthy. I trust my father, so I put my fears aside.

Rafe and Benjamin were sitting cross-legged on the floor near the fireplace, digging into a gigantic bowl of popcorn. Rather than his usual single kernel, Rafe was laughing at something Benjamin said and enjoying popcorn by the handful. I watched as the tense lines faded from his face. He looked happy and relaxed for the first time since we'd returned from our honeymoon.

Chaun was so delighted by his first ever pajama party that no one could help getting caught up in his infectious joy. While I was lost in thought, the team from the Ritz had brought in several pillows and sleeping bags, one of each for each of us.

I glanced over at Newton and nodded my thanks. He'd known exactly what we needed and made it happen. It's no wonder I love him.

We all changed into our new pajamas and then we hunkered down on the floor with our pillows and sleeping bags. Rafe opened his blond superhero sleeping bag up and spread it on the floor. Then we sat on it together, with my pink princess sleeping bag wrapped over our shoulders.

"Sorry," Newton said. "It was all they had."

I would never confess out loud how much I loved my pink princess sleeping bag, but when he grinned at me, I knew that he was well aware of my delight. Newton always did his best to make the people he cared about happy. Another reason to love him and forgive his sometimes single-minded focus on the consortium's goals.

T-8, Chaun, and Benjamin all had superhero sleeping bags, each one dedicated to a different hero. Chaun was thrilled with his spidery themed bag, while T-8 and Benjamin had bags featuring heroes from the pantheon of Norse gods.

Newton had the only plain sleeping bag. It was a simple dark blue with a plaid lining. He rolled it out and sat on the floor with his legs inside the bag and his back resting against the couch.

We spent most of the night munching, chatting, laughing, and telling stories. I felt safe and loved, and I forgot to worry about anything.

Shortly before dawn, one by one we fell asleep. I was the last person awake, and as I looked around at my friends and family, I realized how lucky I really am.

My luck has nothing to do with my ability to escape from dangerous situations or to win at card games. No, my luck truly came from the friends and family that filled my life, and I was grateful for each and every one of them.

Chapter 19
Del

WE SLEPT LATE the next day, and it was only the combination of the enticing fragrance of fresh hot coffee coupled with a persistent sunbeam peeking through a gap in the curtains that covered the window that finally woke me up. I turned my head and nuzzled Rafe's shoulder.

"There you are, Miss Sleepyhead. Here's your coffee." He helped me to sit up and wrapped my fingers around a steaming mug he'd had waiting on a tray on the table beside the couch.

I took a huge gulp of the hot coffee before I could open my eyes fully. Everyone in the room looked like they'd just woken up. I glanced at my dive watch and yelped with surprise. "It's after noon!"

Newton, wearing a chef's apron that was so not his style that I was sure it must belong to Benjamin, bustled in from the kitchen when he heard me. "Then it's about time we had breakfast. Otherwise, we'll miss lunch." He laughed.

I gave Newton's chef getup the once over, and he winked at me. We both knew he couldn't cook to save his life, so I was sure that whatever was on the menu had been prepared by the staff at the Ritz and Newton was simply reheating it.

Even so, it was a feast, and we all stuffed ourselves. I was happy to see Rafe eating like a normal person instead of denying himself more than a bite or two of anything that wasn't either lettuce or water.

As soon as we finished our belated breakfast, Chaun checked all our phones for bugs, turned off the location tracking sensors, and declared them clean and okay to use. But then he gave us each a burner phone from a huge basket of them he had stored in his home office. "Use your regular phone to communicate with your usual friends and business associates. Use the burners if you need to discuss anything sensitive, like where and when you're going to be someplace."

Newton slipped his new phone in the pocket of his bespoke cargo shorts without a second glance, but I looked at the phone in my hand with distaste. I didn't want to think that I needed to keep my whereabouts secret from friends and family, and I didn't even want to try to understand why Chaun had a bushel basket of spare burner phones in his home office.

I nearly jumped out of my skin when my regular phone rang as soon as I turned it on. Caller ID said it was Bari Blackthorne, my assistant. I pushed the button to answer.

"Fin, just wanted to let you know I set up a meeting for you with Del Dunlap later today. Your office. Is that okay?"

"Probably," I said. "But remind me. Who is Del Dunlap again?"

"Interim CEO of Quokka Media. Apparently there's a thing in their bylaws that's automatically triggered if Liam doesn't check in every twenty-four hours. Dunlap steps in until he resurfaces." She sighed. "I thought it sounded weird, but when I couldn't find you or Newton I asked Genevra about it. She said it's legit."

Bari's sister Genevra had worked with Liam for years. She knew a great deal about the inner workings of his businesses, so I wasn't worried about that aspect of Bari's statement. If Genevra said that's how it worked, that was probably how it worked.

But I was worried about the fact that during all the times Liam had been away for months on end—once he'd even been gone more than a year—he'd managed to check in with the business every twenty-four hours so as not to trigger the clause, but he'd only rarely communicated with me while he was away.

I repeated the words in my head, trying to make sense of them. He checked in with work every day, yet all the time we'd been engaged, he'd sworn he couldn't call me or text me when he was away. It was impossible for me to understand.

Anger rose swift and hot, but I tamped it down. Liam and I weren't engaged anymore. I was married to Rafe, and blissfully happy about it. But it still hurt me that Liam had been able to check in with his office every day but he could never manage to find time to check in with me.

Then the real implications of Bari's words sank in.

Liam hadn't checked in with his office.

Therefore, he must be very badly hurt or worse.

"I'll be there," I said. Within minutes I'd showered, dressed, grabbed a muffin to eat on the way, and then I was out the door.

I arrived at RIO with ten minutes to spare before the start of the scheduled meeting, so I was sitting at my desk checking emails when the office phone on my desk buzzed.

"Dr. Fleming, this is Fred—the security guard."

"Hi, Fred. I know who you are. And please call me Fin."

I sighed. Fred and I had this exact same conversation every time we spoke.

"Del Dunlap is here, waiting in the conference room for your meeting."

"Thanks, Fred. I'll be right there."

I closed out my email program, slipped my feet into the red flip-flops I'd kicked under my desk, and walked down the hall. I was dreading this meeting, terrified about what Dunlap's presence meant about Liam's safety.

I was surprised when I walked into the conference room. The only occupant was a stunning, tall woman with red hair, green eyes, and very pale skin. She wore a perfectly tailored grey suit and nosebleed-height stiletto heels. Perfect makeup. Tasteful gold jewelry. If I wasn't mistaken, it was Tiffany.

She smiled at me and stepped forward, extending her hand in greeting. "Hi. I'm Delaney Dunlap, and you must be Fin Fleming. I feel like I already know you because Liam spoke of you so often. He told me all about you." We shook hands.

I'd never heard of her before today, but she seemed to know quite a bit about me. I was confused. For one thing, when I heard the name,

I'd expected Del Dunlap to be male, and for another, I wondered when it was that Liam had the time to tell her all about me, and exactly what 'all' entailed. To cover my confusion, I offered her coffee or lemonade.

She asked for lemonade, so I texted Theresa to request that someone from food services deliver a pitcher and a couple of cookies to the conference room. Noah arrived with a tray within a few minutes, helping to break up the uncomfortable silence which had descended on Del and me like a shroud.

As soon as he departed, Del helped herself to a cookie. She closed her eyes and sighed with pleasure while chewing her first bite. "These cookies are as good as Liam always said they were. I'm so glad to finally have a chance to try one for myself."

I pushed the plate her way. "Have another. Then maybe you can tell me what this meeting is about."

She smiled and reached for the last cookie. After she took a bite, she sighed. "Mmm. So good. Well, the first thing I want to talk about is Liam's disappearance. Rest assured that the full resources of Quokka Media—and all of Lawton Enterprises—are at the disposal of the search teams."

"Thank you," I said. "Right now my father is financing the search, but I'm sure he'll appreciate that generous offer."

She popped the last bit of cookie into her mouth. "Ah, the great and powerful Newton Fleming. Liam admires him deeply." Her smile felt cold.

"The feeling's mutual," I said. "What's the second thing you wanted to talk about?"

"I'm afraid that's a little more delicate." She looked down at her lap, then back up at me, her luminous green eyes trained intently on mine. "You're in breach of your contract. With Lawton Media and *Ecosphere*."

I did a double take. *Ecosphere* is the flagship title at Quokka Media, and I'd done a photo column for them every month for years. But I'd resigned after a blowup with Liam, and in fact, I'd been working on a freelance basis with *Your World*, *Ecosphere*'s chief competitor ever since I'd quit.

I shook my head. "You're mistaken. I haven't worked at Quokka Media or *Ecosphere* for months. I resigned, and Liam knew it."

"Mmm, yeah. About that. Your contract automatically renews annually unless either party cancels in writing. Did you ever send the certified letter required by the contract? I didn't find a copy of it anywhere in the files."

I bit back a growl. "Liam and I had a verbal agreement that I quit working with him. He didn't ask for my resignation in writing, and I didn't send him any certified letter."

I could tell she was trying to look sad, but she failed miserably. "I know. That's why you're in breach of contract with Lawton Media. And I understand you've been working with a competitor, an even more serious breach of your contract. You're not allowed to work for a competitor for two years after your contract with *Ecosphere* ends. We need to find a way to get you back on track."

No question, now she was truly gloating.

I shook my head. "I resigned. Liam knew it. Maybe he forgot to update the paperwork, but we'd both agreed…"

She interrupted me. "You know as well as I do that Liam Lawton never forgot anything when it came to business. He was as sharp as a shark's tooth."

She looked pleased with her metaphor, and I wondered how long she'd been planning to use it.

Then I did a double take because she was referring to Liam in the past tense. I hadn't given up on him, and I never would until we found him one way or another. "I agree Liam is a smart man. But we have a unique relationship…"

She interrupted me again. "Which does not supersede the written and signed contract. Especially since you were the one who ended that unique relationship."

She smiled, cold as ice. "And by the way, congratulations on your recent marriage. Rafe Cummings. My goodness, you must be the envy of every teenage girl in the world."

The way she licked her lips made her look like a snake. How could I have even for a moment thought she was beautiful?

She rose. "I'll expect you to send in your next column by the end of the month. If not, you'll be hearing from our lawyers." She started to walk away, then she turned back, pulling a small sheaf of papers from the leather tote over her shoulder.

"And since you are in breach of contract, I've revoked your privilege to set your own topics and locations for your columns until further notice." She waved the papers she held in my face before dropping them on the conference room table. "Those are your assignments for the next six months. I brought them along because I wanted to make sure you had them in plenty of time since I assume you'll need some lead time to make travel arrangements…"

I stood up, noticing as I did so that we were the same height. "Get out," I said, ignoring the papers she'd tossed my way. I shut the door firmly behind her. When I was sure she was gone, I sat back down and put my head in my hands. Bad enough Liam was missing, but Del Dunlap was clearly going to be a very big problem.

Chapter 20
Newton

I WAS SHAKING with anger from my encounter with the obnoxious Del Dunlap, so I took a few minutes to pull myself together before texting Newton. He's my lawyer as well as my dad, and right now, I needed him in both capacities.

"Need u Where r u" I finally sent.

"Office" he texted back

"OMW"

I popped around the corner to my assistant Bari's office to let her know I was leaving. Horrified, I realized she was sobbing, crying hard with her head down on her desk. She gave no sign she was aware of my presence.

"Is everything okay?" I said softly.

She sat up quickly and brushed the tears off her face with both hands. "Fine. Everything's just fine."

"Is it Austin?" I asked. "Did you two have a fight?" She'd fallen hard for my young photography protégé Austin Gibb as soon as they met. As far as I knew, their budding romance was going very well, but you never could know what went on in someone else's relationship. It's hard enough to manage your own.

But thankfully, Bari shook her head. "No. Why would you say that? Austin is wonderful. I'm just upset about Liam—and Rafe."

"How did you hear about the attempt on Rafe's life? I thought only the people who'd been in Alaska with him knew about it."

Her eyes grew big and round. "Are you saying somebody tried to kill Rafe while he was in Alaska? I only knew about the bottle exploding at Ray's Place! What's going on around here?"

I could have kicked myself. The story would spread around RIO like wildfire, and that meant that sooner or later the paparazzi would find out, and poor Rafe would be under siege wherever he went.

I had to stop that from happening. RIO has been Rafe's refuge.

"If I tell you what happened, you can't tell anyone. Promise?"

She nodded. "I promise."

I'd just finished telling her the story when I heard several gasps and the murmur of shocked voices from behind me.

"Sacre Bleu!" said Christophe Poisson. A handful of students from his current freediving class surrounded him. Their eyes were wide, and their mouths were open in disbelief.

Great. There was no hope of keeping the story quiet now. I groaned. "I gotta go. I have a meeting." I shot off down the hall and out the front door before they could bombard me with the questions I saw in their eyes.

A few minutes later I walked through the main entrance of Fleming Environmental Investments. My brother Oliver's office was empty, and so was the office beside it that belonged to Gus Simmons.

Just as well. I adored them both, but right now I really just needed to talk to Newton.

He was standing with his back to the open door when I reached his huge corner office. As usual, he looked amazing. Perfectly cut hair, flawlessly fitted clothing, the entire ensemble impeccably accessorized. Whatever gene he had that enabled this impossible feat of perpetual perfection had certainly skipped a generation, because I definitely hadn't inherited it.

I blew my overgrown bangs out of my eyes. "Del Dunlap says I'm in breach of my contract with *Ecosphere*. She says I can't work for *Your World* anymore. She says it's all in my contract. I don't understand what's going on. I need your help."

Newton faced me and nodded. "Get yourself a drink of water or some lemonade. Go check in with Oliver and Gus. They're both in the conference room working on a joint presentation they're giving next month. Ask Gus about little Angel's latest antics or convince your brother to tell you one of his silly jokes—which shouldn't be that hard since he has a million of them. Just take a deep breath and relax. Everything will be alright. I'll review the contract, and we can discuss it together in fifteen minutes. Okay?"

I bit my lip, nodded, and left his office without saying anything else. I wandered down the hall to the conference room where Oliver and Gus were poring over a bunch of spreadsheets. I shuddered at the thought of spending my days immersed in financial reports, but for some unfathomable reason they both seemed to love it.

Oliver jumped up and gave me a hug when I walked in. "Hey, Sis, long time no see...except at that photo shoot for the commercial at Ray's Place. We didn't get a chance to talk that day, but you were amazing. You stepped right up and saved that woman's life like it was all in a day's work."

"Thanks, but if I hadn't been there someone else would have stepped in."

"But you're the one who did it, and you're amazing. I'm so proud to be able to say I'm your brother."

I held up my palm. "Enough. You're making me blush, and I actually wanted to ask how Genevra's doing. Is she feeling okay?"

He grinned. "She says she feels like she swallowed an entire watermelon, rind and all."

When we stopped laughing at the image of petite, refined Genevra swallowing a watermelon whole, I turned to Gus. "And how is my little goddaughter Angelica doing? Giving you a run for your money?"

Gus beamed with pride. "She keeps us hopping for sure. Just the other day I was working from home, tied up on an international conference call. She had been playing with her train set in my office. But when I turned my back for a second, she walked out. She filled up the bathtub on her own and threw all her dolls in. Then she wandered away and left the water running."

"I didn't notice until the water ran down the hall and into my office. I dropped the phone and rushed out to make sure she was okay. By the time I tracked Angelica down, she was out in the backyard playing in her sandbox. When I asked her what she'd been doing in the bathtub, she said she'd been teaching the dolls how to scuba dive like Auntie Fin does. And then when Theresa got home and found out, she was so mad she almost killed me."

"Yikes," I said. "Ask Theresa to bring Angel to work one day soon and I'll teach her to swim. At least that way you won't have to worry if she decides to hold another impromptu dive class in the tub."

Gus nodded. "Good idea. Thanks."

Doc no longer allowed poor Gus to dive because of a serious heart condition, and he generally stayed out of the water completely to avoid the temptation to take up his lifelong passion again. Theresa had always hated the water, so their daughter Angelica only got the chance to splash around when she was with me. We enjoyed our time in the shallows together, but I realized it was well past time to teach her the rules of water safety.

We continued chatting until Newton came in. "Fin, I'm ready for you now if you can break away," he said, resting his hand affectionately on Oliver's shoulder. He was always careful not to show any favoritism between Oliver and me.

I sat on the big leather couch in Newton's palatial office, and he took the nearby chair. "I've read the latest version of your contract, and the non-compete clause is only three months, not two years. Other than that, it does say what Delaney Dunlap said it does." Newton's handsome face wore a frown.

"That's not possible," I protested. "Liam and I had an agreement, and besides, he knew I quit my job at *Ecosphere* after the incident with Gary Graydon. Our contract was no longer in force no matter what."

Newton held up a hand to slow down my outburst. "The automatic renewal clause is in there, and it's still in force since neither you nor Liam put your resignation in writing. Last year Liam's office had sent over a new contract changing the non-compete period to two years, but neither of you ever signed it as far as I can tell. I have several pages of notes questioning the changes in terms from your original contract that I had sent in an email to Liam for comment. He never responded. So the version of the contract that Del is quoting from isn't legit. But there's also no record of you and Liam agreeing to end the prior contract, which does have the automatic renewal clause she cited."

"What does all that mean?" I was used to negotiating contracts for RIO, but somehow it was different when it was my future on the line.

"Technically you may actually be in breach of contract because of your work with *Your World*. But maybe we can get Will Graham, the publisher over there, and Gary Graydon from *Ecosphere* to vouch for the fact that you had resigned from *Ecosphere* and waited the required three months before you joined *Your World*. I'll put in some calls."

I sighed. "Fat chance Gary will come to my defense. Remember I tried to get him fired."

Newton made an airy hand gesture that implied it didn't matter. "Water under the bridge. And worst case, we'll buy out your original contract. The annual renewal is only a few months away, so it'll be little more than pocket change."

Newton's idea of pocket change differed considerably from most people's, but I was relieved to hear that he thought he could easily fix the problem. "What about *Your World*? Do I need to resign?"

He shook his head. "Probably not, but I'll call Graham and let him know what's going on. You may have to skip a few months of your column, but maybe we can figure out something that works for everyone. I have a few ideas."

I took a deep breath that felt like the first time I'd inhaled since Del Dunlap had shown up unannounced.

"Thank you. I love you, Dad."

He smiled. "I love you too, Sweetheart."

He looked at the Patek Phillippe watch on his left wrist. "Dane and I have a meeting with Peter Roberts of the Coast Guard to talk about how we can track down that diamond smuggling ring. You're welcome to join us. In fact, I think it would be a good idea if you did."

"Okay," I said. "I haven't had a chance to talk with Peter Roberts since I left Kraken Island."

He smiled. "Don't let Rosalina hear you call it that. She owns it now, and she calls it Alonzo's Island. Although come to think of it, everybody else calls it Rosalina's Island."

Chapter 21
Captain Roberts

It didn't take long to get to Coast Guard headquarters. Captain Roberts offered us coffee when we joined him in his office, and then he and Newton spent a few minutes catching up. I was restless, and wanted to get the conversation over with so I could get back home to Rafe and Penny.

Bored with their chitchat, I abruptly stood up and restlessly stepped over to the bookcase against one wall of the office. The shelves were stuffed full of plaques and awards, as well as personal mementos from Peter's travels scattered among small groupings of family pictures.

I leaned over to one of the lower shelves and peered at a small clay statue that depicted one of the fierce Caimans that gave the Cayman Islands their name. Caimans, part of the family of Alligatoridae, once roamed the island and made their homes in the quiet inlets and mangrove forests along the shore. While today the islands are generally free of the dangerous predators, they still form an important part of its history.

As I stood back up, my gaze landed on one of the framed photos. The picture included Peter Roberts and another man—one who looked familiar. I couldn't place the face, but I was certain I'd seen him somewhere, sometime.

After wracking my brain for a moment, I shrugged. I'd probably seen him around town at some point. No big deal. I tuned back in to the conversation between Peter and Newton.

Peter was agreeing to step up surveillance of small boats that might be smuggling the contraband cases of Ice Water—the ones containing the smuggled conflict diamonds.

"I'm sorry," I said. "I was admiring your little caiman statue and missed the earlier parts of the plan you discussed. I know about blood diamonds, but what are conflict diamonds."

I was embarrassed. It wasn't like me to tune out of important meetings like this.

Peter looked annoyed, but Newton merely smiled.

"No problem. Those are just different names for the same thing. Here's a quick recap. We had some top-notch gemologists test the diamond that Adriana choked on. The gemologists and the geologists all say it likely came from an area where small blood diamond mines continue to operate. And since it's illegal to import diamonds without a 'Kimberley Process' certification, when you find a diamond that doesn't have the right paperwork, you can be pretty sure it wasn't mined ethically. Those uncertified diamonds are conflict or blood diamonds, and they are a source of a great deal of human misery and environmental damage. But they can also be very lucrative if you can smuggle them out and then sell them to unscrupulous jewelers or consumers."

I nodded. Human rights and the environment are two of my biggest passions. I hated the very idea of conflict diamonds. The damage to the humans involved in the mining operations is horrendous, and the toll of the environmental damage it creates is just as bad.

My dislike for blood diamonds is part of the reason I'd been thrilled when Rafe bypassed the traditional diamond engagement ring and offered me the perfect wedding ring I wore—a slender band set with several randomly placed gemstones in varying shades of blue. The ring had paperwork attesting to the safe and ethical mining of the stones.

"Go on," I said.

Newton leaned back in his chair and continued. "We've cleared Ice Water's manufacturer of any involvement in diamond smuggling.

There is no record of them ever ordering packaging with red lettering like the bottles we—I mean you—found the diamond in. We've had agents watching the authentic product as it's loaded on ships to come here, and we didn't see any point where the legit product came in contact with the counterfeit bottles."

He shook his head, obviously puzzled by the smuggling process. "We're assuming that only a few of the cargo ships are rendezvousing mid-ocean somewhere nearby to take on the faux cargo. They unload it as usual in Georgetown, and then the distributor splits the goods, sending cases of water to various outlets. All the product with the blue labels is going to stores and food service, exactly as it should. We haven't found any more red labeled cases, so we haven't been able to track where they pick up or siphon off the red-ink product."

"Makes sense," I said. "They must know we're investigating after the mix-up during filming. And I imagine they are always pretty careful about when and where those transfers take place. What are we doing about that?"

Newton looked at me in a way that let me know what he was about to say next was important. "Peter has committed that the Coast Guard will step up its patrols to see if they can catch the boats in the act of transferring the pallets of Ice Water that contain the diamonds."

I nodded and then thought for a minute about his hidden meaning. "Good. Maybe Vincent and the *Omega* can help out with that. Vincent can go anywhere around the islands without causing suspicion, and the *Omega* is fast enough to give chase or possibly even get to a suspicious location before the Coast Guard can."

Newton nodded. "Good idea. Will you discuss that with Maddy and Vincent? I don't want to interfere with RIO's important research, so if they have other priorities, I can get another boat to handle that part of it."

I nodded that I understood.

He nodded back. "I have someone working on the inside at the distribution center so we can uncover the point person in the supply chain—the people diverting the bottles containing the diamonds. If we can manage to identify the lower level culprits, it should get us at least one step closer to the big guns in this game."

"Got it," I said. "Sounds good. Who do you have undercover?"

He looked away. "Your brother. Oliver."

Chapter 22
Suspicion

My mouth fell open in surprise. Newton had dragged me into his undercover work, and our relationship had barely survived it. We'd JUST gotten back on an even keel, and now Newton wanted to pull my lovable but way too trusting brother into the dangerous world he inhabited.

Oliver's twin sister Lily is a murderer. His mother was a con artist and a drug dealer. She'd lied to him about his birth father's identity, telling him multiple versions of the story of his true parentage.

After his mother died and his sister fled the Caymans to avoid going to jail, Oliver had been alone and on his own, trying desperately to finish his education, working part time jobs at both RIO and Fleming Environmental Investments to earn his keep, and trying valiantly to make his way in the world all on his own.

Maddy and Newton had grown to love him as he worked odd jobs at RIO and Fleming Environmental, and they'd been worried about him because he was all alone in the world. He didn't become part of our family until he was an adult when my parents legally adopted him.

And yes, you can adopt an adult. They legally took him into the family to ensure that he had a next-of-kin with his best interests at heart in case he was ever sick or injured. We shuddered to think of him at psycho-Lily's mercy if he ever became incapacitated and needed someone to make decisions on his behalf.

And Oliver seemed happy being a part of our family, although he still went back and forth between believing that Ray Russo, my late stepfather, was his biological dad as his mother had told him, and feeling certain that she'd lied to him about his true parentage.

Which I knew she had.

I was one of the few people who knew the truth, and I was certain that if Oliver learned that Seb Lukin, the very worst of all possible bad guys, was his birth father, it would kill him. Although Newton and Maddy both knew that Ray hadn't been Oliver's biological father, I didn't think they had an inkling as to who his father had actually been. As far as I knew, Oliver's twin sister Lily and I were the only people he was likely to come in contact with who knew the truth.

Lily would keep quiet as long as there was nothing for her to gain by telling him. Then again, she might also decide to tell him at any point just because she was mad about something and wanted to hurt him by striking out. I don't think the twins are in contact anymore, but that didn't keep me from waking up in a cold sweat after bad dreams in which she maliciously told him the terrible secret we both kept. Luckily, she'd dropped out of sight a while ago, and I fervently hoped she'd stay gone forever.

I was so startled by the info about conflict diamonds and Newton's plan to enlist Oliver in undercover work that I forgot all about asking Peter Roberts about the identity of the other man in the photograph. I was anxious to get Newton out of Captain Roberts' office so I could beg him to leave sweet Oliver out of the dangerous world my father navigated so effortlessly.

I looked at the dive watch on my wrist. "Look at the time. Newton, we have that meeting we need to get to. We'll be late if we don't leave right now."

Newton blinked once, but he played along. He glanced quickly at the gold Patek Phillippe watch on his wrist. "You're right, as usual. Thanks for the reminder."

He turned back to Peter Roberts. "I think we're done here anyway. If you wouldn't mind, please let me know when you have the details of your part of the surveillance worked out."

Captain Roberts stood up and shook Newton's hand. "Will do. Thanks for stopping by, and thanks for the extra resources. See you both soon, I hope."

He smiled, and something about his smile struck a familiar chord in my brain, but I didn't know why. I put the thought aside to focus on convincing Newton to choose anyone but Oliver to do the dangerous undercover job.

As soon as we left Coast Guard headquarters, I stopped walking and turned to Newton. "Please don't drag Oliver into your undercover work. He just got married, and you know there's a baby on the way. It's way too dangerous."

Newton's face was impassive. "I appreciate your concern, and I know Oliver would too if he knew. But it doesn't matter now anyway. He's already working undercover and has been at it for a couple of weeks. He's doing a fine job."

I gaped at him. "I can't believe you sent your own son into danger without even a second thought."

"He's strong enough to handle it and smart enough to stay out of trouble. You've been on several missions now, and you did fine on each one. What's your concern?"

I closed my eyes, wondering where my father's head was right now. "Do you even remember the last mission you sent me out on? I was nearly assaulted; the bad guys almost killed me more than once; they did manage to shoot Rafe; and they tortured Liam. They even tried to hurt Penny, a defenseless little dog, and I couldn't do a thing to stop them. What part of all that was fine?"

Newton shrugged. "The world is full of bad people. What we at the consortium do helps rid the world of some of the worst of them. It can be dangerous sometimes, but it's worth the risk. Need a ride home?"

I shook my head. "Sometimes I feel like I don't even know you anymore. This is one of those times, and I don't take rides from strangers. I'll walk." I turned away, leaving Newton behind.

Chapter 23
Liam

I FLAGGED down the public bus that was just passing and paid my fare. The bus traveled down South Church Street, past the Paradise Restaurant by the Sea and Sunset House, then continued on toward RIO. The driver let me off at the entrance to our parking lot.

I stuffed my hands in my pockets and trudged toward the main entrance with my head down. It was between start times for the aquarium shows, so the beautiful glass ceilinged atrium was cool and uncrowded. I breathed a sigh of relief as I crossed the lobby to the hall leading to my office.

"Afternoon, Dr. Fleming," Fred said from his security station near the aquarium entrance.

I sighed. "Hi, Fred. Please, just call me Fin." Fred had an exaggerated sense of my importance in the world, and he always addressed me with the utmost respect. By now I was sure that no matter how many times I asked him not to, Fred would always call me 'Dr. Fleming,' but even so, I would never give up trying to get him to call me Fin.

I waved at Fred and strode down the hall to my office. Before I went through the door, I poked my head into the office next to mine. "Bari, I'm here, but please don't let anyone know unless it's an emergency."

She smiled when she saw me. "Sure thing." Then with another quick smile, she turned her gaze back to the spreadsheet she'd been working on.

As I always do when someone takes on managing one of those dreaded spreadsheets, I thanked the universe for sending that person into my life. I hate numbers, and spreadsheets just have so many of them.

I threw the raggedy old canvas tote bag I used as a purse into my bottom desk drawer, kicked off my flip-flops, and sat at my desk. Groaning, I put my head down on crossed arms and shut my eyes.

I was wrestling with how I should handle Newton's desire to drag Oliver into his undercover international law enforcement activities. I was convinced that it would be too dangerous and too stressful for gentle Oliver to live undercover. His wife, Genevra Blackthorne, was one of my closest friends, and she was carrying their first child. Whatever Newton's objective in this operation might be, pulling Oliver into it was surely a recipe for disaster.

Newton seemed so certain it was the right thing to do that trying to find a way to change his mind seemed like an impossible task. I was mentally running through all the arguments I could think of to get him to see how wrong he was when my cellphone buzzed.

I lifted my head from where it rested on my crossed arms and used my left hand to push the phone away. There was no one in the world I wanted to talk to until I had this figured out.

But then I saw the caller ID.

Liam Lawton.

I grabbed the phone in shaking hands, fumbling to answer the call.

"Liam? Liam, are you okay?"

"Help me," his familiar voice rasped through the speaker.

"Where are you? We'll come get you. Just tell me where you are." I pulled out a pen to write down an address.

"G..." there was a sound like the phone had fallen to the floor. The call disconnected.

I pushed the callback button, but the caller had masked the number, and there was no answer. Not even voicemail.

I bit back my anger at Newton. We could continue our discussion about Oliver going undercover later. Right now, I would need his help to find Liam and bring him back. I hit his speed dial on my phone.

"What's up?," he said. He sounded distracted.

"Liam just called, but the call disconnected before I could find out where he is. He sounded in a bad way. We have to help him."

I could feel Newton's concern even through the phone. "Of course. I'll be right there."

"I'll call Chaun. Maybe he can help us trace where the call came from." My friend Chaun has amazing technology skills.

"Maybe so," Newton said, but I could plainly hear the doubt in his voice. "See you in a few."

I didn't have a moment to waste, so I hit the favorites button for Chaun. His phone rang but switched over to voicemail after a few seconds. I left a message, letting him know I needed his help. But just to make sure he knew it was urgent, I added "It's for Liam" to the end of the voice mail.

Chapter 24
Chaun

I STILL HAD a few minutes before Newton was likely to arrive, so I went around the corner and down the hall to Maddy's office. My mother, Maddy Russo, is the founder and Executive Director of RIO, and she always knows everything going on in the institute and in her field of oceanography.

I knocked on her door. She pulled off her reading glasses and looked up from her computer with a warm smile. "Hi, Fin. What's up?"

I went in and sat at the small round table in the corner of her office and looked out at the stunning view of the Caribbean Sea. "It's about Liam. And maybe some smugglers. I need your help."

"Tell me." Maddy was very fond of Liam, so I knew she'd give me whatever help she could muster.

I explained Newton's theory about conflict diamonds, smugglers, and setting up the surveillance. "Any chance Vincent and the *Omega* could help out with that?"

She nodded. "Of course. I'll give him free rein and ask him to contact Newton and Peter Roberts to work out the details. Now what else is bothering you?"

I sighed. Maddy knew me so well she could always tell. I'm not sure how much she knows about the international law enforcement consortium Newton is a part of, and I didn't want to out him if she didn't know anything.

I bit my lip and looked into her stunning turquoise eyes. I saw love, support, and understanding there. "You already know, don't you?" The realization surprised me.

But then again, of course she knew. How could she not? She and Newton had been divorced for years, but they were still incredibly close friends.

She nodded at my words. "I don't think Newton knows that I do, but I've always known—even long before he abandoned you. Leaving you behind was so unlike him. I was distraught at his frequent disappearances, and I worried about how his rejection would hurt you. Ray ended up telling me why Newton eventually felt like he had to leave."

Ray Russo, my late stepfather.

Just thinking of him brought a pang to my heart. I missed him so much. "Ray knew about Newton's undercover work?"

She nodded. "And Vincent does too. Newton left him in charge of my safety. He wasn't supposed to tell me but not letting me know didn't feel right to him."

"Vincent's your guardian?" I'd suspected that Newton had charged Doc with keeping Maddy safe. Vincent had never even crossed my mind as a possibility.

She smiled. "You never suspected?"

I bit my lip. "I thought he was in love with you."

A frown crossed her face. "The two states are not mutually exclusive, but I don't think that's the case. Vincent's in love with the sea."

I thought she was deluding herself, but I didn't say anything. The arrangement apparently worked for both of them, so who was I to question it?

"Something else brought you in here though, didn't it?" she said.

I wrung my hands together as though I were trying to wring out my stress. "I'm worried. Newton has dragged Oliver into his undercover operation. I'm afraid they'll hurt Oliver if they figure out he's undercover. He's not good at subterfuge."

"Genevra won't let anyone hurt him," she said.

"Genevra's pregnant, remember? This time she may not be able to swoop in at the last minute to save him with her martial arts kicks or even her big rifle. Oliver will be in there all on his own."

She sighed. "You're right. I'll talk to Newton about sending someone else in undercover. Consider it handled. Now, how are we going to rescue Liam?"

"I called Chaun to see if he could trace the call, but he hasn't called me back. That's not like him. He usually returns my calls right away, and I told him this was about finding Liam..."

Our gazes met across the table, and we realized the problem at the same time. "They have Chaun," we each said, practically in unison.

There was a moment of stunned silence while we thought about feisty Chaun in the hands of bad guys. He was smart and sassy, but he was physically and emotionally fragile, and he wasn't at all tough in any way. He wouldn't last long under rough or intense questioning, and his bravado and sass might even earn him a harsher interrogation than necessary.

I opened my mouth to speak, but before I said anything, Benjamin Brooks broke the silence. "Who has Chaun?" His voice sounded strangled. He and Chaun were very close and they had been best friends and business partners since college. Benjamin knew Chaun better than any of us, which meant he would know exactly how much danger Chaun was in if the bad guys had him.

"We don't know if anyone actually has him," I said. "I got a call from Liam..."

"Liam called? Where is he?" Benjamin asked. "Is he okay?"

"I don't know. All he did was make a hard 'G' sound before the phone disconnected. The caller ID said Liam Lawton. If it really was Liam, he wasn't calling from his own phone. I figured Chaun would know how to track down his location from the call. That's why I was looking for him."

"I think you're right. Sounds like something's really wrong. Chaun would've called you back immediately if he could have. He'd drop anything else on his plate for you or for Liam." Head down, he paced the length of Maddy's office and then back again. "We have to rescue him."

"I agree. There's just one problem...well, actually, there are lots of problems. But the first one is a doozy. I don't even know who has him or where he is. How will we find him?" My voice cracked. Chaun was a good friend, and I was very afraid for him.

Benjamin pulled out his phone. "We track each other's locations on our phones…" he flushed. "Not for spying. Just for fun. Chaun was intrigued by the technology."

"Of course he was," I said with a smile. "So where does it say he is?"

Benjamin frowned. "It looks like he's in Ray's Place. But that doesn't make sense. I just walked by there, and I didn't see him."

I shivered as though somewhere a goose had walked across my future grave. Very superstitious, but Chaun's disappearance had me spooked. "Maybe he was in the restroom when you went by. Let's go see."

Maddy picked up her own phone. "I'll join you as soon as I've talked to Vincent. I want to get things rolling."

Benjamin looked puzzled, but wisely, he didn't say anything. I nodded and scurried out of her office and through the rear door, Benjamin not far behind me.

Noah Gibb was polishing glassware behind the bar as we skidded to a stop across the stone patio. "Have you seen Chaun?" I leaned over with my hands on my knees as I panted to regain my breath.

Noah put down his cloth and frowned. "No, I haven't seen him, but he left his phone here. Must have forgotten it when he was here for lunch. It's been ringing constantly." He reached under the bar and pulled out Chaun's phone. "Here," he said, handing it to Benjamin. "You can give it back to him when you see him."

Benjamin and I stared at each other. It was definitely Chaun's phone, which was easily recognizable by its thick heavy metal case, which he said was for security. He called it a Faraday cage.

Benjamin reached out for the phone. As soon as his hand touched the case, the phone began to blare out its distinctive ringtone— Beyonce's *Single Ladies*.

Chaun had always laughed at what he considered a hilarious pun, since the song admonished listeners to "put a ring on it."

Benjamin jerked his hand back as though the phone burned him. His face was deathly pale, making it obvious he was very, very frightened for his friend. "You answer it. I can't." He handed the phone to me just as Maddy arrived.

I hit the answer button. "Chaun's phone."

An electronically altered voice clicked on. "We have them both. Back off on the diamond smuggling investigation, or we'll ice your friends. It won't be pretty." The call disconnected.

I tried to find the number that had placed the call, but it came back as Chaun's own number. I remembered he'd told me once that he knew how he could spoof anyone's phone number. He'd said it was easy, but to Chaun, any kind of technology was easy.

Me? Not so much.

I wondered if Dane or Newton had access to the technology that could "un-spoof" the call and identify the actual number that had placed it. At the very least, maybe they could identify the call's point of origin, which would narrow down the search area and help us locate our missing friends.

When the call disconnected, Benjamin's face was an ashy grey color. His terror for his friend was obvious. "What are we going to do? We have to help them."

Maddy took Benjamin's hand. "Come with me. You'll be no help to Chaun if you're this scared. I'll take you to Doc and she'll help you calm down. It's okay to let Fin handle this." She tugged gently on his arm. Moving like a zombie, he followed her along the crushed shell path back to RIO's rear entrance.

Seemed like I was on my own once again.

From his position behind the bar, Noah looked at me, fear and puzzlement on his face. "What's going on?"

I shook my head. "I wish I knew. But don't worry. I'll find out, and I'll get our friends back safely."

Chapter 25
Newton Calls in the Cavalry

I TURNED AWAY from Noah and with my head hanging down with misery and fear, I trudged along the path to the back door. My head was spinning, and I felt paralyzed by my terror about the fate of my friends. I couldn't think straight, so it startled me when I bumped into someone.

Stewie's strong arms grasped my shoulders and held me upright when my muscles turned to wet noodles and lost their ability to keep me standing. He smoothed my hair down as he spoke soothingly into my ear. "It'll be okay, Fin. You'll find them and bring them home safely. We all have faith in you."

I stepped back and brushed tears off my cheeks. "I don't know where they are or who has them. I don't even know what the people holding them want. How can I save them? How can I go on living if we lose Liam and Chaun because I went blundering around and made stupid mistakes?" Even to me, my voice sounded panicky.

Stewie nodded. "I understand. But you won't make a mistake and you will save them. I'll help with whatever you need. Let's go to your office and make a plan." He slung an arm over my shoulder and together we walked through the door and down the hall to my office.

Del Dunlap was standing behind my desk, looking up at the

famous photo of Maddy staring down the great white shark. She turned to face us when we walked in, a nasty smile on her face.

"You'll need to deliver more shots like this one to regain your reputation when you come back to *Ecosphere*."

She turned to face the opposite wall. "I like that one too." She gestured toward the equally famous image of Rafe hovering eyeball-to-eyeball with a hammerhead.

I sighed. "Go away, Del. I don't work for *Ecosphere* anymore, and I..."

Her lips tightened. "I have a contract that says otherwise."

"No, you don't have a contract. Neither Liam nor I ever signed it. Now go away."

Her face was like steel. "There's an automatic extension clause in your original contract. The contract is very clear that you must deliver your decision in writing by certified mail if you don't want the automatic extension to go into effect. You never sent anything in writing, not even an email, never mind a certified letter. I can and will make you very sorry for not living up to the terms if you keep this up. You may think you didn't agree to those new terms, but..."

Stewie took two steps toward her and stood up as straight and tall as he could. She was still a good two inches taller than him, same as me. "Fin told you to get out. Now go. Get out of here before I carry you out myself."

In a voice like ice she asked. "And you are?"

I could see Stewie fighting for control in the face of her arrogance. "Doesn't matter who I am. Fin asked you to leave, and I'm here to see that you do."

She looked at me. "I thought you were at least strong enough to fight your own battles. I can see I was wrong."

Newton's soft but commanding voice cut through the tension in the room. "She is strong enough, but even so, there's no rule that says she has to do it alone. Go away, Del. Now." He stood in the doorway, pointing to the lobby. His face was like thunder.

"Newton Fleming," she said cooly. "How lovely to see you again."

He didn't say anything, but he crossed the office to my desk and picked up the phone. I saw him dial the security office.

Fred was the only person on duty today. Although he'd been with

RIO for years and I liked him, he was long past retirement age, out of shape, and in general, pretty inept. I knew there wasn't likely to be any resolution by bringing Fred into the fray.

Newton barked into the phone. "Fred, call Roland and Morey at police headquarters and ask them to come to Fin's office ASAP. There's an armed intruder holding her hostage." Obviously Newton knew Fred wasn't up to the task too.

"Yes, sir, Mr. Fleming. I'm calling right now. Do you need me to come down there as soon as I finish the call?" For once Fred sounded strong and determined.

When she heard Fred's response to Newton's request, Del gasped. "What makes you think I'm armed?"

"I always figure it's better to be safe than sorry." Newton put his hands in his pockets and smiled, a cold and nasty smile. "If I'm mistaken about you being armed, we'll just have to let the police figure it out."

Del stood perfectly still, staring at Newton. He stared right back at her, his face harder than I'd ever seen it before. Stewie and I were unable to figure out what was going on between these two, or how we should deal with removing Del from the RIO grounds if she didn't agree to leave on her own. Nobody moved for at least a minute. We were all frozen, as though we were figures in an ice sculpture tableau.

Luckily, we didn't have to go it alone for long. A mere second before the tension in my office got bad enough to snap everyone's last nerve, Dane Scott, Vincent Pollilo, and Peter Roberts all walked in.

Captain Roberts said, "I came over to meet with Vincent about how we would split up the area for surveillance and I overheard the security guard calling the police. What's going on here?"

Del smiled. "Uncle Peter. How nice! I didn't expect to see you here. Would you please explain to Newton and his daughter that I'm no threat to them."

Peter lifted his hands in a conciliatory gesture. "I'm sure it's a simple misunderstanding…"

Newton spoke without taking his eyes off Del. "Dane, she's armed, and she threatened Fin with violence. Stewie and I both heard her. Please pat her down and disarm her."

Dane stepped forward just as his lead detectives entered the room.

Since Fred had forewarned them, both men wore bullet proof vests. Morey already had his weapon drawn, although he held it with the business end safely pointed toward the ground.

"I'll handle it, Boss," said Roland as he edged past the crowd in the office.

Del raised her arms, holding her hands palm out. "Back waistband. Right ankle." She let out a deep sigh.

Roland nodded and pulled two small guns from the locations she mentioned. He carefully handed them to Dane. "I still have to pat you down."

She shrugged. "Knock yourself out."

He found her keys and a multi-tool in a front pocket. The multi-tool included a pull out knife, and the keys he found dangled from a set of brass knuckles. Roland put them both on the table beside my desk, just out of reach.

Dane sighed. "I don't suppose you have permits for the weapons?"

Del smiled brightly. "Nope."

Roland reached for his cuffs, but Peter Roberts put a hand on his arm to try to stop him. "She's my niece," Roberts said. "Can't you give her a break?"

Dane shook his head slightly.

Roland gave a quick nod to his boss to show that he understood. "Sorry. No can do. The law is the law." He snapped the cuffs on Del's wrists and then he and Morey each took hold of one of her arms and walked her out of my office and down the hall, while Peter Roberts frowned and chewed his lip.

Chapter 26
A Respite

THE LAW ENFORCEMENT TYPES—DANE and Peter—had planned a meeting with Newton and Vincent, and the last thing I wanted was for my father to drag me into their undercover machinations.

I left as quickly and as quietly as I could. I picked up my car in RIO's parking lot and headed for home. I needed time and space to think.

But when I arrived at my house, I was pleasantly surprised to find Rafe lounging by the pool in the backyard. Penny was napping on his lap, snoring softly in the sunshine.

I was delighted to find him there, looking happy and at ease. Rafe rarely took time to relax or be lazy. When he wasn't on set, he was always working out, reading scripts, or memorizing lines.

"Nice to see you taking some time to recharge," I said planting a kiss on his forehead while I rubbed Penny's furry belly. "Did you walk home from Benjamin's this morning?" It was odd to think that just this morning we had been eating a big breakfast after the impromptu pajama party.

Rafe shook his head. "Chaun dropped me off on his way somewhere. He was in a gawd awful rush to get there, wherever it was."

My ears had perked up when he mentioned Chaun. "He didn't say where he was going?" I asked. I tried to sound casual, but I couldn't fool Rafe. He knew me too well.

"What happened?" he asked.

I sighed. "Chaun's missing. We found his phone at Ray's Place, but nobody's seen him. And I got a scary call on my burner phone. The caller masked the number, and it's untraceable. The caller sounded nasty, threatening to 'ice" Chaun and Liam both if we don't stop investigating the diamond smugglers."

Rafe's lips tightened with anger. "Chaun had nothing to do with any of that. And he's more or less defenseless. What kind of monsters would go after a sweet guy like him? It's like threatening to hurt a child because you don't like something the parents did."

He stood up. "C'mon. Let's go. We've got to find him and bring him back before they hurt him."

A wave of love for this man washed through my heart. He didn't just play act at being a hero. He truly was one in real life. He'd do whatever he could to save his friend Chaun, and he wouldn't think twice about his own safety while doing it.

I adored Chaun—and I'd once loved Liam. I didn't want anything to happen to either one of them while the smugglers had them in captivity. It was especially upsetting because the bad guys had hurt my friends before. I couldn't keep the tremor out of my voice when I spoke. "But we don't have any idea where to start looking."

Rafe straightened his shoulders. "Then we'll search until we get an idea. We'll start at Ray's Place, see if we can figure out who dropped off his phone. And we'll just keep looking until we find them, no matter how long it takes." He grabbed my hand. "Let's go."

"What about Penny?" I asked. "We don't know how long we'll be gone. Maybe we should drop her off with Gus and Theresa."

He shook his head. "Sure. If we have to. But let's keep her with us for a while. Her skills might just come in handy."

Dachshunds like Penny were originally bred to hunt small burrowing animals, and they are brave and tireless in pursuit of their quarry. They have a great sense of smell, and like most hounds, they can track whatever they decide to track. Penny's ability to track might conceivably come in handy.

But the bad news about dachshunds is that they have minds of their own, and it can be virtually impossible to convince one to do something they don't feel like doing. If we found a clue, it was possible that Penny would want to track Chaun's scent, but it was equally possible that she'd just want to roll over and have her belly rubbed.

It could go either way.

The thought occurred to each of us at the same time.

"Uh, maybe it would be better if we leave her here," said Rafe.

I laughed in agreement. "Okay. Let's go," I said.

We headed to RIO in Rafe's beat up junker car as quickly as we could. He uses the junker car when he wants to remain anonymous—which is most of the time. We parked in a shady corner of the back parking lot at RIO, and cut through the pool house, the gym, and the executive offices to reach RIO's back door.

Before we exited, I poked my head out to scan the crowd at Ray's Place. Luckily it looked pretty quiet, and I recognized most of the patrons as regulars. "The coast is clear," I whispered over my shoulder.

Rafe pulled a floppy wide brimmed hat with ear and neck flaps out of a pocket in his cargo shorts and put it on to hide his face. Then he hunched over like an old man and limped along the crushed shell path to the tiki bar. He waved to Noah as he went by and sat down at a table behind the bar, next to the door to the kitchen. I followed a few seconds later.

As soon as I walked in, Candy, our Cayman parrot, squawked a greeting. "Hello. Look, it's Fin Fleming." I walked around to an open spot at the bar near her perch and gave her a seed from the small dish we keep there for her treats.

Noah put down his bar towel and joined me. "What's going on?" he asked as he poured two glasses of lemonade.

"Chaun and Liam are both missing. Rafe and I want to find them, but we aren't sure where to start. Do you remember anything at all about who was here just before you found Chaun's phone?"

Out of the corner of my eye I saw Rafe pretending to read the menu, but I could tell he was using the menu primarily to hide his famous face. He was actively listening to my conversation with Noah.

Noah shut his eyes and raised his head, the better to run his memories of this morning through his mind. He sighed with frustration. "Sorry. I got nothing. The place was crazy right up until a half hour ago. I had to call Austin in to help, even though it was supposed to be his day off. Maybe he saw something while he was here."

I took my phone out of my pocket and hit the speed dial for Austin. "Got a minute for me? I'm at Ray's Place."

He groaned. "I'm working a shift in the dive shop now, and I just finished a shift out there at Ray's. I haven't had anything to eat all day and I'm starving."

"I'm sorry. It will only take a minute, and I'll buy dinner for you and Bari after we talk. Deal?"

"Deal," he said, sounding much happier. "Be right there."

It didn't take Austin more than a minute to scurry over from the dive shop where he'd been helping Stewie with scuba tank inspections. "What's up?"

I crossed my fingers, hoping that this time—when I really needed it —my famous luck would be with me. "We're looking for Chaun. Any chance you saw him around today?"

Austin stared at the thatched ceiling above us. I could almost see him running a high-speed mental movie of his shift through his mind's eye. After a minute, he shook his head. "Sorry. It was crazy today, but I'm pretty sure I'd remember if he'd been here. I don't recall seeing him at all." He paused a moment. "You don't think anything bad happened to him, do you?"

I shook my head. "If you don't remember seeing him then he probably wasn't here today. He might have left his phone here last night," I lied. "Maybe he doesn't even know it's missing."

Everyone, including Austin, is fond of Chaun, and I didn't want to cause the young man undue angst for not remembering seeing Chaun. And who knows? Maybe Chaun really hadn't been here at all, so that gave me twice the incentive to be sure I didn't give Austin any reason to blame himself if any harm befell Chaun.

"Okay, maybe. I guess that's possible," Austin said sounding unsure of himself. "If you say so."

I tried to smile. "I do say so. Now, where do you want to take Bari for dinner tonight? Here, or should I make arrangements for you somewhere else?"

He grinned. "Right here is fine. It's Bari's favorite spot—and we might do a sunset dive from shore before we eat, so it'll be nice to be close by."

"Excellent plan." I laughed. "I saw Noah prepping what looks to be an amazing lobster dish for tonight's special. You guys have a wonderful evening, and order anything you want." I turned back to the bar to let Noah know that it was okay to comp Austin and Bari for anything they wanted this evening and to put it all on my tab.

When I'd finished with the arrangements, Rafe and I grabbed a pitcher of lemonade and walked down the dock to my boat. Rafe poured icy cold lemonade into a stainless-steel RIO branded mug for each of us. We sat on a blanket on the *Tranquility*'s deck with our backs supported against our gear bags, which we'd stored under the benches. This way we were relatively comfortable while enjoying the sunset and the ocean breeze. Rafe wasn't visible from shore, so we didn't have to worry about fans chasing after him for an autograph.

I was way too stressed to sit still, so I stood up after a few minutes and started pacing back and forth across the deck. "Where could they be? Why would anyone want to hurt them?" I muttered over and over again. "They're not the ones investigating the diamond smuggling. Why go after them?"

About the fifth time I'd said it, Rafe took my hand as I passed him and gently tugged me down beside him. "You can't work out the puzzle when you're like this. You've gotta get a grip on your fear so you can think clearly. I know exactly what you need."

I looked at him, wondering what he had in mind.

"Let's go diving," he said with a laugh, and I laughed right along with him.

He did know me well, even better than I knew myself. Nothing else in the whole world cleared my mind like a dive.

"Where to?" I asked, hopping back up to my feet.

"Trinity Caves," he said. "The rigor of diving in those tunnels will require our full conscious attention, and maybe if we give up struggling to figure something out, a plan will form itself in the back of one of our brains."

"Brilliant. Let's get a move on." I climbed the ladder to the flying bridge while Rafe unhooked us from the cleat on the dock. Within a few minutes, we were on our way.

Trinity Caves is a relatively easy dive site off the northeast tip of Grand Cayman, an area known as West Bay. While divers can access the site from any of three mooring buoys, two of them are more convenient to the site known as Round Rock than they are to Trinity Caves.

We chose to tie up at the mooring ball directly over the Trinity Caves site, which is about 300 feet from the other moorings at the end of a reef finger that points toward shore.

Trinity Caves is a fairly shallow dive, since most of the interesting sights are above eighty feet of depth. There are several swim-throughs and tunnels that meander through the abundant corals and sponges. Although many of the swim-throughs are open to the surface, coral growth completely encloses some of them, forming small caves. The diverse terrain gives divers multiple options and lots of variety, one of the reasons the site is so popular.

Some portions of the swim-throughs are extremely narrow, so safe passage requires a diver's full attention to avoid bumping the delicate corals with a too vigorous kick or an errant floating hose. Skillful careful diving is normally second nature to me, but today I gave it my full concentration, which was exactly what I needed to take my mind off my missing friends.

I gave myself completely over to monitoring my dive skills and enjoying the sights. I used a small flashlight I took out of my BCD pocket to bring out the vibrant colors of the corals and sponges I passed.

I saw thick schools of both blue and brown chromis, a couple of hogfish, several yellowtail snappers, two hawksbill sea turtles, and one enormous giant barrel sponge which must have been at least 1,000 years old.

In a small crevice, we noted a shy Caribbean reef octopus, who pretended to ignore us while keeping one wary eye pointed our way. We pretended to ignore him right back, although we were thrilled to see him as well as the Caribbean spiny lobster in the crevice next to his.

We exited the last tunnel we'd planned to traverse on the sandy side of the reef and saw a vast field of garden eels waving in the current. Nearby, we saw three southern stingrays—my favorites— buried in the sand. I think they assume the thin coating of sand they hide under prevents you from seeing them when you pass by—which always makes me laugh.

We hovered over the reef at fifteen feet for our safety stop, checking out the teeming sea life below us. I took a deep breath through my regulator and realized the tension of the last few days was completely gone. I could see the situation a lot more clearly, and at last I felt ready to make a plan. Rafe had instinctively known exactly what I needed to get my head back in the game. Just one of the many reasons I love him.

When we'd completed our three-minute safety stop, I climbed the ladder to *Tranquility* and slotted my tank into an empty spot in the rack behind the bench. Then I helped Rafe aboard, and we sat down to talk about how we could find and rescue our friends.

Chapter 27
An Old Enemy

We hadn't come up with any real ideas by the time we decided to head back to RIO. We had to get back to Penny and feed her, and I wanted to check in with Noah and Austin to see if they'd remembered anything new.

I held the *Tranquility* steady in her slip while Rafe tied off the mooring line. By the time I'd climbed down from the flying bridge, he had the excess line neatly coiled next to the cleat, and I smiled to myself thinking of how much I love him. One might think that as big a star as he is, he'd be a spoiled entitled prima donna, but that's not the case. He's as sweet and down to earth as he could possibly be.

He was waiting on the dock when I reached him, and he extended a hand to help me step up onto the gunwale. As soon as I hopped down, we held hands and strolled toward Ray's Place to see if we could find Austin.

The place was hopping, with lots of couples dancing to the loud music. It was so loud that nobody heard Candy when she announced my arrival, which was fine by me.

Besides everyone was giving all their attention to our newest attraction, Taz, a white cockatoo. Taz was dancing up a storm on his perch, bobbing his head in time to the music and picking up his feet along with the bobbing. He had a very happy smile on his face, especially when people formed a circle around him and clapped along with his dance moves. He was adorable, and a natural born ham.

Because he was new to us, we only brought him out for brief intervals so as not to overwhelm him with too much attention and noise. Although from the look of joy on his face as he danced, I didn't think the audience bothered him in the least.

Rafe and I had just threaded our way through the crowd to an empty table in the back when Stewie came to pick up Taz and bring him back to the dive shop for the evening. You could see by the look of disappointment on his face that Taz wasn't quite ready to quit dancing, but he's a good boy. He didn't try to resist leaving, but he did keep dancing all the way across the recreation area while perched on Stewie's shoulder.

I was watching Taz dance when I noticed a familiar figure slip out of the bar and head toward the parking lot. The woman was petite, dressed in a pink sarong and matching bikini top, and she had glossy dark hair hanging in rich curls down her back. At first I couldn't put my finger on where I knew her from. She was long gone by the time I realized it was Oliver's homicidal twin sister, Lily Russo.

Chapter 28
The Chase

I grabbed Rafe's arm. "I just saw Oliver's sister Lily." I hissed. "What do you think she's doing here?"

He craned his neck to see over the crowd. "Do you want to say hello? Should I run after her?"

I realized that Rafe had never met Lily, and although he knew Oliver had a twin sister that nobody talked about, he probably didn't actually know the whole story. "No. I want you to call Dane and let him know she's here. Call Newton too. I'm going after her. I'll explain later." I raced off toward the parking lot while Rafe fumbled to get his phone out of his pocket.

The sun had already set, and the parking lot was shadowy, but I saw Lily's white kicks flash in the glow of the mercury vapor lamps on the far side of the lot. Redoubling my effort, I chased after her as fast as I could.

Thanks to all the training I do, I was moving fast and I wasn't even breathing hard, but training doesn't help when you step on a loose stone and twist your ankle. I fell to the ground, and I hit hard, bruising my right hip and ripping the skin from my knee. I rarely swear, but this time I let loose with a stream of words that might have made a sailor blush. I wasn't angry about my injury, but I was mad at myself for letting Lily get away from me.

I fought to get back up and resume the chase, but I couldn't put my weight on my knee or my ankle. Still, I never give up. I struggled to keep moving forward, determined to catch up to her.

I was still limping ahead when Rafe and Stewie ran up. Rafe grabbed my arm and placed it over his shoulder. "C'mon. I'll help you to the infirmary," he said.

"And I'll keep looking for the evil one. Which way did she go?" Stewie asked.

I pointed in the direction she'd been heading, but she was long gone. Then a few seconds later, the headlights of a car parked on the main street switched on, and we could hear the roar of its engine as it peeled away.

There was no way we would be able to catch up to her at this point. Her head start was just too great, and none of us had seen any details of the car she'd escaped in.

She was gone.

Chapter 29
Dane Arrives

I WAS STILL LEANING on Rafe and limping across the parking lot toward the infirmary when Dane's unmarked police car screeched to a halt beside me. Newton's electric Mercedes pulled up silently beside it. The doors of both cars slammed shut at the same time. The loud bang was startling in the still night.

"Where is she?" Dane asked.

I shrugged. "Gone."

"You let her get away?" Newton asked, sounding incredulous.

Rafe stepped forward. "Cut the crap. She didn't let anyone get away. She fell. Her knee, her ankle, and her hip are all badly bruised. She might have sprained her knee and her ankle. She might have even broken them. Thanks for asking. Your concern for your daughter is touching."

Newton looked abashed. "I'm sorry. You're right. Fin, I apologize. It's just we've been trying to get a handle on her location for so long, and she outsmarts us every time we get close to her. She's a danger to all the people I care about as long as she's free, but that doesn't mean it's okay for me to take my frustration out on you."

I reached out and touched his arm. "It's okay. I get it. Like you I want her locked away someplace where she can't hurt the people I love anymore."

Newton frowned. "You're right that I want her locked away, but that doesn't give me license to hurt the people I love. I've been doing that way too much lately. I'm sorry."

I stepped forward and gave him a hug. "You need to stop every now and then to take a deep breath. Focus on the big picture. I understand how easy it is to forget to do that because sometimes I'm the same way. But don't worry about hurting my feelings. I know you love me, and I hope you know I love you."

He smiled. "Thank you for saying that. And I do love you too."

Dane cleared his throat. "If this love fest is going to continue much longer, Lily will have had more than enough time to disappear into thin air, and we may not ever have a chance to find her again. Now can one of you point out which way she went?"

I'd had my back turned away from the road after my fall, so I wasn't sure, but just then Stewie jogged back into the pool of light cascading from the mercury vapor lamps above the parking area. "I think she's headed toward the harbor. Maybe she's got that submersible working again and it's docked somewhere in town. Can you get someone down there right away to see if they can spot her?"

I held up a hand. "If Lily's back and she's using that submersible again, there's only one place she's going. She's on her way to the *Golden Kelp*." With a deep breath and my eyes closed, I continued. "Seb Lukin's back."

There was a shocked silence before Newton spoke. "Well then, I guess we know where those conflict diamonds are coming from and who's behind the smuggling and the attacks on you and Rafe. He's probably got Liam and Chaun stashed on the *Golden Kelp*. Now all we have to do is find his mega-yacht, and we'll have solved the crimes."

Dane nodded. "I'll see if we can get Peter Roberts to deploy the Coast Guard helicopter in the search. It'll be the fastest way to pinpoint that accursed yacht. While he's searching, we'll put together our plan for retrieving Liam and Chaun and locking up Lukin and his crew of sleazebags. It's past time we stopped that devil for good."

Chapter 30
Failure is Not an Option

By now it was late. Rafe and I needed to take care of Penny and make sure that Chico and Henrietta had plenty of seed and water, so we took our leave and drove home. Penny greeted us ecstatically when we came through the gate into the back yard.

After we'd rubbed her silky ears and furry belly sufficiently, Rafe fed her and refilled her water bowl while I set out seeds and water for the birds. Once we'd taken care of our pets, we looked into the refrigerator, wondering what we'd be having for our dinner. We were both ravenous.

Rafe took out a bowl containing some ribs he'd been marinating since yesterday and carried it out to the grill. I decided to zap a couple of potatoes in the microwave, which is the upper limit of my culinary skill.

The food was nearly ready when we heard a car pull into the yard. Oliver and Genevra came through the gate, wearing big happy smiles and carrying a couple of large pizza boxes. I greeted them warmly before slipping back inside to place a couple of additional potatoes in the microwave. Ribs, potatoes, and a veggie pizza—a perfect balanced meal in my opinion.

Rafe handed Oliver the barbecue tongs and went inside to mix up a pitcher of lemonade. Now we had the makings of a feast.

Half an hour later, we were all leaning back in our chairs, well-fed and at ease with each other. My cellphone rang, breaking into our happy mood.

I pulled it out of the pocket of my cargo shorts to silence it and noticed that Newton was the caller. "Sorry. I need to take this." I went inside with the phone.

"What's up?" I asked as I closed the sliding door behind me. I put the phone down on the counter and turned on the speaker while I rummaged through the freezer to see if we had any ice cream for dessert.

"Peter did a helicopter sweep a couple of miles wide around Grand Cayman and saw no sign of the *Golden Kelp*. Maybe we jumped to the wrong conclusion."

I pulled a tub of chocolate ice cream out of the freezer and a basket of fresh strawberries from the fruit drawer and placed them on the counter before I responded.

"I don't think we're wrong. You know if Lily's around that means Lukin's around here too. They have to be somewhere nearby."

"That could be true, but it's not very easy to hide a mega-yacht, especially one as big and showy as the *Golden Kelp*," Newton said.

"If Lukin managed to evade Peter's search team, we have to at least consider the possibility that we're wrong. Maybe we should look at some alternative theories. I'm on my way over to you now—just a couple of minutes away. We'll talk then."

I still had my phone on speaker while I was searching in the back of the refrigerator for some whipped cream, so I didn't notice when Oliver came inside.

"Okay, but I don't for a minute believe we're wrong. If Lily's back, then so is Lukin."

It was only when I heard Oliver drop the pile of dirty dishes he'd been carrying that I realized he was right behind me.

Chapter 31
Family Fight

"You knew my twin sister was here, and you didn't think to mention it to me?" Oliver sounded really upset.

I slowly turned around to face him. "I didn't know until just a few hours ago. And I'm still not absolutely sure it was her anyway. All I saw was the back of a woman who could have been her. Whoever she was, she ran away from me before I could identify her for certain. And I thought you and Lily were in touch with each other. Wouldn't she have mentioned it to you if she were here?"

I was babbling. I love my adopted brother, and I didn't want to see him hurt. And one thing I knew for sure about his sister Lily was that she was jealous and vindictive, and she loved to hurt people. Any little thing could set her off, and the deeper the pain she caused, the more she seemed to enjoy it. She'd killed Ray Russo, my beloved stepfather, and she'd tried to kill me multiple times out of pure jealousy.

Luckily, I'd figured her out before she succeeded in doing me in.

But the thing that terrified me most was that she knew the terrible secret that would cause poor Oliver very deep pain. If he ever did anything to set her off, I felt sure she'd use the secret to hurt him without giving it a second thought. I was pretty sure that if anyone in the family did something she didn't like, she'd pull out the secret she wielded and use it to hurt Oliver, just because she hated us that much. I knew I had to protect him from her.

I don't know if Newton knows the awful secret Lily and I share, but I do know he loves Oliver and he'd give up his own life to protect him. Now it was even more imperative that we find out who the conflict diamond smugglers could be and figure out the connection between Lily and them. If we didn't get a handle on this and bring the smugglers to justice soon, Lily might use the horrible secret to hurt Oliver.

And even once we did find the evidence we needed, she might use the secret to hurt her brother just to make herself feel better. She was a ticking time-bomb of pain.

I didn't realize that Newton had arrived until he, Genevra, and Rafe came through the slider in time to hear my words to Oliver. Rafe immediately put the tray of leftovers he was carrying on the counter and took Genevra's tray from her.

She thanked him with a nod and took Oliver's hand. "I don't think Fin was trying to hurt you. You heard her. All she saw was a woman who from the back looked like she could possibly be Lily. She can't be sure it was your sister. And you know your twin has a history of sneaking around and getting involved in bad situations. I'm sure Newton and Fin were only trying to protect you by not saying anything until they knew for sure."

He pulled his hand out of hers. "I should have known you'd be on their side." He stomped out through the sliding door, angrily slamming the heavy glass against the stops as hard as he could. We heard a loud splash from the backyard, and I guessed Oliver had jumped into the pool.

Good. The cool water might help him calm down.

I took a step forward to follow him out, but Rafe put a hand on my arm. "You won't be able to talk to him right now. He's too angry to hear you."

I bit my lip, but I knew he was right.

Rafe opened the refrigerator and pulled out two cans of the bitter IPA Oliver enjoyed. I smiled, knowing Rafe wouldn't drink more than a sip from his can, if he drank even that much. He was bringing the second can along purely for bonding purposes.

Genevra stepped forward. "I should go too."

Rafe smiled kindly. "It's up to you, but I don't think he's happy with anyone right now. Since I'm the only one with no skin in the game, why don't you let him take it out on me?"

We both knew that Rafe and Oliver were close friends, so Oliver could comfortably vent his feelings without worrying about causing a rift in his marriage or his relationship with me. She stepped back and nodded.

Rafe smiled gently at her and followed my brother outside.

A few seconds later, the sound of two pop tops popping carried across the still night. Penny went to the door, whining for me to let her out. I knew how comforting she could be if someone around her is upset, so I let her go. Oliver needed her calming presence.

"Let's go diving while they settle down," I said, before remembering Genevra's pregnancy.

She grinned ruefully and patted her burgeoning belly. "Can't. But I can snorkel. You coming, Newton?"

Newton shook his head. "Thanks to Fin I can swim now—barely— but I still hate the water. The ocean at night is definitely not my idea of fun. I'll stay here until Oliver cools down, or I may just head home if it gets too late. But you two go on and have fun."

Genevra and I went out to the breezeway where Rafe and I stored our dive gear when it wasn't in use. I had an assortment of masks and fins that I used for classes and demonstrations, so Genevra rummaged through the piles until she found some things she liked. She selected one of my shorty dive skins—she was so petite that one of my full-length suits would have swum on her. As it was, the suit's short legs, which hit me mid-thigh, reached well below her knees.

We giggled about that for a few minutes. Then I handed her a snorkeling vest from the rack and an underwater flashlight from the shelf above the hanging area. We lugged our stuff out to my KIA Niro EV and took off for the nearby beach at Rum Point.

No one was on the beach at this time of night, but the patio bar at the nearby restaurant was hopping. We waved at our favorite waitress as we walked by on our way to the water, already wearing our dive suits and snorkeling vests, but carrying our fins. We waded into the warm water. When we were about waist deep, we lent each other an arm to balance on while we slipped on our fins.

When it was her turn I held on tight to Genevra to make sure she didn't slip or fall. I would never have forgiven myself if she fell and something happened to my future niece or nephew, whichever the case might be.

Once we had our fins on, we pulled our masks up and swam lazily across the surface. Normally I head immediately out of the roped off swimming area at this site because I love to see the stingrays who have settled just beyond the line of buoys, but tonight for once, I stayed inside the lines.

We aimed our flashlights toward the bottom, delighting in the vibrant colors and darting fish revealed by the light. We saw a brilliant turquoise parrotfish, wrapped in a mucus bag she'd spun for protection while sleeping, and Genevra's light caught an octopus slinking across the sand, hunting for the evening's dinner. Several crabs scuttled around the scattered coral heads, and we saw a few sea stars and a conch inching along at a barely perceptible pace.

In deference to Genevra's condition, I swam slowly and mostly stayed on the surface with her so she wouldn't be tempted to dive down or overexert herself. I knew that Doc had given her the okay to swim and snorkel, but just to be on the safe side, she'd strongly cautioned Genevra against diving to any depth. Since we weren't breathing compressed gases tonight, there was little cause for concern.

But one of the reasons I'd chosen this spot for our snorkeling is because the water is shallow enough that we could see everything below us very clearly from the surface. Even though Genevra wasn't breathing compressed air, I didn't want to tempt her to swim down for a closer look at any sea horses we might encounter. Genevra loves sea horses the way I love stingrays.

After a while I noticed she was flagging a little bit as she swam beside me, so I popped my head up and spit out my snorkel. Genevra immediately bobbed up beside me.

"It's been a long day and I'm kinda tired," I lied. "Is it okay with you if we cut the dive short and head home?"

Although she tried to hide it, I could tell she was relieved.

She spit out her own snorkel so she could reply. "Absolutely fine. I don't want to leave Oliver alone for too long anyway, even if he is with

Penny and Rafe." She grinned at me, looking like a little pixie with her new shorter haircut.

We surface swam to shore and rinsed off our gear with the hose hanging from a hook behind the restaurant. While we let our equipment drip dry a little bit, I bought Genevra a mango milkshake for the ride home. Once the waitress delivered it to her, we packed up our gear and loaded everything in the car for the trip back to my house.

Nobody enters my house without Penny sounding the alarm or barking out a greeting, so I wasn't surprised to hear her loud and surprisingly deep woofs as we came up the walk. I swerved over to the left and dropped off the gear in the breezeway. Then we went inside where Newton lounged on the couch with his feet up, reading an old copy of *Your World* magazine.

Penny was waiting for us just inside the door, and she greeted me as though I'd been gone for days. When she turned her attention to Genevra, Rafe came over and gave me a hello kiss.

"Short snorkel?" he asked.

"I was tired," I said. I almost never get tired, and if I do, I never admit it.

Rafe looked puzzled by my words, but then he nodded when he remembered Genevra's condition.

Oliver was standing behind Rafe, and when Penny was through greeting Genevra, he stepped forward. He took her hand and I heard soft murmurings as he whispered his apology. My brother is a very sweet man.

A beautiful smile spread across her face as she heard him out, and she squeezed his hand before turning to Rafe and me standing awkwardly nearby. "Thanks for dinner. We've taken up enough of your time. I think we're going to head out now."

Rafe and I were arm-in-arm. "Thank you for the pizza and the company," I said. "You two—soon three—are welcome anytime."

We watched them get in their car and drive away before we turned off the outside lights.

Newton sat up straight when we went back in the living room.

"You leaving too?" I asked.

"Nope. We have a meeting in Peter Robert's office right now. We need to figure out what's next."

"They found the *Golden Kelp*?" I asked.

"No. Just the opposite. That's what's puzzling me. We need another plan." He stood up. "We can take my car if you want. Then you can stay at my place. Penny's welcome to stay over too." He patted her furry neck. "Rosalina loves Penny and she will jump at the chance to spoil her rotten."

Chapter 32
In Peter Robert's Office

Rafe quickly packed an overnight bag, which took him all of two minutes. He is a whiz at packing because he travels so much. I didn't need to pack at all, since I already have everything I need in the suite Newton keeps for me in his penthouse condo.

I made a mental note to invite Rafe to keep some of his things there too. Newton wouldn't mind at all, and it would simplify our decisions about where to stay when we have late night meetings like this but don't want to sleep on the *Tranquility*. Or even if we ever need to don business clothes for an unexpected daytime meeting but didn't have enough time to go all the way home to Rum Point to change.

And besides, we're a couple. Our jobs keep us apart enough as it is. We try to do whatever we can to be together whenever possible. I felt bad that it hadn't occurred to me before this to invite Rafe to share my suite at Newton's penthouse as well as my home.

Once we were ready, we headed out. Rafe took his "junkmobile" to provide a small degree of anonymity, and we followed Newton's black Mercedes EV. We parked side-by-side in his building's ground floor garage, and then we all piled into Newton's car for the short jaunt to the Coast Guard office.

Peter Roberts was sitting at his desk when his assistant ushered us in. The assistant was obviously a little bit in awe of Rafe. He never looked directly at him, and when he tried to talk, he could barely speak above a whisper. He seemed shocked when Rafe pulled a large color photo out of his canvas duffle bag and proceeded to autograph and personalize it for him. The man stammered his thanks with a huge happy smile and left us to the meeting.

Peter had watched the whole episode with a face like granite.

Once the assistant had walked out and shut the door behind him, Newton and Rafe sat down at the small conference table on one side of Peter's office, and Penny sat on the floor next to Rafe.

I was uneasy and way too restless to sit still, so I prowled around looking at all the knickknacks and photographs Peter had on display. My gaze was repeatedly drawn to the photo of a young Peter standing beside another man, their arms slung across each other's shoulders. I was sure I knew the other man in the photo, but no matter how hard I tried, I still couldn't place him, and I didn't want to pry into Peter's personal life.

After a few minutes, Newton loudly cleared his throat. I knew that meant he wanted me to sit down so we could start the meeting. We were all anxious to hear what Peter had to say, so I reined in my anxiety and sat down between Newton and Rafe. Peter was alone on the other side of the table.

He opened up his computer and projected a map of the area around the Cayman Islands. I noticed he'd used a combination of red and white lines to shade most of the ocean portions of the map, and I was interested in learning what the lines signified.

Once he was sure he had my attention, he began to speak. "So far, we've put in close to one hundred person-hours in the copters looking for the *Golden Kelp*, and Vincent has put in another large chunk of time circumnavigating the island with the *Omega*."

He used a laser pointer to draw our attention to the white lined area, which was equal to a little more than half of the total search zone. "This is the area we searched with the helicopters." He leaned back in his chair. "And this is the area the *Omega* covered." He waggled the beam of his laser pointer over the red lined area.

"Nobody in either group saw any sign of the *Golden Kelp*. We didn't see any ships that could support a submersible like the one Lily Russo has been known to use in the past. Nothing we saw seemed to be out of place or unusual."

He leaned back and folded his hands on the table. "With all that searching, and all the area we've covered, you'd think we'd have seen something if there was anything to see. But we came up with nothing. I think we're barking up the wrong tree."

We all stared at the map with deep intensity. I was trying desperately to see any likely little corner the searchers might have missed. I was sure Lily and Lukin were in the area and that they were the evil brains behind the conflict diamond smuggling.

If they were the masterminds, it made sense that they'd targeted both Rafe and me during the ad shoot. In fact, it made so much sense that I couldn't believe the theory was wrong no matter what Peter said about the lack of success during the search.

I noticed Newton's eyes darting across the map, just as mine had, and I knew he was looking for something we'd overlooked too. As soon as he had given in to the inevitability of Peter's conclusions, he slumped down in his seat. "Let's regroup tomorrow. I'm too tired to think straight tonight."

Peter nodded. "I get it. We were all so sure we had the answer. But I guess it's possible that the woman you saw wasn't Lily Russo after all. That means there's no reason for us to assume that Seb Lukin is in the area. And really, he's not the only bad guy in the world. It must be someone else behind the diamond smuggling. We'll just have to keep working on it until we figure out what's really going on."

"Of course," said Newton, "Maybe we'll think of something after a good night's sleep." He turned to Rafe and me. "You two ready?"

I nodded, but then I had another thought. "Peter, can you please send us the map showing the areas you've already searched?"

He frowned. "It's just a standard map…"

I nodded. "I know that. I just thought it would help our thought process to see what we've already covered so we don't waste time trying to think of another way to accomplish the same thing all over again. And even if it's not Seb and Lily behind the diamond smuggling, whoever it is has to be around somewhere."

He frowned and thought for a minute. When it became obvious that he couldn't think of any reason to turn down my request, he hit a few keys on his computer. "Done. It's a large file, but the map should be in your inboxes within a few minutes. And you're right, Newton. It's late, and we're all tired. Let's check in again tomorrow."

We said goodnight and left the Coast Guard headquarters.

Newton parked his car in his reserved spot in his condo's garage, and we rode the elevator up to the penthouse without saying a word. We were all lost in thought, except Penny, who was still trying hard to understand elevators.

When the elevator stopped, Rosalina, Newton's friend and temporary housekeeper, greeted us at the door. She kissed my cheek and gave Penny lots of belly rubbing time. She was still a little shy with Rafe, but he leaned over and kissed her cheek when she stood up after finishing with Penny.

She blushed like crazy.

Rafe dropped his duffle bag in my suite and then we both headed to Newton's immense living room. Newton had already hit the button to slide open the teak doors that hid the massive built-in screen. He was projecting the map Roberts had sent him onto the wall-sized screen, and he looked utterly perplexed by what he saw.

Rafe and I flopped onto the couch beside him so we could stare at the screen too. I couldn't see any areas the searchers had missed, and I was beginning to think Peter was right when he said my belief about Lily, Lukin, and the *Golden Kelp* was way off base.

The thought that we were no closer to figuring out who was smuggling the diamonds—and targeting my husband for death—made me crazy with fear.

In my mind, the theory that the nasty father and daughter Lukin duo were behind all the illegal activities was the only one that made any sense at all. Lily hated me, and in the past, she'd shown no compunction at all about hurting me or the people I love.

For some unknown reason, Lukin detested Newton just as much as Lily loathed me, and he'd tried to hurt my father by hurting me before. Lukin also hated Liam and Chaun, because in the past they'd helped me best him while he was engaged in his evil schemes.

And although Lukin was incredibly rich, he was always interested in gaining more wealth, and he wasn't too concerned with whether his methods were legal. I knew for a fact he'd been involved in distributing illegal drugs and that he dabbled in human trafficking. Simply smuggling conflict diamonds seemed a little tame in comparison to some of his other businesses.

We had to be missing something, and I knew Lukin had to be around here somewhere. I could almost smell the evil emanating from him and his crew.

I sighed with frustration just as Rosalina wheeled in a cart loaded with snacks and drinks. She didn't even have to ask what I wanted before she handed me a plate with a half dozen of her homemade cookies—based on the famous recipe used at RIO.

Don't tell Theresa I said so, but if anything, Rosalina's version was maybe a teensy smidgen better than RIO's—but I'd take either variation in a heartbeat. Next, Rosalina placed a glass of icy cold lemonade on a coaster on the table beside me.

Rafe received a crystal glass of ice water along with two cookies and a small bowl of raisins on the plate. I tried not to gloat because my snack was so much better than his, because I also knew he wouldn't eat the cookies, making them mine by default.

Without realizing I was doing it, I smiled. He winked at me as though he'd followed my entire thought process, which he probably had.

Like Rafe and me, Newton rarely drank alcohol, but this evening he had a small glass of beer. He sighed after his first sip, and I could hear his frustration in the sound. "What are we missing?"

Chapter 33
Rosalina Chimes In

I WAS on my second cookie and still staring at the screen. I hadn't made any progress in alternate theories about the perpetrators yet, so I was starting to get antsy. Rafe put one of his cookies on my plate and smiled at me.

I love him, but right then I needed more than a couple of cookies if I were going to keep him safe and stop the flow of conflict diamonds.

I was about to give up and go to bed when Rosalina came back into the room. "Can I get anyone anything else?"

There was a chorus of "No thank you," from us all.

Newton added "Why don't you turn in for the night? We probably won't need anything else, and if we do, we're perfectly capable of getting it ourselves."

This made me smile. Newton and I had abysmal kitchen skills. I could just about manage to make a cup of tea or heat up a can of soup. I wasn't sure Newton possessed even that much culinary expertise.

Rosalina smiled at him. "If you're sure you won't need me..." she started to walk out of the room, but then she turned back. "Before I go, is it okay if I ask a question? Just one?"

Newton smiled. "Rosalina, you're a member of the family for as long as you want to be. Feel free to say anything or ask any questions you want. We'll do our best to answer whatever you want to know."

Rosalina nodded, then she walked over to the map projection. "I see the three Cayman Islands—Grand, the Brac, and Little. But where is my island? I don't see it on the map. Is it just too small to show?"

The tiny island was Rosalina's and always had been. It had been in her family for generations, and her father had willed it to her and her alone when he passed away. She'd inherited it before she married her lout of a former husband, so she still held full title. Neither the no-good husband nor either of her sons had a claim to a slice of the pie. But that hadn't made much difference when Kraken Industries had insisted they'd bought it fair and square.

The legal case over ownership of Rosalina's Island was still wending its way through the courts after the syndicate of bad guys had tricked one of her greedy sons into selling it for a pittance, but since he'd never actually owned the island to begin with, the deal wasn't legitimate. It should have been a cut and dried decision, but legal systems move incredibly slowly.

And although I'd shot Kraken's head bad guy in a heated under-water struggle, I'd never seen his dead body. And for that matter, it was entirely possible that the syndicate consisted of multiple teams of bad guys—not just the odious Brock Moran. And one of those other criminals might conceivably be Seb Lukin, who was an even bigger scumbag than Moran.

There was a lot of deep water at Rosalina's Island—plenty deep enough to float Lukin's mega yacht and there was abundant solar power to charge his small fleet of submersibles.

Several small outbuildings still stood on the island, any one of which might work out well for a charging shed for submersibles. There was a long sturdy dock that led to deep water. And the entire island was outside Cayman territorial waters. Best of all, nobody lived there anymore.

It was ideal.

I slapped my forehead, amazed at how stupid I'd been. The search area on the map stopped just a few miles short of Rosalina's Island. Was that merely a coincidence, or had it been deliberate on his part?

Newton had obviously had the same thought. "Rosalina, I don't know what I would do without you." He walked over to the map and swept his hand over the open ocean area where her ancestral home was located. There wasn't even a dot on the map to show it. "It's right about here, isn't it?"

Our gazes met and I saw in his eyes he'd come to the same realization I had. Rosalina's Island had to be Seb Lukin's new headquarters, the center of the smuggling operation. And Peter Roberts had to be the mole in Newton's organization.

Chapter 34
Brothers

ROSALINA SMILED, happy that Newton had asked her to point out where her family home should have appeared on the map. She practically caressed the spot on the screen where her ancestral home was located, then she took her leave and went to bed.

The rest of us stayed up late, trying to make a new plan and discussing whether failing to search the area around Rosalina's Island had been deliberate or just an oversight on the part of Captain Roberts.

I had a very strong opinion that it had been deliberate.

"I've known him for years," said Newton. "I'm sure it was just an innocent mistake."

I wasn't anywhere near as sure as my father, and I could see the same question in Rafe's eyes that I knew showed in mine. Captain Roberts had been instrumental in developing the operational plan for the mission that had nearly claimed my life when I tangled with the nasty crew from Kraken Resorts and Industries.

I'd thought at the time the oversights and omissions were the result of simple incompetence or maybe arrogance, but now I wasn't so sure. The tiny hairs on the back of my neck stood up, and a chill ran down my spine, but I knew Newton wasn't ready yet to believe my concerns about his friend.

I stood up and yawned. "It's late. We've had a long day and tomorrow promises to be just as bad. We should get some rest. I'm going to bed."

Rafe stood up and took my hand. "I'm with you."

Newton smiled. "I'm just going to give Joely a call before I turn in."

Joely Wentworth, Newton's significant other, is RIO's CFO, and one of my closest friends. She was away right now traveling on fundraising business in the states. Both Newton and I missed her.

I kissed his cheek. "Okay then. Don't stay up too late. We should get an early start tomorrow."

He nodded. "I'll be good."

The next morning Rafe and I were up early, well before the sun, but not before Rosalina. She was just taking a tray of fresh baked muffins out of the oven when Rafe and I tiptoed into Newton's gleaming gourmet kitchen looking for coffee.

Rosalina wasn't expecting us to be up so early, so our arrival startled her. She nearly dropped the hot tray of muffins, but Rafe used his left hand to steady her before disaster struck. With his other hand he grabbed a towel off the counter and deftly slid the scalding hot tray onto the massive stovetop.

It could be very handy being married to an action hero superstar. His reflexes are amazing.

Rosalina smiled her thanks at him and bustled over to the massive, wickedly confusing stainless steel coffee maker at the other end of the counter. She quickly set it up for two cups of American coffee.

I was impressed. I usually pulled out Newton's old French press when I stayed over, because the machine Rosalina used so effortlessly was complicated as well as temperamental. At least for me it was.

Luckily, Rosalina had tamed that complex beast because the coffee she served us at the kitchen counter was amazing. Rich, smooth, and the perfect temperature. I took a huge slurp and sighed with contentment.

Rafe laughed so hard at my slurping that he nearly choked. He wasn't actually choking, but I playfully thumped his back.

Rosalina smiled benignly at us, enjoying our antics. She put a basket of warm muffins on the counter in front of us, and added silverware, napkins, and small dishes of butter and assorted jellies and jams. "What else would you like? Eggs? Bacon? Oatmeal?"

"No, thank you," Rafe said. "This is perfect just as it is."

My mouth was full of warm buttery muffin, so I just nodded along with Rafe. I smiled when I noticed that for the first time since I'd known him, he'd eaten an entire serving of something on his plate. It had been less than a minute since Rosalina had put the plate in front of him but already there was nothing left of his muffin but a few crumbs.

"Would you like another muffin, Mr. Cummings?" she asked.

"No thanks, but I would like you to call me Rafe. You saved my wife and dog from some very bad men, and that makes us family."

She stared into his eyes for a second or two before nodding. "Okay. Family. Rafe."

They both smiled.

At that exact moment, Newton entered the kitchen. He was wearing gray silk pajamas and a matching robe. The pajamas looked like they'd just come from the dry cleaner, and every one of his hairs was in place. Not a single whisker had dared to sprout on his chin overnight.

I had no idea how he did it, but I'd almost never seen him look even a little bit disheveled.

"Morning, everyone," he said, smiling as Rosalina handed him a large mug of coffee tricked out with lots of cream and two sugars.

He took a sip. "Perfect, as always. Thank you, Rosalina." He sat on the stool next to Rafe's and helped himself to a warm muffin from the platter on the counter.

After he'd finished the first muffin, Rosalina brought him a second muffin, nestled on a plate of bacon and scrambled eggs.

Newton ate whatever he wanted and never seemed to gain an ounce. It was another gift he had, like the secret of his always perfect clothes and hair. It didn't matter to me. I sometimes got angry at him, but I loved him anyway. I always had and always would. I just wished he had passed that elusive 'neat' gene down to me along with my height and misty grayish blue eyes.

Rafe returned to our suite to shower and get ready for the day. I had another cup of coffee while Newton finished his breakfast. As soon as he put down his fork, I said "What's the plan for today's meeting with Roberts?"

"No plan. We'll play it by ear." He lowered his voice. "Let's not mention the omission of Rosalina's Island to him when we meet, okay? Whether or not he brings it up, either way we'll just act like we didn't notice anything."

I nodded my agreement. "That's what I was going to suggest. I'll fill Rafe in on the plan when he gets out of the shower. What time are we meeting Roberts?"

"As soon as you and Rafe are ready. And after I have another cup of this excellent coffee."

"Ah, so no rush then?" I asked.

"Nope. I don't want to alarm him by going over too early." Newton winked and sipped from his stainless-steel RIO branded mug.

It was a good two hours later before we rode down the elevator to the parking garage. Newton drove slowly to Coast Guard headquarters, but we were still early because we'd all gotten up at the crack of dawn. In fact, we were so early that we bumped into Peter Roberts on his way in from the parking lot.

Peter led us into his office. "Coffee?" he asked.

We all declined, but he asked his assistant to bring him a cup.

I smiled smugly. It was petty, but I was secretly pleased that his coffee wouldn't be anywhere near as good as ours had been. I'd never liked him much because I felt like he'd sent me into danger without a well-thought-out plan, and now that I suspected he was secretly one of the bad guys, I liked him even less.

Once his assistant had delivered his beverage, Peter took a sip and sighed with satisfaction. "Okay. What's up? And why so early, without even an appointment?"

Newton sat down, looking as relaxed as if he were sitting on his own couch about to read the morning's *Wall Street Journal*. "We need to split up today. Rafe has filming. Fin's teaching a class. I have investments to make. We want to get an update before we have to go our separate ways."

Roberts looked at Rafe. "Where are you filming today?" he asked.

Rafe smiled. "It's just rehearsals. We're doing it at my place. One of the perks of being the star."

Roberts smiled. "Nice." He paused. "Any chance of getting an autograph for my wife? She has a bit of a crush on you. Even bigger than the one she has on Ryan Gosling."

"Sure thing." Rafe reached into his canvas bag and pulled out a glossy photo. "Who should I make it out to?"

Roberts turned red. "Uh, actually, it's for me. I'm not even married."

Rafe never blinked, just wrote 'To Peter' and signed his name before handing the picture to Roberts. "Here you go."

Newton spoke up. "Now that we have that settled, can you give us the update we need please? You're not the only one who has a busy day planned."

Roberts scowled. "Not much happened overnight. The choppers will be heading out around mid-morning to see if we missed anything in the rush yesterday."

Newton nodded. "Good. Where will they be searching?"

Roberts' face grew hard. "Same territory as yesterday. Maybe a little lower and slower, just to be sure we don't miss anything."

Newton put a puzzled expression on his face. "Can you show me again?"

Roberts sighed with exasperation, "For heavens' sake...Oh, all right." He opened up his computer and projected the map on a blank wall beside his desk. Using a laser pointer, he outlined the search area. Just as it had before, the pointer carefully stopped just a little bit away from Rosalina's Island.

I was practically bursting, my nerves stretched tight. In my mind, his omission of the area around the island seemed willful. I considered it proof he was playing for the bad guys' team.

I opened my mouth, ready to blurt out my suspicions, but Newton made a shushing gesture in front of the desk, where Roberts couldn't see it. I nodded, but I was too overwrought to sit still.

I jumped up and took the few steps to the bookcase where Captain Roberts displayed all his mementos and glory photos. Something about that photo with him and the unidentified man still weighed on my mind.

I didn't want to broadcast my interest in that specific picture, so I picked up the framed photo next to it to get a better look at the one I was interested in. "Is this really the Queen?" I asked.

Roberts looked up, obviously annoyed. "No. Actually, it's my mother dressed for a costume party."

I thought he was kidding and I was just about to laugh when I realized who the man in the bothersome photo was.

I paused a second to think of a way to get the information I wanted without letting him know I was on to him. "She looks great. It must have been fun growing up in such a fun family. Do you have any siblings?"

He turned pale and swallowed before speaking. His voice was shaking. "No. I'm an only child." He didn't meet my eyes.

I didn't say anything out loud, but I thought, *"LIAR! I have you now."*

Ostentatiously looking at the dive watch on my left wrist I said, "My goodness. Look at the time. I have to run if I'm not going to be late. Newton, you promised to drop me off in plenty of time…"

He looked up and smoothly covered his surprise at my sudden and previously unannounced need to depart. "You're right. Let's go. Sorry to rush out, Peter. We'll talk later."

He picked up his Hermes Sac à dépêches leather brief bag and walked calmly out of Peter's office and the Coast Guard headquarters. He didn't speak until we were in his car and on the way to RIO. I was bursting to tell him what I'd realized.

When we were finally on South Church Street, he said. "Okay. What?"

I inhaled slowly. "Peter Roberts has a picture of Bert, one of the guys from the Kraken Resorts and Industries crew in his bookcase. They're both a lot younger in the picture, so I didn't recognize him right away, but when Peter started talking about his family, I just knew. They look enough alike to be brothers. If Bert and Peter are friends or relatives, Peter must be one of the bad guys. That's why the search doesn't extend to Rosalina's Island. The *Golden Kelp* must be anchored there."

Newton nodded. "I think you're right about the *Golden Kelp*'s location. Peter certainly went out of his way to keep anyone from searching the surrounding area. But I thought the police killed the entire Kraken crew in the raid."

I shrugged. "I didn't see the aftermath, and I didn't look at the names of the people who died that day. Is there a way we can check the records?"

Newton was concentrating on parking his car in the lot at RIO, so he didn't speak for a minute. "Maybe," he said. "Dane might have the list, although the incident happened outside his jurisdiction. And it was a madhouse, as you'll recall." He stared into space. "So many injured. I feared I'd lost you…both of you." His voice broke, and my heart broke along with it, remembering that awful day.

He recovered himself during the walk across the parking lot. "Let's call Dane and see what he can dig up."

I opened RIO's heavy glass front door. "Remind him to be discreet. We don't want to alert the bad guys if Peter is one of them."

When we went inside, Fred the security guard was too tongue tied by Rafe's presence to say anything, so for once we walked across the lobby and down the short hall to the glass-walled conference room unannounced. We sat huddled at one end of the massive table while Newton called Dane.

After a brief conversation, Dane agreed to pull out the file and see if he had a list of the victims. He promised to email it over to us as soon as he found anything. While we waited, we sat in silence except for the drumming of our fingers on the table.

Maddy came in. "There you are, Fin!" she said. "I was looking for you to see if you wanted to go diving with me this afternoon. Doc and Oliver are coming. Rafe, you're welcome to come too."

We all knew there was no sense inviting Newton. Although I'd finally managed to teach him to swim a short distance, he still wasn't comfortable in the water, and it was unlikely he ever would be. That meant scuba was off the table for him.

Rafe smiled his glorious smile at my mother. "Thanks, Maddy. I'd love to tag along. We're kind of in the middle of something here right now though. What time were you thinking of heading out?"

"No specific time. Just give me a five minute warning and Doc and I will meet you on the dock."

"Perfect," he said.

She turned and walked down the long hall that led to her corner office.

Once she was far enough away that she wouldn't be able to over-hear our conversation, I said, "There's something I've been meaning to talk to you about. It's been on my mind for a long time, and I don't know what to do about it."

"Spit it out," said Newton. "We'll figure it out together."

"Okay. Remember a few years ago when Lily caught me snooping around looking for her sub?"

"You mean the day she tried to kill you?" he said.

"Yeah, it was one of them anyway. I heard something that day that that's been weighing on me ever since. Especially now that Oliver and Genevra are having a baby together. I think they have a right to know." I took a breath. "Lily told me that Seb Lukin is her father. That means he's Oliver's father too."

There was a crash from behind me, and a torrent of ice cold lemonade splashed against my bare legs. I turned around.

There was Oliver, his face as white and drawn as a sheet of paper. "You knew who my biological father was all this time and you never said anything? I can't believe you let me marry Genevra and father a baby knowing the horrible genetic legacy I'm carrying."

I was so shocked that I couldn't speak—and I was scared for my brother,

Rafe stood up and went to him. "Genes don't carry evil. People learn their evil behavior, and there's no reason to assume your baby will be anything except sweet and caring, just like you and Genevra."

"And like my twin sister Lily? We all know she's pretty evil, and we had the same upbringing. If she learned it, then maybe so did I. If she inherited it, then maybe so did I. Either way, my legacy would doom any child of mine."

He punched the wall, leaving a dent in the plaster. "Fin, you should have told me as soon as you knew. I never would have married Genevra, never agreed to have a child…"

Rafe put a hand on his brother-in-law's shoulder. "My parents were pretty horrible, but I didn't catch evil from them. My brother Dougie has problems, but they're not genetic. Our dad used to beat him with a broomstick until his face was black and blue and his ears bled. Dougie learned to be a malicious criminal—he wasn't born that way. Now he's learning a different way to live. Your baby won't have to go through anything like that. Relax. Everything will be fine."

Oliver wrenched away from Rafe and practically spat his next words at me. "None of that stuff matters. You should have told me. I had a right to know." He spun away and stormed out of the room and down the hall.

Chapter 35
Maddy and Doc

HALF AN HOUR later we were still waiting for Dane to send over the names of the casualties from that horrible day on Rosalina's Island. Newton drummed his fingers on the tabletop for a minute before he spoke. "They say a watched pot never boils, and I think the same rule applies here. Emails won't come if you're sitting around waiting. Why don't you two go take that dive with Maddy and Doc? You don't want to keep her waiting too long."

"Good idea," Rafe said. "We won't be gone long. You'll probably have the names by the time we get back, and then we can decide on our next steps over dinner. Sound good?"

Newton agreed, so Rafe and I walked down the hall and around the corner to Maddy's sunny office.

"Still up for that dive?" I asked.

"Yup. I'll text Doc to meet us on the *Sea Princess*. I don't know why, but Oliver decided not to join us. It will just be us four."

Rafe and I shared a glance, worried about Oliver's reaction to the news about his parentage. It had always been a sore spot with him. His late mother had first told him his father was dead. Then she changed her story and claimed his father was Ray Russo, my late stepfather. Neither story was the truth.

But Oliver had always idolized Ray, even long before they met.

He'd been thrilled to think his idol might also be his father when Cara told him the lie.

Shortly after Ray died, Oliver learned that his fondest wish had not come true. Ray was definitely not his father. Then Cara died, without ever telling him the truth about his genetic background.

Maddy and Newton both loved Oliver, so they'd gone ahead and adopted him. He was already an adult at the time, but they'd wanted to be sure he would always have someone looking out for him in case of an accident or illness. We'd all shuddered to think of what his fate might be if he'd ever been ill and Lily was the person designated to make medical decisions on his behalf.

I had learned the truth about his parentage during a dangerous encounter with Lily, but I'd never wanted Oliver to find out. He loved Newton, but I knew he still sometimes fantasized that the genetic test Doc ran had somehow been wrong and that Ray really had been his bio-dad. Now that dream was truly shattered, and the reality of his parentage could hardly have been worse.

I assumed my sensitive brother had gone off someplace where he could be alone to try to come to grips with the awful truth. It was probably for the best that he'd decided not to join us on the dive. He'd need some time to digest the bad news.

Maddy, Rafe, and I went out the back door and walked along the crushed shell path to the dive shop.

Stewie was inside, doing some maintenance on the shop's rental gear. "Doc's on her way," he said smiling. "I loaded tanks on the *Sea Princess* for you, Maddy. Do you need anything else?"

She looked at us, and Rafe and I shook our heads. "I guess we're all good then. Thank you, Stewie." We went around the shop to the employee gear storage area and picked up our gear bags.

Maddy's tiny, but even after her bout with melanoma, she's tough and still very strong. Although she didn't need the help, Rafe insisted on carrying her gear bag along with his own. I loved that Rafe took such good care of my mother.

We boarded Maddy's boat, the *Sea Princess*, and stowed our gear. We'd just finished when Doc arrived. It took her less than a minute to set up her rig and stow her own gear bag. We were good to go.

"Is Hammerhead Hill okay with you two?" Maddy asked.

I smiled. It was Rafe's favorite dive site, and I knew she'd suggested it to please him. When he and I dove with her she almost always chose it despite the nearly 400 other amazing dive sites available around Grand Cayman. "Fine with us," I said.

Most commercial dive operations rarely dive Hammerhead Hill because it's a little further out than the sites they typically visit. The fact that divers are so seldom here means that the site is beautifully pristine, with abundant healthy corals and larger sea life than that found at other sites.

It used to be almost a given that a diver would see a hammerhead on this site, but the great beasts are no longer here as often as they once were. Still, a lucky diver has an excellent chance of seeing one—or on occasion three, four, or even more.

Maddy pulled up to the permanent mooring ball at Hammerhead Hill and Doc grabbed the line with the long-handled gaff. She had us secured in less than a minute. Once Doc had signaled Maddy that the line was secure, Maddy climbed down from the flying bridge. She and Doc used the bench on the port side of the boat to gear up while Rafe and I stuck to the starboard side. We dove together so often that we knew each other's rhythms, so everyone was ready to go at about the same time.

The *Sea Princess* has a deep and wide dive platform on its stern, with two ladders for reentry. There was a little chop here today, so we wanted to get in the water and away from the surface waves as quickly as possible.

Doc and I did our giant stride entries first. As soon as we'd popped up to the surface and given them the okay sign, Maddy and Rafe quickly joined us.

Visibility today was superb, reaching to more than 250 feet through the clear water. There was a mild current. We headed into it and swam toward the deep wall, which starts at about seventy feet and drops to more than 1,000 feet.

It was definitely our lucky day, because a gigantic hammerhead swam right past us as we reached the drop off. Two marginally smaller specimens of hammerheads followed right behind him.

I hadn't brought my bulky professional camera and light setup, but I had a small point-and-shoot camera in my pocket. I pulled it out quickly and managed to get a shot of the three sharks. When the flash lit up the area, the big shark turned around to check out the unusual light. I quickly clicked off several head-on shots of him as he glided toward me.

Once he got close enough to ensure I knew he was the boss around here, he veered off and swam placidly away with his two friends.

I was thrilled to have seen him and thrilled to have managed to grab a few photos. I hoped the quality of the shots would be good enough to include in my next column for *Your World*.

My fellow divers were hovering a little way down along the wall. Once the big guys were gone, it was time to settle down and explore the channels, tunnels, and overhangs that made the site so spectacular and so welcoming for a myriad of sea life.

We admired the large and healthy corals and sea sponges growing on the wall, but as we went deeper the growth flattened out. Because the sights were more interesting at a shallower depth, we ascended a few feet. We immediately saw a school of perfectly matched creole wrasse pop out of one of the overhangs. They swirled around Doc for a minute, making her laugh with delight before they took off.

As we continued, we saw a glasseye snapper hiding in a crevice, and then a trio of glassy sweepers in a tiny cave formed by a large sponge overhanging the coral wall. A gigantic Nassau grouper swam by, ostentatiously ignoring us as though our presence meant nothing to him. To be fair, it probably didn't.

By now we had crested the top of the wall and we swam out to explore the shallower sandy areas. Two pairs of southern stingrays swam right in front of Rafe, coming so close that the leader brushed him with its wings.

As we headed over the reef top to return to the *Sea Princess*, we were thrilled to find a tiny fairy basslet, so curious and so cute that I'd have sworn she was smiling a welcome at me. We glided by a gorgeous sea fan, and Maddy pointed out a flamingo tongue feeding on its delicate lacy fronds.

We noticed a red lionfish grazing on some small reef shrimp. Lionfish are an invasive species, and their venom is extremely toxic. Sadly, we didn't have our lionfishing gear with us, so we gave him a wide berth.

Just before he would have been out of our sight, the large Nassau grouper we'd seen earlier snuck up on him and attacked. The grouper won himself a nice lunch, and we let go of our guilt that we hadn't been able to remove the invader.

We rose up to about twenty feet and swam across the coral toward the mooring line. We went slowly, watching the terrain beneath us for any final sightings of interesting sea life.

Just before we reached the mooring line, the trio of hammerheads we'd seen earlier rose up over the wall from the deep side. They swam right by us without a second glance, but their reappearance made a nice bookend to the dive.

We took our safety stop at fifteen feet, hovering in place for the recommended three minutes so we could watch the abundant life on the reef below. Once we completed our stop time, Rafe and I each climbed one of the twin ladders. We sat on the bench under the gunwale on the starboard side, slotting our used tanks into the rack and wiggling out of our BCDs. Then we scurried back to the dive platform in case Maddy or Doc needed a hand getting aboard.

Of course, they didn't.

Doc and Maddy had dinner plans, and Rafe and I wanted to get back to RIO to peruse the names of the people who had died during the shootout on Rosalina's Island, so we opted not to do a second dive. Maddy climbed the ladder to the flying bridge and we headed for home.

Chapter 36
Plan B

NEWTON AND DANE were sitting at a secluded corner table in RIO's public café when Rafe and I went looking for them. We went through the line and picked up a couple of glasses of icy cold lemonade, a dozen chocolate chip cookies, and a bowl of sliced fruit before we joined them.

My best friend Theresa—RIO's VP of food services—was on duty, so I stopped to chat with her for a minute while Rafe carried the tray of food over to Newton and Dane's table.

While she updated me on Angel's latest antics, Theresa kept a watchful eye over all the café's patrons to make sure everybody had everything they needed. After a few minutes, she glanced over at Dane and my father and laughed. "Newton's eating all your cookies."

"Oh, no!" I said. "I've been thinking about those cookies for hours."

She laughed again. "There's plenty more where those came from." She placed a half dozen on another plate and sent me on my way.

I put the new plate in the center of the table next to the original one, and the three men started laughing.

"I knew the fastest way to get you over here would be to start eating your cookies," Newton said.

I looked at the plateful of crumbs in front of him, all that remained of the dozen cookies that had been there just a few minutes ago.

"Looks like you did more than start eating my cookies," I said grumpily.

Rafe placed a folded napkin on the table in front of me. "I saved you a couple," he said. "But I had to act fast. These guys could give the Cookie Monster a run for his money."

"Thank you." I unfolded the napkin and took a bite of my first cookie. "Do you have the list?"

Dane slid a sheet of paper across the table toward me. It was a list of names segregated by each individual's status after the melee on Rosalina's Island.

Confirmed Dead:

Ken Rawls

Arthur Getty

Missing, Presumed Dead:

Brock Moran

Garth Jones

Cuthbert Roberts

Injured:

Liam Lawton

Finola Fleming

Rafe Cummings

I looked up at Newton after perusing the list. "I knew I recognized the man in the picture in Peter's office. They were both a lot younger in the photo, so I couldn't quite place him, but Bert is Peter Roberts' brother, isn't he?" I asked.

Dane nodded. "Looks like it. We should have picked that up right away, but with all the confusion that day, it slipped through the cracks. We didn't know the names of any of the Kraken crew—except for Brock Moran—until we had to identify them after the raid. If I'd known there was a traitor on our team back then, I'd never have allowed you to take on the undercover role."

Newton put his hand on mine. "I'm so sorry. We're lucky you're so resourceful that you made it out without even worse injuries."

I shrugged. "Water under the bridge. Does Peter know that we know?"

Dane shook his head. "No. And we're going to keep it that way for as long as we can. Our first priority is to recon the area near Rosalina's Island. Just to see if we can find the *Golden Kelp*."

I already had a plan in mind. "Okay, then here's my plan. We leave at first light, on the *Tranquility*. We should all try to act casual—so it looks like it's just a recreational trip. Rafe and I can dive in a couple of spots to lend credibility to the idea. Once we've located the *Golden Kelp*, we'll figure out how to get Liam and Chaun safely off the mega-yacht."

"One problem," Dane said. "Nobody's going to think this is a casual trip if both Newton and I are on board. How can we get around that?"

I thought a minute. "No problem. You can stay here. Christophe's in town. He can be my backup muscle and keep a lookout for bad guys."

Christophe Poisson is a champion freediver and he heads up RIO's global network of freedive training facilities. "And I'll bring Doc and Stewie in case we need medical help or someone to captain for me. Newton, you can come along but you should probably stay out of sight in the cabin."

They mulled it over for a few minutes, looking for flaws in the plan. There were a million. Like how we were going to get on board the *Golden Kelp* if we did find it. Or how we'd get Chaun and Liam safely off the yacht if they were injured or incapacitated.

But eventually we concluded there was no other way to meet our objective.

"Okay then. We sail at dawn." I bit into the last remaining cookie.

Chapter 37
Assembling the A-Team

As soon as we left the café, Rafe and I strolled down to the dive shop to ask Stewie if he'd be willing to go along with us as backup captain. He and Chaun were good buddies, and he'd been worried about his missing friend. I felt sure he'd do anything he could to help rescue Chaun.

But I did have one big concern. Stewie had told me once that he still had nightmares about that day on the beach when Rafe and I had been shot along with all the bad guys.

He was a brave and loyal man, and a true friend to Chaun and me both. He swallowed hard before he spoke. "Okay. Count me in. But don't expect me to shoot anyone."

"Never," I said. "Thanks for agreeing to come along. Do you think you could convince Doc to join us too? Just in case we need her medical skills?"

He nodded. "I think once she knows your plan she'll insist on going. I'll take care of asking Austin and Benjamin to cover the dive shop for me, so don't worry about that. You know that Doc's team can handle any run-of-the-mill patients that show up at the infirmary while she's away, and if there's anything they can't handle they know enough to send the patient to Cayman Island Hospital. I think we're good."

"Thank you, Stewie. I'm going to ask Christophe to join us too. Have you seen him around?"

Stewie grimaced. "I think he's doing an apnea class in the pool house. That's one water sport I don't understand at all, but it's his most popular. Go figure."

"Thanks, Stewie. We're leaving at dawn. Let me know if you think of anything we might need before we go." I walked out of the dive shop and headed to the pool house with Rafe at my side.

Christophe's class was just finishing up. When they climbed out of the pool, he gave each of his students a high five and a towel. Every one of them grinned and thanked him before they rushed off to the locker room.

Christophe took a towel from the top of the stack and used it to dry his slightly too long—but sexy in a very French way—dark brown hair. "To what do I owe this honor, Madam Cummings?" he said in his alluring accent.

Christophe had been the only person besides Rafe and me to know we'd decided to get married. He'd been instrumental in convincing me to follow my heart, and I would be forever grateful for our late-night conversation at Ray's Place. That conversation led directly to Rafe and me eloping in the middle of the night.

Christophe took every opportunity to call me Madam Cummings, even though he knew I continued to use my birth name both personally and professionally. I didn't mind. Secretly, I liked it.

I quickly filled him in on all the facts. Chaun and Liam missing. Millions of dollars in smuggled conflict diamonds. My sighting of Lily. Oliver's paternity secret. Our growing certainty that Seb Lukin was behind it all.

I finished by telling him my suspicions about Bert, my co-worker while I'd been undercover at Kraken Resorts and Industries, and Captain Peter Roberts of the Cayman Island Coast Guard.

"I don't think Bert Roberts died during the shootout, the way we thought. Now Peter Roberts supposedly sent choppers out to look for the *Golden Kelp*, and he may very well have sent some choppers out. But none of them went anywhere near Rosalina's Island, and I suspect we'll find the *Golden Kelp* somewhere very near the area. We're heading out at dawn tomorrow to bring our friends home, and I'd like you on the team."

He didn't hesitate for a second. "Merci. Count me in. I will bring them home or die trying."

I rolled my eyes. Christophe could be so dramatic, but I knew that in his heart he truly meant what he'd said.

Chapter 38
Searching

SHORTLY BEFORE DAWN the next morning, I was making final preparations to the *Tranquility* when Stewie pulled up with one of RIO's jet black rental Zodiacs. His boat was towing my submersible. We hadn't used it much since I'd fired Davy Jones, who at one time had been RIO's primary submersible pilot.

Stewie tied up the Zodiac and hopped onto the dock. He quickly turned around to give Doc a hand to steady her as she stepped aboard. Doc had been around boats all her life, and she was a credentialed boat captain and a scuba training course director. She didn't need any help, but the expression of love and caring on his face made my heart melt.

Once she was safely on deck, he headed back to the Zodiac's stern and untied the float he'd rigged up for the submersible. He hauled the float over to the *Tranquility* and attached it to my boat.

He saw me watching him, a puzzled look on my face. "We know the *Golden Kelp* has at least two subs and two pilots. We may need a submersible of our own to keep tabs on them. Or we might find a sub is the best way to get aboard that accursed mega-yacht. Anyway, bringing it along shouldn't slow us down, and we might find out that we need it. Same for the Zodiac. Better to have it and not need it than to need it and not have it. Once they know we're onto them, we won't get a second chance to recover our friends."

"You're right," I said. "Good thinking."

Stewie grinned and set to unloading several underwater scooters from the Zodiac and then securing them aboard the *Tranquility*. "Same reason," he said as he passed me with the third scooter.

I smiled to myself. I loved it when the new improved Stewie thought things through and took on responsibilities without my having to ask him for every little thing. For too many years he'd been too drunk to think at all.

By now he'd been sober for a few years, and Doc had made it clear right from the start that their relationship was totally dependent on him staying that way. His deep love for her was a very strong incentive for him to stick to sobriety.

Newton arrived next, carrying a gear bag that I assumed contained his usual assortment of high tech gadgets and weapons. Since Dane was with him and wouldn't be joining us on our voyage, I didn't ask Newton what he'd brought just then. He'd show me once we were underway. A few minutes later, Christophe and Rafe boarded together, bearing coffee and muffins for the whole team.

I took my RIO branded mug up on the flying bridge with me and started the *Tranquility*'s engines. Mindful of the submersible I was towing, I backed out of my slip carefully. As soon as we were clear, I pushed the throttle and we took off in a sparkling spray of seawater.

Once we were well underway, Rafe climbed up the ladder and joined me on the bridge, bringing me a fresh hot cup of coffee and another warm muffin. He held the wheel steady, keeping us on course while I ate. I popped the last morsel of muffin in my mouth before speaking. "Do you have any suggestions on how we should approach Lukin if we do manage to find him?"

"Nope. I know you'll come up with the best possible solution on the spur of the moment. You always do. It's one of the things I love about you. I know I'm always in good hands." Rafe smiled and winked at me, and I could feel myself blushing.

"Then let's go see what new toys Newton brought along. That may give me some ideas on the best way to approach the rescue." I engaged the autopilot and climbed down the ladder.

Newton, Stewie, Doc, and Christophe were soaking up some sun on the rear deck. When I jumped down off the last step of the ladder, Newton stood up.

"Ready?" he asked.

We all went into the cabin, where Newton had stowed his gear bag on the daybed. He unzipped it and handed us each a pistol.

Stewie immediately handed his back. "Nope," was all he said.

I remembered how devastated he'd been after the shootout with the Kraken team, so I understood his reluctance to carry a weapon on this mission. "You don't have to carry a gun if you don't want to, Stewie. But if you won't, then you'll have to stay on the *Tranquility* if we board the *Golden Kelp*."

He bit his lip. "Can I think about it?"

I nodded. "Of course. We don't want you to do anything you're not comfortable with."

Doc reached out and took his hand. "We'll need someone who knows how to handle a boat to be on board in case we need to make a fast getaway. That's an important role too, and you're the best person for that job. No gun required."

Stewie looked relieved.

I realized that she was right. Other than the first time I'd boarded the *Golden Kelp*, I'd never again been aboard Lukin's boat when I hadn't had to leave at a run. The first time, I hadn't really known how bad Lukin was, but now I realized that having Stewie ready at the *Tranquility*'s helm was a great idea. Chances were good they'd give chase and we'd have to get away fast.

Newton cleared his throat. "May I proceed?"

"Go ahead," I said.

He handed out dive watches to everyone. They were similar to the ones he'd provided to me in the past. I knew they acted like a walkie-talkie and also had a rescue beacon built in.

"Anyone on the team will be able to hear anything you say, and so will the people near them, so keep speech to a minimum unless you know for certain everyone is in a safe spot. And remember you have to hold down the button to broadcast. Otherwise, nobody will hear anything."

Assuming this new batch of watches operated on a different frequency from the last one he'd given to me, I removed my existing watch from my left wrist and strapped on the new one. "What else do you have for us?"

"Nothing," he said. "We have the scooters, the sub, the watches, and the guns. We don't know what we'll be up against, and we don't have time to practice working with any new tech. I thought it would be best to keep it simple on this operation."

Doc stepped forward. "I have my full medical kit on board, and a small supply of sedatives in my waist pack in case we need them to get Chaun and Liam onto the *Tranquility* without causing them undue pain. I also have some bandages and antiseptic if any of you are wounded, but I won't be with you on the *Golden Kelp*. Try not to get injured." She smiled.

I nodded. "Christophe, you're the point person for spotting the *Golden Kelp*. Binocs are in the middle drawer in the galley. Everybody, keep your eyes peeled just in case we come up on them quickly."

About an hour later, we approached Rosalina's Island. My search plan was to circumnavigate it in ever widening circles until we either found the *Golden Kelp* or reentered the zone already searched by Peter Roberts' team.

We were only on our second circuit of Rosalina's Island when Christophe spotted the *Golden Kelp* anchored off toward the east.

Chapter 39
Boarding

I TURNED the *Tranquility* around and once we'd hidden from view behind an outcropping that formed the cove on Rosalina's Island, I cut the engines. "Any ideas how we get aboard?"

Newton said, "I'll go and try to negotiate for their release if one of you will drive me over in a boat."

Newton's lack of facility with boats and water was legendary, and Lukin hated him. He wasn't anybody's first choice to lead the boarding group.

Hoping someone else would be the first to speak, the entire team stayed quiet for a minute.

Finally I answered. "That won't work, Dad. You know how much he hates you. He'll be angry right from the start."

Doc spoke up. "I'll go. Lukin doesn't know me at all."

Stewie tightened his grip on her hand. "No, you're way too important. We may need your medical skills." That was true and we all knew it.

"Fin and I can go together," Rafe said. "She's the best at thinking on her feet, and I'll be there to watch her back."

At his words I realized how Stewie's heart must have shrunk with terror when Doc volunteered to go. I couldn't imagine being okay with putting Rafe in harm's way.

Christophe spoke for the first time since we'd spotted the mega-yacht. "Rafe has the right idea. There needs to be at least two of us, and better if we have three, because we need to rescue two people and we don't know what shape they'll be in. Fin does think fast on her feet. She and I have the best water skills. It should be the three of us together."

I nodded and opened my mouth to agree with him when we heard a splash from the stern. We hurried outside to see what was going on.

Standing on the dive platform and looking down into the clear water, I recognized Oliver heading toward the *Golden Kelp* using one of the dive scooters. He must have stowed away on the *Tranquility* some-time last night. He'd chosen this moment to make his move.

I grabbed the nearest scooter and was ready to jump in after him when Rafe grabbed my arm to hold me back. "You can't stop him, and we need you with us to execute the plan."

"Lily and Lukin will never let him go once they have him. I have to stop him before he gets there." I tried to shake off Rafe's grip.

Christophe put a hand on my shoulder. "Rafe is right. And now we have three hostages we need to rescue. Let it be us three who go." He twirled his finger around in a small circle that included Rafe, himself, and me. "We'll take your sub. It seats six, non?"

My shoulders slumped. He was right. It had to be us three.

"Wait," said Stewie. "I'll go. Rafe can stay here in case Doc or Newton need anything."

I wanted to agree with him. I'd be so much happier knowing Rafe was safely tucked away on the *Tranquility*. But it wasn't right.

"That won't work," I said. "We need someone that can pilot the boat back to RIO to stay on board, just in case. Although I know without question that Doc can do that job, it's possible we'll need her medical skills at the same time as we need a captain. It has to be both Doc and a boat captain who stay behind. And Newton should stay here too."

I looked at my team. "We'll use the sub, and let's bring the other two scooters with us, just in case we need them." The scooters Stewie had brought aboard were top-of-the-line professional models. They were lightweight, fast, battery operated, and they had a long range.

Even so, I begged the universe to ensure we wouldn't need to use them.

We loaded the scooters into the sub along with a couple of extra tanks, our masks and fins, and our BCDs. With all that, there wasn't a lot of room left for the team even though the sub ostensibly seated six passengers plus a pilot.

I shrugged. I couldn't see a way to safely avoid the overcrowding, and we needed to be on our way right away.

Rafe, Christophe, and I scrambled through the sub's overhead access door. I started the engine and turned on the ventilation system before I closed the hatch. I set up a nav route that led directly to the *Golden Kelp*'s last known location and then gave Stewie the okay sign through the huge clear acrylic viewing window. Stewie, Newton, and Doc slid the sub off its platform and into the ocean.

I let us sink to about twenty feet before I revved up the engine. The sub had a top speed of about three knots per hour, which meant it would take us about an hour to reach the *Golden Kelp*. "You guys might as well sit back, relax, and enjoy the sights," I said. "It's gonna be a while."

My companions leaned back in their plush recliners and watched the wonders of the ocean unfurl around us. We saw several lemon sharks cruising by, and I was happy to see that the undersea area around Rosalina's Island once again looked healthy and robust.

We soon left the island behind. My plan was to try to board the *Golden Kelp* through its underwater docking port, which was a pressurized room below sea level that was open to the ocean through a portal in the hull. The docking port had space and charging capabilities for at least two subs, and it emitted a homing beacon on a specific frequency to ensure its subs could rise through the water from underneath and go directly through the opening without fear of bumping into anything.

I'd erased the yacht's beacon frequency when Seb Lukin had given me the sub, but I still remembered it because the numbers had coincidentally been the same as my birthday. When we neared the destination, I entered the frequency into the sub's homing device and let the autopilot bring us home.

My biggest concern with the idea of rising unannounced through the portal was that there might be crew members in the docking room when we arrived. That could be extremely dangerous for us, not only because we would lose the element of surprise when we confronted Lukin, but also because we'd be defenseless for several minutes as we exited and secured the sub.

We'd just have to wait and see what the future held.

Just before the one hour of travel mark, the homing beacon began beeping, so I knew we were near the destination. I briefly wondered why we hadn't seen Oliver through the viewing dome during the trip. We should have been following the same trajectory, and the sub was slightly faster than his scooter. I didn't think we'd procrastinated for very long after he jumped ship. I crossed my fingers for luck and begged the universe to protect my brother.

A few minutes later, I could feel the sub starting to rise, and a bright light lit up the water that surrounded us, so I knew we were on target for the docking area.

"Get ready, team. We'll want to move fast as soon as the sub reaches its final position." I showed Christophe how to open the hatch so he could take care of that while I stabilized the sub.

I'd decided that Rafe would be the first one out of the sub because he was the most agile. If necessary, he'd be able to climb out and jump to the deck to finish securing us. He would also be able to get back inside quickly if there was trouble. I explained the procedure to him and made him repeat it back to me.

He sounded confident. Then again, he's an actor. It's his job to sound like he knows what he's doing.

When I was sure they each understood their respective roles, I added, "If the docking room is manned, the bad guys may shoot at us. If that happens, I'm going to reverse direction and submerge as quickly as I can so that the sub doesn't sustain any damage. Until I give the okay, make sure you hold onto something to stay stable. I don't want either of you to fall and hurt yourselves, or even worse, fall and damage the instrumentation. Remember the old adage. 'Always keep one hand for the boat.' In this case, it may be imperative."

We broke the surface of the water and emerged into the docking area. I looked through the 360 degree viewing window, hoping to see a deserted docking room. While I looked, Rafe climbed the ladder to the hatch and Christophe positioned himself to push the button that would open it as soon as I gave the word.

Before I'd finished my reconnaissance, I heard a clang and the sub lurched.

Drat. The yacht's lift mechanism already had hold of the sub. Obviously, they'd expected our arrival.

Chapter 40
Un-Welcoming Committee

"Change in plan. Let me exit first," I said. "They know who I am, and for some reason Lukin seems to have a soft spot for me." I set the nav system to return automatically to the *Tranquility* in case Rafe and Christophe had to leave without me. Or if we had to leave in a hurry, the precaution might shave a few seconds off our departure time.

Christophe and Rafe exchanged glances and shrugged. They knew there was no sense arguing with me about it. No matter what they said, I'd insist on being the first one out of the sub, even though it might mean I'd be the first one shot.

Christophe spun the wheel that unsealed the hatch and I pushed the locking lever aside. Then I opened the heavy hatch cover and peeked out. Several of Lukin's crew stood on the steel decking, high powered rifles trained on me.

I turned and looked back down into the hatch. "Prepare to leave as soon as I get out. I'll try to make it look like an accident when I knock the grappling hook off while I'm exiting. As soon as you feel the lurch, shut the hatch and submerge quickly. The sub will find its own way back to the *Tranquility*. Newton will know what to do next. Don't worry about me in the meantime. I'll be okay,"

Rafe stared at me. "Are you crazy? I'm not running away and leaving you here alone."

Christophe joined him at the bottom of the ladder. "Me either. So get out of the way. We're coming up with you." He put his foot on the bottom rung of the ladder.

I heard a familiar voice from near the charging control board. "You can never resist being the hero, can you, Fin? You're so predictable."

"Hello, Lily," I said. I finished climbing out of the hatch and stood on the sub's exterior for a second while I looked around the room. The members of Lukin's gang completely surrounded the sub. Most of them I already knew, and the ones I knew were scum.

Davy Jones, my ex-employee and former friend, stood beside Lily. On his other side stood Garth Jones, my supervisor from my time undercover at Kraken Industries. Now that I saw them side by side, I recognized the resemblance between the two men. Given that and their common last name, they had to be brothers.

Brock Moran from Kraken Resorts and Industries stood in front of the heavy steel airlock door, holding a high-powered rifle pointed my way. Several other people I didn't recognize had guns aimed at me as well.

Oliver sat by himself on a stool near the elevator doors, his hands cuffed together. He looked miserable and ashamed.

With a whoosh, the elevator doors behind him slid smoothly apart. Seb Lukin entered the docking room with all the pomp and manifest evil of Darth Vader walking onto the bridge of a starship.

"Welcome back," he said, his smile exuding malevolence. "I hear congratulations are in order. You and your new husband have my very best wishes. I hope your time together is happy, although I fear it may end up being a great deal shorter than you had planned."

My blood ran cold at the sight of him, but I knew the worst thing I could possibly do would be to show this man that I feared him.

I smiled. "Thanks. Nice to see you too, Seb."

I scrambled down the portable steps that one of the crew had wheeled up to the sub. I sensed Rafe and Christophe behind me, but I didn't dare take my eyes off Lukin. After hopping off the last step onto the steel deck, I walked over to stand in front of the kingpin of evil.

I looked him right in the eye and willed my voice not to shake. "We've come to take back Liam and Chaun. Would you have them brought here, please? Right away would be good." I glanced at my brother. "Oh, yeah. We'll be taking Oliver too."

"Oh no you won't. My brother stays here with me," Lily screeched.

"He's my brother too," I said. "And I'm taking him back to people who love him and don't want to see him hurt."

Lukin smiled. If he'd had a moustache he'd have been twirling the ends like an old time cartoon character. "Nobody's going anywhere," he said. "At least, not until we've worked out a deal."

"What deal?" I said.

"Diamonds. Tell Newton and his buffoon friends to back off. Get the idiot Keystone Kops to look the other way. Do that and I'll even let your husband keep his endorsement deal with the Ice Water folks. No more exploding bottles. No more nonsense with colored labels. We bring the diamonds in. We trade the illegal ice for money. You and your people stay out of it. The deal is simple enough that even you and Newton should be able to understand it."

"I'm puzzled," I said. "You purposely brought us into the smuggling operation in the first place, didn't you? The whole set up with Kraken Resorts. The attempt on Rafe's life in Alaska..."

Brock Moran stepped forward and sneered. "I have to hand it to you, Cummings. You're hard to kill. I thought for sure you were a goner on that last dive in Alaska. You have more lives than a cat." Garth Jones stood beside him nodding vigorously.

"Are you saying you guys were the safety divers who tried to kill Rafe?" I said.

They both nodded, modest smiles on their faces.

"Another failure," I said. "Too bad. Nice try though."

I turned back to Seb. "And you were behind the Ice Water endorsement deal and Liam's plane crash. That was all you, wasn't it?"

He smiled. "You overestimate my skills. And my interest."

"I don't think so," I said. "But I don't understand why you do it. What are you after?"

He stared at me with glittering eyes. "My motive doesn't matter."

I pressed the issue. "What's driving this feud between you and Newton? What do you have against my family?"

"You forget, some of them are my family too."

I pretended not to hear Oliver's heartbroken moan. "Okay. None of that background actually matters to me. Just bring my friends down and we'll be out of here for good."

He smirked. "Unfortunately, they aren't very mobile right now. They need medical care. You might have to stay here quite a while until they're well enough to travel."

I smirked right back at him. "No problem. I've got medical expertise standing by. They'll be fine leaving with me right now."

"Ah, yes. The beautiful and incredibly smart Doctor Annie Warren. They would indeed be in good hands with her. But I can't put that kind of burden on her." He grinned, and it was so evil that I was glad we'd left Stewie behind.

Rafe was standing beside me now, and Christophe was at my back.

I stood up tall and tried to look large and very fierce. "Doc wouldn't consider it an imposition to care for her friends. She doesn't mind. She's ready to take them on as patients."

He nodded. "But the patients are in a really bad way. I don't think they'd make it off my yacht if you try to move them right now."

Rafe put on his superhero persona. "Say what you will, but they are coming with us. Right now. Even if I have to carry them all the way down here on my back."

I walked over to Garth and held out my hand. "I'll take the key to Oliver's cuffs please."

He reached into the pocket of his shorts like he was actually going to give me the key, which surprised me.

I should have known better.

What he pulled out of his pocket was a gun.

He grinned. His ugly crooked teeth were a dingy yellow in the overhead light. "The key is in my other pocket. Can you reach in and get it? As you can see, my hands are full."

He aimed the gun at Rafe. He knew that was more likely to make me stand down than if he'd pointed it at me.

Rafe didn't care. "I'll get it." He reached for Garth's pocket.

Garth stepped back with a horrified expression on his face. "Here," he said, pulling the key out and holding it up so it caught the light. When he was sure we'd all seen it, he stepped forward like he intended to hand it to Rafe. Then he pretended to trip. "Oops,' he said.

I watched the key fly into the open docking port and sink to the bottom of the sea. So much for easily freeing Oliver's hands before our departure.

Christophe had had enough. He walked over and pushed the button that called the elevator. "What floor are they on?"

Lukin didn't answer, but he stared a dare at the Frenchman.

Out of the corner of my eye, I saw Davy Jones flash three fingers behind his brother's back. "Third floor," I said.

If anyone was surprised that I knew where they were keeping the prisoners, they didn't say anything. Christophe was holding the elevator door open with one hand. I walked across the room and helped Oliver to his feet before escorting him into the opulent lift.

When I turned to face the front of the car, I expected to see Rafe getting in with us. Instead, I saw him keeping everyone in the room at bay by holding a gun to Seb Lukin's head.

"Go on," he said. "I've got this."

I started to step out of the elevator to go to him, but Christophe pulled me back inside just as the doors slid shut.

Chapter 41
Rescue Attempt

THE ELEVATOR STOPPED SMOOTHLY when we reached the third level. The doors slid open without a sound. Christophe put his arm in front of me to keep me from rushing into the hall without looking and poked his head out for a quick survey.

"Okay," he said. "It looks safe." We stepped out onto the thick carpet.

I paused a moment to get my bearings. I'd been on the *Golden Kelp* before several times, but it had been quite a while and it was a very big boat.

"I think it's this way," I said finally, pointing to the left. We scurried down the hall. Oliver trudged sullenly beside me, but Christophe and I walked back-to-back so we could see if anyone was approaching from the stairs at either end of the long hall.

About halfway down the corridor, we saw the door marked Infirmary. I reached behind me and swung through the door, my gun at the ready.

The *Golden Kelp*'s infirmary was nowhere near as comprehensive as the one at RIO. For one thing, it was little more than a closet. Aboard the *Golden Kelp* your first aid remedies seemed limited to your choice of either a Band-Aid or an aspirin.

Liam was lying on a pile of blankets in the center of the floor.

Chaun curled up next to him, shivering. Neither man was conscious. They both wore an assortment of bruises, burns, cuts, and scrapes. I attributed most of Liam's injuries to the plane crash, but I shuddered to think that they had tortured poor sweet Chaun.

I fell to my knees and checked each of them for a pulse. Thankfully, they were both alive, but their breathing was so shallow I knew they were deeply unconscious and probably heavily drugged.

"How are we going to get them out of here?" I asked. "We can't carry them both at once, and we don't have enough time to do it one after the other. It won't be very long before those thugs downstairs try to make a move on Rafe…"

Christophe heard the rising panic in my voice as well as I did. "Let me see what I can find," he said. He opened a nearby closet door and found a manual stretcher. It was only a sheet of canvas with two poles stitched into it along the sides.

The stretcher required two people to carry it, one supporting each end. It didn't have wheels, so we weren't much better off with it than we were without it. We couldn't just load both men into it and assume the stretcher could absorb their combined weight.

The stretcher's poles were so far apart that Oliver couldn't carry it with his hands cuffed together, which meant Christophe and I would have to be the ones to haul it. That meant we'd be defenseless if the bad guys decided to strike out at us.

Christophe raced out of the infirmary and rushed up and down the corridor flinging open every door he passed to see if he could find anything of use. I searched the drawers and cabinets in the room while Oliver watched without comment. A few minutes later, a rattle and a bang at the door announced Christophe's return with a waiter's room service cart. He had also found a meat mallet in the kitchen.

Christophe pounded the short chain between Oliver's hands with the mallet, while

I used some surgical tape I'd found in one of the drawers to try to attach the stretcher to the cart. Once Oliver's hands were free, I held the cart steady while he and Christophe lifted Liam onto the stretcher.

Christophe rolled Liam onto his side before he picked Chaun up and added him to the board. I wrapped more surgical tape over the two patients, hoping it would be strong enough to keep them stable during transport.

Christophe and I grabbed the poles on the ends of the stretcher and rolled the cart through the door, with Christophe in front pulling while I managed to push from the rear. Oliver followed us out. We all winced when the cart banged against the infirmary's door frame, but neither of our patients stirred.

While we'd been working, the elevator had moved. That was worrisome, and it felt like forever before the elevator returned to the third floor. When the doors slid open, revealing an empty elevator, I wondered who'd been using it while we'd been working, and what they'd been up to. There was nothing I could do about it anyway, so we rolled our makeshift gurney inside.

As soon as the soles of Liam's feet had cleared the door, I pushed the button for the submersible docking area. I pointed behind Christophe. "The doors open on that side," I said.

He nodded. "Merci." He turned around so he'd be facing into the submersible maintenance area when we arrived. Oliver said nothing, just stared straight ahead at the door.

The elevator arrived at the docking level, but the doors didn't open immediately because the elevator functioned as an airlock as well as a lift. The air pressure in the submersible area was always slightly greater than the ocean pressure to keep the room from flooding, and the elevator wouldn't open until the atmosphere inside had reached the correct pressure.

My ears popped a second before the doors opened. At first glance, the tableau in the maintenance area looked just as it had when Christophe and I had left.

Then I noticed the new arrival.

Newton was standing in the center of the room with his hands in the air. A couple of Lukin's guys had their weapons trained on him, but Rafe still held his gun to Lukin's temple. The two groups were at a standoff.

Christophe and I hurriedly pushed our rickety cart over to the laddered platform that enabled easy entry to a docked submersible. Oliver followed right behind us. I stepped on the cart's brake, and then I pulled my own weapon out of a pocket in my cargo shorts.

Before anyone could make a move to stop me, I aimed the gun at Brock Moran. It was encouraging to see him wince when the red light danced across his forehead. Newton's face twitched with a little bit of a smile at the sight of the man's discomfort.

Now I just had to get everybody on my team into the sub before someone's trigger finger spasmed. "Oliver, will you help Christophe get Liam and Chaun into the sub please?"

He scowled at me, but I didn't care. He was still my brother, and except for Christophe, he was the only person I could trust who wasn't either currently holding a weapon or pinned in place by the sights of someone else's weapon.

Oliver walked over to the ladder platform. He helped Christophe unwrap the surgical tape from the cart and carry Chaun up the ladder. Once on the platform, he climbed down the sub's inside ladder, holding on to Chaun as Christophe lowered him.

"Put him on the back row of seats, please," I called out. "There should be enough room for both of them in that row."

Oliver's only response was a grunt of effort. I took that as a signal that he'd understood my request.

I stood so I could keep Moran in my gun sights and still see through the sub's viewing window when Oliver gently placed Chaun at one end of the back row of seats. Then he climbed back out to assist in transporting Liam.

He and Christophe teamed up again to get Liam off the makeshift gurney and up the ladder to the platform. Liam is much bigger and heavier than Chaun, so it took both of them to get him down the inside ladder and laid out on the other half of the back row of the sub's seats.

When they had finished, I watched through the portal as Christophe blocked the exit and gestured for Oliver to remain in the sub. Oliver was obviously trying to convince Christophe that he had no intention of coming back with us.

At last Christophe moved away from the ladder he'd been blocking, and Oliver wasted no time climbing out. He even jumped down from the top of the platform rather than take a few extra nanoseconds on the external ladder. Once he was back on the steel decking, he returned to the corner where he'd been sitting before and sat down on his stool without meeting my eyes.

I saw Newton biting his lip. He really loved Oliver and had done a lot for him. This outright rejection in favor of a nogoodnik like Lukin must have been painful for him.

I walked over beside Rafe and caressed Lukin's ear with my own gun. "Your turn, Rafe." I said.

"Not without you. We'll go together." I could hear the worry in his voice.

"No, I need you in there now watching out for Chaun and Liam. The rest of us will be joining you as quickly as we can."

Rafe sighed and let his gun hand fall. He dragged his feet as he walked across the decking. As he climbed the platform ladder, Garth Jones lunged forward to try to push him into the water. Rafe managed to stay upright, and he quickly twisted Garth's arm behind his back.

Garth seemed to resign himself to being outmanned. He shrugged and stepped forward as though he were going to resume his spot in front of the ever-changing submersible status board. After two steps, he spun around and leaped at Rafe.

Rafe had superb reflexes. He was able to step aside and avoid an entanglement with Garth. He pushed Garth away.

Garth fell to the steel deck. He managed to catch himself before he hit his head, but he surprised me by jumping back up to a standing position, facing away from Rafe.

He lunged forward, tackled Newton, and pushed him off balance.

For what felt like an eternity, Newton teetered on the edge of the deck, his arms windmilling in a vain attempt to regain his balance. Almost in slow motion, he fell over backward and immediately sank under the water.

Newton could barely swim at the best of times.

The water here in mid-ocean is cold.

Dark.

Deep.

Newton had been taken by surprise when Garth pushed him. He'd had no time to psych himself up for a deep-water swim or even to take a breath.

I lunged forward. "Dad!" I yelled.

I was about to dive in after him when Christophe reached for my arm. "I'll get him. I'm a better freediver than you are, and you're the only one who knows how to pilot the sub. Get out of here. Now."

He stepped forward off the steel decking and sank into the dark water. He was out of sight within seconds.

I was shivering with fear. Newton. Christophe. Rafe. Liam. Chaun. Oliver.

I had to save them all.

I couldn't save them all.

"Rafe, get in." I gestured with my free hand.

He climbed up the ladder to the platform and lowered himself into the waiting submersible.

I twisted Lukin's arm behind his back. "Move it."

I half dragged him to the platform and up the ladder, never moving my gun away from his ear.

Poised atop the platform, I looked across the room to my brother. "Last chance, Oliver."

He took a step toward me.

Lily called out, "Don't leave me."

He paused, one foot in the air.

His eyes met mine.

He shook his head and stepped back.

I could have cried.

I shrugged and pushed Lukin down prone on the platform.

I stepped through the hatch to the first rung of the ladder, daring a quick glance below. I still had my gun aimed at Lukin. "On three," I whispered.

Rafe was already standing by the control that closed the hatch.

I took one last look into the dark oily water of the docking port. No sign of either Christophe or Newton. It had been several minutes by now. I had to assume they were gone.

Quietly, I gently kicked the rung I was standing on.

Once. Twice.

The third time I kicked, I fired my gun into the charging panel and jumped down rolling away from the hatch when I landed. By the time I stopped rolling, Rafe had shut the hatch and activated the engine. I sprang across the front row of seats to the pilot's chair and slapped the lever to begin our descent.

We were under water and moving away before anyone on the *Golden Kelp* had time to react.

Chapter 42
A New Search

I KNEW the team on the *Golden Kelp* would be unable to deploy either of their own subs for at least a few hours since I'd destroyed the electrical panel that controlled the winch that raised and lowered the subs through the deployment portal.

That meant I had some time to search for Newton and Christophe. I flipped on the exterior lights and dove.

Once we were far enough away from the *Golden Kelp*, I spun the sub in circles.

I piloted the sub in a matrix pattern at various depths, looking for any sign of Newton and Christophe.

Nothing.

I brought the sub up almost to the surface and deployed the periscope. Rafe stared intently out at the empty water, just as I did, while we made circles around the *Golden Kelp*, looking for Newton and Christophe.

We saw nothing.

Meanwhile, whatever the bad guys had given Liam and Chaun to keep them unconscious was beginning to wear off. They were both moaning, obviously in great pain.

They needed medical help, and they needed it fast.

But my father. My brave friend Christophe.

Liam and Chaun writhing behind me.

My father.

My *father*!

Tears streamed down my face as I wrestled with the decision I knew I had to make.

Finally, Rafe put his hand on my shoulder. "It's been too long. They're gone," he said. "Now you need to take care of the living. Chaun and Liam need you to be strong."

I shuddered as I set a course to take us back to the *Tranquility* with all the speed my little sub could muster.

We hadn't gone very far when I heard the thrum of the *Golden Kelp*'s engines cycling on. The sound moved away from us. They were leaving.

I didn't know where they were headed but I could only hope they were gone for good.

Tears leaked from my eyes the whole time I was piloting the sub, but I didn't waver for even another minute while we were traveling back to the *Tranquility*. I didn't want to take a chance on losing Liam and Chaun as well as Newton and Christophe.

Back at the *Tranquility*, I brought the sub to the surface near the floating platform Stewie had fashioned to transport it. He was waiting on the *Tranquility*'s stern with a long gaff.

He used the hook to grab one of the sub's mini-cleats and pulled us toward the platform. Doc came out of the cabin to help him.

They could see through the acrylic window that neither Christophe nor Newton was sitting in the front row with us. I recognized the exact moment when Doc realized what this meant.

She used one hand to brush tears from her eyes, but she kept hauling the sub. At last, between the two of them, they managed to wrestle the submersible back into position on the platform and secured it for travel.

I pushed the hatch release and stumbled out. I rushed past Stewie and threw myself into Doc's arms, sobbing like a baby. She patted my back and whispered soothing sounds in my ear.

Stewie and Rafe managed to get Chaun out of the sub and Stewie carried him gently into the *Tranquility*'s cabin and laid him down on the day bed. Then he went back to help Rafe move Liam.

Doc stopped rubbing my back. "C'mon. Chaun needs us." She turned and went into the cabin to see to her first patient.

I took a deep breath and followed her.

She'd finished her initial examination by the time Stewie and Rafe brought Liam in. They took him into the captain's quarters and put him on the bed.

Doc gave me some instructions for taking care of Chaun while she went below to evaluate Liam. Luckily, most of Chaun's injuries were relatively minor and I could treat them with antiseptic, calendula, aloe balm, and bandages.

There were a few places I wanted to leave for Doc because they looked pretty bad. When I'd done what I could, I called Benjamin Brooks on my cell to let him know we had Chaun and that he was safe.

"Thank you," Benjamin said, breathing a deep sigh of relief. "He can be an annoying little twerp, but he's been my best friend for years. I don't know what I'd do if I ever lost him."

"Well, you don't have to worry. He seems fine. Still sleeping though. I'll ask him to call you when he wakes up so you know for sure he's okay," I said.

Since he wasn't awake yet, I worried about what they might have given Chaun to keep him quiet, but I wasn't about to say anything about that to Benjamin.

At least, not yet.

I could plainly see the terrible things they'd done to Chaun. I recognized several of the sores on his body as cigarette burns. He also had a large number of shallow cuts that looked like someone had used a knife on him.

Not to injure. Just to cause pain.

My blood boiled. There were sick people aboard the *Golden Kelp*.

I left Chaun sleeping on the daybed and went below to see if Doc needed a hand with her other patient. She was just finishing resplinting the last of Liam's broken fingers, and I could tell she'd managed to reseat his dislocated shoulder all on her own. One of his legs looked broken, and I assumed that would be next on her priority list. Liam also had several burn marks and small cuts that Doc hadn't even had a chance to address yet.

"Want me to handle the cuts and bruises?" I asked.

"Yes, please, if you can do it without getting in my way while I work on his leg. Maybe start with his arms and upper body," she said.

I nodded, pulling fresh tubes of antiseptic, aloe, and calendula from her bag, along with a big pile of adhesive bandages. I set to work on his face, chest, and arms. They were a mess. The damage made me want to cry.

I applied the last bandage to his chest about the same time Doc finished splinting his leg, so she took over from there to manage the rest of his minor injuries. I went out on the deck, passing a still comatose Chaun with a worried glance.

I climbed up to the flying bridge where Stewie had been piloting the boat. Glumly, I plopped into the chair beside him and burst into tears.

"Your brother wouldn't come back with you?" he asked gently.

I shook my head. "He started to, and then Lily begged him not to leave her. They're twins. How could he say no?" I sighed deeply. "But it's not like she really wants him there out of love. She just wants him around for a punching bag—and to spite me."

Stewie patted my hand. "He'll come to his senses soon. I can practically guarantee it. Don't you worry about him. Right now, we need to go pick up Christophe and Newton. Do you know how to track their beacons?"

My mouth fell open. I'd forgotten both of them were wearing dive watches with rescue beacons built in. "Oh no! I forgot all about those. I just sailed away and left them behind." I bit my knuckle.

Stewie looked at me kindly. "I know you. I'm sure you spent time you didn't have available to waste looking around for them, and I'm also sure you didn't leave them behind without beating yourself up for it. But you did the right thing bringing Chaun and Liam to Doc first. They obviously needed her, and they needed her fast."

He paused a moment. "And Christophe is practically a fish himself he's so comfortable in the water. He'll be fine."

I sobbed. "But Newton is terrible in the water. He's so bad he could drown in a puddle. And I don't know how to track the beacons. I didn't ask because I thought he'd be here."

Stewie said nothing for a moment. Then, "You'd better call Dane and find out how we can find them. Christophe will take care of

Newton as long as he can, but if Newton panics, it could be bad for them both."

I'd seen my father panic over nothing in the shallow end of the pool when I was trying to teach him to swim. Eventually, he'd learned a basic dog paddle, but anything unexpected could still send him into a panic.

Loud noises. Splashing. An unanticipated touch. A flooded mask. There were an infinite number of triggers just in the pool. How was he going to fare in the open ocean?

I pulled out my cell and called Dane.

He breathed a sigh of relief when he heard my voice. "Did you get everyone out safely?"

"No. Oliver refused to leave, and we lost Newton and Christophe at sea. I need you to tell me how to track their rescue beacons so we can go pick them up."

He sounded puzzled. "How did Newton get in the water? He was supposed to stay on your boat so he could monitor your homing beacons himself." He paused a moment. "You know he can't swim very well, right?"

Sighing, I said, "I know all too well how uncomfortable he is in the water. He didn't go in voluntarily. He was standing on the edge of the sub deployment port when one of the crew pushed him in. Christophe dove in after him. That's the last time I saw either of them."

"The tracker must still be on the boat somewhere. Did you check out Newton's bag?"

"Not yet. I'm sorry—I'm not thinking straight right now. I'll go look. Will you hang on?"

I thrust my phone into Stewie's outstretched palm and raced down the ladder. Rafe was sitting on the daybed, putting a cool cloth on Chaun's forehead. Chaun's eyes were still closed.

"Where's Newton's gear bag? The tracking device for their beacons may be in it."

Rafe jumped up and crossed the cabin. He pulled Newton's bag out from under the table and handed it to me.

I dumped everything out on the floor and searched through the pile. Newton had brought a gray hooded sweatshirt, two pairs of cashmere socks, his cellphone, a leather notebook with a matching pen, a tiny packet of mints, a rolled-up bucket hat with the RIO logo on the brim, and a shiny featureless black box.

I picked up the box and shook it in frustration. "This must be it. I don't know how it works though."

From the daybed, I heard Chaun say, "But I do. Hand it to me please. I'll get you the info you need." His voice was weak, barely above a whisper.

Chaun was awake at last. My heart swelled with happiness while at the same time I was consumed with terror for my father and my friend.

Chaun's hands were shaking as I handed him the black box. "You're sure you're up to it? I don't want you to overdo it."

I lied, of course. I didn't want to seem heartless, but I desperately wanted him to solve the problem immediately to help save my father. I knew Chaun had been through a lot, and he was fragile to begin with.

But Newton is my father.

And Chaun was on the *Tranquility*, safe and warm, while Newton was floating somewhere in the vast ocean, unable to swim more than a few strokes and probably paralyzed with fear. It seemed to me that asking Chaun to figure out how to make the black box work was a reasonable request if it could help save Newton and Christophe.

"Of course," he said in a weak and raspy voice. "Lives are at stake, and they risked themselves to save me. What kind of friend would I be if I didn't do all I could to save them in return?"

He ran his hands along the sides of the box. It was sleek and smooth. I hadn't even been able to find anything that seemed like an on/off switch, but Chaun found it right away.

The shiny black surface panel slid back and lifted up to form a screen. A keyboard rose out of the box's depths. The screen lit up, displaying six pulsing lights spread across a map. Four were clustered together, and I realized those were the beacons Stewie, Rafe, Doc, and I wore. Two beacons pulsed together at the far edge of the screen. That must be where Christophe and Newton were. And it looked like they were still close together—maybe even side by side.

Chaun touched one of the two pulsing lights. Numbers appeared on the screen. I recognized them as GPS coordinates, so I raced over to the bridge. "Please read those out loud for me."

Rafe took the heavy black box from Chaun and read the coordinates aloud while I typed them into the GPS. As soon as I finished, I cranked the engines up to max and we took off like a hungry shark after a chunk of chum.

Rafe was scanning the horizon with the binoculars to see if we could discover what the *Golden Kelp* was up to, but the boat wasn't anywhere along the horizon, no matter how hard he looked.

I was a nervous wreck, and I couldn't decide whether it was good or bad that the *Golden Kelp* had left the area. I could only hope that Newton and Christophe had been far enough away to avoid the engine's powerful churn as the yacht moved away. If they'd been too close, the vortex would have sucked them in and hacked them to ribbons.

Of course, that was only a problem if they'd still been alive when the engines started.

Keeping my eyes anxiously on the NAV, I crossed my fingers, hoping that my famous luck would come through for me one more time.

Chapter 43
Discovery

RAFE and I had moved up to the flying bridge to give Doc more room to work on her patients. He was still scanning the horizon for signs of Newton and Christophe, while Stewie helped Doc with the patients below.

Rafe wasn't having any luck catching sight of them, even though we were nearing the coordinates shown on the GPS. The waves were getting higher and choppier. I flipped on the NOAA weather radio. As I'd suspected, there was a storm coming our way.

Now it was even more imperative that we find them—and we had to do it fast before the storm broke.

We were so close to the coordinates that I was puzzled about why we weren't seeing any sign of them yet. I'd had to use the beacon myself twice before, and both times my rescuers easily came to within a few feet of my location.

Rafe was biting his lip. "Shouldn't we be there by now?"

I nodded. "Check with Chaun. Maybe there's something he missed."

Rafe grabbed the black box and scurried down the ladder. I squinted, trying to sharpen my vision, and carefully scanned the water ahead.

Rafe climbed back up the ladder carrying a new set of coordinates written on a scrap of paper. "Chaun says they're moving. He says this is their new location."

I gritted my teeth, angry that I hadn't considered that they were moving. Of course they'd be drifting with the wind and the currents, and I should have been keeping a constant watch on their movements, tuning our course as needed to intersect with theirs.

I plugged the new coordinates into my autopilot's NAV, and the *Tranquility* turned a few degrees to the north. Rafe picked up the binoculars and resumed scanning the horizon.

I resumed chewing my lip. I was missing something. I just couldn't figure out what it was.

The wind was picking up even more, and the first drops of rain bounced on the deck just as we reached our destination. There was no sign of them.

Back to the black box. They had drifted, but not as much as I expected. I corrected the course again. Rafe resumed scanning.

Still nothing.

My heart stilled. I remembered when Newton had said they could tell my beacon was underwater the last time I'd used it. He'd told me how scared he been that he might have lost me.

I knew exactly how he felt.

My voice cracked when I spoke. "Rafe, ask Chaun if he can read the depth on that black box."

Rafe rushed off to do my bidding. When he came back, Stewie was with him.

"Sea level, not at depth. They're still on the surface," Stewie said. He took the black box from Rafe and made a slight adjustment to the NAV. Again, we swung a few degrees, this time to the south.

The wind was whipping the waves into a frenzy, and the rain made it hard to see anything past my nose. We'd never be able to find them in this weather. And they'd never be able to survive the storm if we didn't.

I turned to Rafe in despair when I suddenly realized why we weren't seeing them. He'd been scanning the horizon, which was fine while we were far away from them. But as we drew nearer, and the waves grew surlier, we needed to be scanning closer to the water's surface.

I grabbed the binoculars from Rafe. "Stewie, please take the wheel," I said. "Rafe, please bring me the bullhorn and then go below where it's safer. And dryer."

I sloshed through the fat raindrops and the water washing across the bridge to the railing. I used one hand to hang on, and the other to scan the water's surface, about twenty-five or thirty feet away.

Rafe came back in less than a minute with the bullhorn. "I'm not leaving you up here. If it's too dangerous for me, then it's too dangerous for you."

I could hear the concern in his voice.

"Okay, given this wind, we should all clip in anyway." I showed him how to clip himself to one of the D-rings on the boat's hull. Stewie had already secured himself to the wheel.

Once I knew they were both safe, I grabbed a line of my own and clipped onto the hull. Once more, Stewie had nudged the course, and we turned a few degrees north again. I resumed scanning, using one hand to hold the binoculars. With my other hand, I held the bullhorn to my mouth.

"Newton! Christophe! Are you out there?"

Thunder rolled, and it drowned out any possible reply they might have made.

Frustrated, I tried again.

No response.

The *Tranquility* shifted its course again.

I scanned the surface ahead of us.

The rain poured down with the intensity of a waterfall.

The wind blew.

The boat changed course.

I yelled through the bullhorn.

And then I saw them. Christophe was holding Newton up by the back of his shirt with one hand, waving his arm in the air with the other.

I could tell he was shouting, but the wind and the rain drowned out his voice.

"Slow down, Stewie. They're just ahead. I'm going in."

I started to scurry down the ladder, but Rafe grabbed my arm. "It's too dangerous," he said.

"My father," I replied. I shrugged off his restraining arm.

I threw a couple of life rings their way and then I quickly pulled on a pair of fins and my mask. I grabbed two life vests and one of the dive scooters we had brought and stepped overboard.

The water was freezing, and I felt like I was inside a washing machine that was tossing me around like an old sock. I fumbled with the scooter's switch. When it powered on, I had a little more control against the crazy waves, but not much. I pointed the scooter toward Christophe's upraised arm, sank down a few feet to get away from the powerful surge, and took off.

It took less than a minute of swimming underwater to reach them, and I'd held my breath the whole way. Back on the surface, I inhaled deeply and handed Christophe one of the vests while I held an unconscious Newton above the water's surface. Once I'd secured Christophe in his vest, we teamed up to get Newton into a vest of his own. It was a struggle, but we finally managed to get him into it.

Now I just had to get them back aboard the *Tranquility*.

Stewie was holding my boat steady about ten feet away. It might as well have been a mile. The current was pushing against us with more force than we could overcome.

I could easily make it back to the boat with the scooter. Christophe could do it too. But we only had one scooter. Then I had an idea.

We didn't have to swim against the current to reach the boat. If we could get ourselves and the *Tranquility* to reverse our positions, the current would do all the work for us. I signaled to Stewie to move past us, but since there's no official signal for leaving your divers behind, I wasn't sure he'd get what I meant.

But I watched in amazement as Stewie piloted the boat about twenty feet past us and turned her around so the dive platform and ladder were facing us. If we could just hold on, the ocean would take us right to my beautiful boat.

I bellowed to Christophe to hold onto the scooter with one hand, and to keep hold of Newton with the other. He nodded his understanding.

Once I saw his strong hand close around the scooter's handle, I turned it on again. I aimed it under a few feet to get out of the current, but I immediately headed for the surface again so we could all take a breath. We were rising and sinking almost like we were swimming using a dolphin kick. I hoped that even though he was unconscious, Newton's body would automatically know enough to breathe each time we surfaced.

I did the maneuver again.

The third time, we were there at the platform. Christophe and I lifted Newton as high out of the water as we could.

Stewie and Rafe were there to pull him aboard. As soon as he was safely on the boat, Rafe picked him up and struggled into the cabin, where Doc was ready to take on her next patient.

Christophe started to climb, but the boat bounced and he fell back into the water. He sank, too exhausted to fight any more.

Still holding the scooter, I dove down and grabbed him around his chest with my left arm, and I pointed the scooter to where I hoped the *Tranquility* was with my right arm. I couldn't tell for sure where the boat was because of the tossing waves and because I'd turned my back so I could hold Christophe tight.

I'm not ashamed to admit I was scared as cold ocean water splashed across our faces, blinding us and making it hard to breathe.

Even though it hurt like mad, it was a relief when I bumped my head against the *Tranquility*'s dive platform. I hadn't realized I was that close to the boat until I banged into it. Stewie and Rafe reached down and pulled Christophe aboard. This time Stewie carried him into the cabin.

I climbed the ladder with shaking limbs. Rafe put his arms around me. "Let me get you into the cabin before you fall down," he whispered. "My beautiful, brave, amazing wife."

He put his arm around me and we battled the wind as we crossed the deck to the relative safety of the cabin.

Stewie had already pulled out a couple of inflatable air mattresses and was busy blowing them up with a small portable compressor. When the first one was ready, he placed it on the floor. He gently lifted the still-unconscious Newton from the end of the daybed and laid him on the mattress. Then he covered him with a silvery rescue blanket before turning to the next mattress, this one intended for Christophe.

Christophe was sitting in one of the captain's chairs, slumped against the wall. He was wearing one of Rafe's sweatshirts, but he was still shivering violently. When the mattress was ready, he rose unsteadily and we helped him lower himself onto it. We covered him with another rescue blanket, and I rolled a thick pair of Rafe's wool socks onto his feet.

The boat was still at the mercy of the wind and rain, but Rafe braved the rolling seas to make a pot of hot coffee. When it was ready, he poured it into some of my collection of RIO-branded stainless-steel mugs and added a cover to each mug to keep the contents from sloshing out. He and I served the hot coffee to the injured team members first.

Then he rummaged through the cabinets to see what we had aboard to feed the patients, all of whom must have been desperately hungry. Back when it was just me living on the *Tranquility* there would have been nothing edible on board, but Rafe was good about keeping the boat stocked with staples. He pulled out some instant oatmeal, zapped it in the tiny microwave, and covered it with canned milk and sliced fruit.

As he finished preparing each bowl, I picked up a spoon and a napkin and delivered the steaming bowl to the injured team members, serving Christophe and Chaun first, since they were the worst off. Liam and Newton were still unconscious, so the next servings went to Doc and Stewie, both of whom had been working tirelessly to save our friends.

By the time it was my turn, I was shaking with fatigue. I sat at the small galley table next to Doc and wolfed down the warm food. I felt one thousand percent better when I'd finished.

My next priority was to get the team back to safety.

Stewie and I debated whether we should head to the lee side of Rosalina's Island to wait out the storm or brave the weather and go straight back to RIO. We'd just made the decision to head to RIO because of the medical facilities there, when like magic, the storm broke.

The clouds rolled away, the waves evened out so the surface looked as smooth as glass, and the sun shone as it does nearly every day in the Caymans. A few drops of rain tried to keep the storm going, but even they soon petered out. I pushed the *Tranquility*'s engines to max, and we headed for home.

Chapter 44
Homecoming

We were still about an hour out from home port when Liam woke up. He was coherent, but in great pain from his broken fingers and the burns he'd sustained both in the plane crash and from lit cigarettes at the hands of Lukin's sadistic crew while he'd been in captivity.

Doc radioed ahead to her team, and I was sure they were scurrying around making sure they had everything they'd need to treat our injured comrades and preparing for our return.

Newton was still unconscious, breathing oxygen from the small rescue tanks I keep on board. He was nearing the end of the last of the three tanks I had available, and he still hadn't stirred. I was utterly terrified for him.

Chaun was doing well physically, but he was extremely subdued, very unlike his usual exuberant self.

Christophe had stopped shivering, but he stared moodily into the distance and unusual for the outspoken Frenchman, he didn't speak unless spoken to. I was worried about him. The ordeal he'd been through seemed to have sapped his usually abundant self-confidence.

Rafe brought me another mug of coffee and sat beside me in the mate's chair. He reached out and stroked my hair. "Everything will be fine," he said. "You were—no, you ARE—absolutely amazing."

I smiled absently at him. Even I recognized that the hollow smile I mustered hadn't reached my eyes, but it was the best I could do given all my worries about my father and my friends—and my brother. I wasn't looking forward to telling Genevra about his decision to stay with his twin sister and the Lukin gang rather than to return home to her and their unborn baby.

As we rounded the point at the edge of RIO's cove, I radioed ahead to let them know about our approach. Austin was manning the dive shop radio, and he took the call.

"Please ask Theresa to have plenty of hot, hearty food delivered to the infirmary. Oh—and coffee. Lots of hot coffee. And let Doc's team know we'll be there in under five minutes. Ask them to be on the dock, ready to act fast. We've got quite a few injuries."

"Will do," Austin said. He signed off, and knowing him, I felt sure he was dashing around making sure he did everything exactly as I'd asked.

When I pulled into my slip on the dock at RIO's marina, four EMT's rushed forward with wheeled gurneys. They formed into teams of two to lift the non-ambulatory patients onto the assigned gurney,

They quickly rolled Liam and Newton down to a waiting ambulance, but Christophe refused to make the expected trip to Cayman Islands Hospital.

"Non. No other doctor is as good as Doc. I will be fine with the treatment here." He waved the EMTs away with a Gallic shrug of his broad shoulders.

The remaining EMTs loaded him and Chaun onto gurneys they rolled to our in-house infirmary. They moved at a run, and although she must have been as exhausted as I was, Doc ran beside them, easily keeping up. Rafe loped along with her.

While they were maneuvering the gurneys through the door, she turned back and shouted to me. "You and Stewie come see me as soon as you get *Tranquility* buttoned up."

I nodded and waved, watching her go inside.

I packed all my stuff into my gear bag while Stewie finished coiling the excess line holding the *Tranquility* to the dock. At the last minute, I put one of the guns Newton had brought aboard with him into my canvas tote bag.

I snapped the bag closed a nanosecond before Stewie looked up at me. "Ready?" he asked.

I was just about to agree when I saw Oliver's wife Genevra hurrying down the crushed shell path to the dock. She raced toward the boat, holding her pregnant belly with both hands to keep it stable.

"Where is he?" she asked, panting. "Is he okay?"

I took her hand. "He's fine. Let's go have some tea and I'll tell you all about it."

The excited look on her face fled. "He stayed with Lily, didn't he?'

I nodded. "I think it may just be for a little while. Let's go inside and I'll tell you all about what happened."

She brushed tears from her eyes and stood up straight—all five feet of her radiating an aura of angry hurt. "It doesn't matter what happened. He chose to stay with a known criminal and his homicidal twin sister rather than come home to me and our baby. What more is there to say?"

"Seb Lukin is his father, and you know how much he's always wanted a dad. And he has a twin sister—who can even understand what that bond is like?"

She grimaced. "In case you've forgotten, he already has a father who loves and respects him. It's your own father, Newton Fleming. Newton turned his life upside down to adopt Oliver, put him through school, set up an amazing trust fund and gave him a dream job at an incredible company. What more can Oliver expect from any father? He certainly won't get anything like that from Seb Lukin."

"Probably not," I agreed. "But Lily…"

Genevra interrupted me. "The homicidal maniac?" Her voice held scorn.

"Yup. She's his twin sister. They were very close growing up…"

She interrupted me again. "Don't try to defend his choice. Knowing how much not having a father hurt him growing up, he still chose to desert his own son. It's unforgivable."

Privately I agreed with her. The very least he could have done was talk it over with her before running off to join the bad guys on Lukin's team. In my opinion, that's the bare minimum he owed to his wife—his sworn life partner.

Although Genevra and I were close friends, there'd been a wall between us since I found out she'd worked for Newton's international law enforcement group, which had assigned her as my guardian. Thinking she'd spent all that time with me because it was her job rather than because we were friends rankled—even after she swore it hadn't been like that.

We stared at each other, neither saying a word. Then her chin quivered and tears spilled from her eyes. I threw my arms around her and drew her close. It didn't matter how our relationship had started. We'd grown into friends and my friend was hurting. I would do what I could to help her.

I patted her back and smoothed her hair, murmuring "there, there'" and "It'll be alright." I knew that what I said didn't matter to her. It was having someone who cared that made the difference.

I vowed I would always be there for Genevra and my future niece or nephew.

After a while, Genevra's sobs slowed down. Eventually she stepped back and wiped her eyes. "Thank you," she said. "I know you're angry with me, but I really needed a friend just then."

I looked into her stunning green eyes. "I'm not angry anymore. And we are friends. Friends forever. Sisters even. Now let's go get that cup of tea and figure out what we're going to do next.

She nodded and walked with me to my office. I called Theresa to ask her to have someone on staff send a tray with a couple of pots of tea and some scones to my office.

"Is Genevra okay?" she asked. She knew from the food order that it must be Genevra. I loathe tea and I barely tolerate scones, but they are both Genevra's favorites.

I was happy when a few minutes later, Noah brought in a huge tray laden with tea and scones but also cookies and lemonade, my own favorites. It was handy that Theresa, my best friend, was RIO's VP of food services. She knew my likes and dislikes as well as she knew her own.

I poured some tea into a pretty china mug that I knew came from Maddy's personal collection and handed it to Genevra. Then I offered her the small plate of lemon slices before I pushed the plate of scones her way.

Genevra raised an eyebrow at me.

"I'm not hungry," I lied, although I felt famished.

Genevra broke off a small piece of her scone and nibbled daintily. "Let's see how long that lasts," she said.

She was right.

I had a cookie in my hand before she swallowed her first bite of scone. What can I say? It had been a very tough day.

We sipped and munched for about twenty minutes before Rafe knocked on the door and poked his head in. "Doc sent me to find you. She says if you don't report to the infirmary within the next ten minutes, she'll come out to get you herself."

Genevra and I giggled.

"Doesn't she have enough patients on her hands?" I asked. "She should have plenty to keep her busy."

He smiled his famous smile. "She wants one more, and she asked for you by name. She told me if you wouldn't come on your own, I should throw you over my shoulder and carry you down there or else she'd come up here and drag you to the infirmary herself." He winked at Genevra. "So, Doctor Fleming, it's up to you. Which would you prefer?"

I laughed, as I always did when he called me Doctor Fleming. "I'm coming." I stood up, but then I turned to Genevra. "Maybe you should come along and keep me company."

"I'd like that," she agreed. "Let's get going before Doc makes good on her threat."

Chapter 45
Recovery Area

WHEN I WALKED into the infirmary, Benjamin Brooks, RIO's VP of business development, was sitting on the edge of Chaun's bed. He stood up when he heard me enter and walked over to give me a hug.

"Thank goodness you're okay and thank you for rescuing Chaun. I was worried sick about him."

I smiled at Benjamin. "Of course you were. He's your best friend. But I think he's a lot stronger than we sometimes give him credit for."

Benjamin laughed. "I agree. He's already threatening Doc that if she doesn't discharge him within the hour he's leaving anyway."

"He's a brave man if he thinks he can get Doc to back down on what she believes is right for one of her patients."

Just then Doc bustled over to Chaun's bed. Benjamin excused himself to listen to her instructions since Chaun had a maddening tendency to daydream about some technological wonder rather than paying attention to what was going on around him.

Doc handed Chaun tubes of several different salves. Some were for the burns and others for the cuts he'd sustained. She counted out a few pills for the pain, and then she explained the complicated dosing instructions. At last, she cautioned him to keep the bandages dry and to change them daily.

Chaun nodded through the whole recital. Benjamin took copious notes as he always did when he was hearing important information.

When she finished, Doc asked, "Any questions?"

Chaun looked at Benjamin.

"No questions," he said.

Doc smiled at Benjamin. "I'm holding you accountable." Then she turned to Chaun. "You're free to go, but please take it easy for the next few days."

Chaun didn't answer, but he jumped off the bed and scurried toward the exit, still wearing his RIO scrubs.

Benjamin turned to Doc. "Thank you," he said. Then he followed Chaun out the door.

"You're next," Doc said.

She gave me a thorough exam while Genevra and Rafe waited outside the cubicle. "I'd feel better if you'd stay here overnight where I can keep an eye on you," she said when she finished.

"But I'll feel better if I go home with my husband and my dog."

"That's probably true, and I could go along with that plan, but only if you promise to get plenty of rest, drink lots of water, and eat healthy food. Can you promise me that?"

I bit my lip, and she laughed.

"Lucky you have a handsome live-in caretaker. Did you hear all that, Rafe?"

He laughed. "I did, and I'll see to it."

Doc nodded. "Then you're free to go, as long as you go straight home."

"After I check on Christophe, of course." I knew I was pushing my luck.

She bit back a smile. "Of course."

Christophe was in the furthest cubicle, lying in bed under a silvery thermal blanket. When I walked in, his mesmerizing brown eyes looked huge in his unusually pale face.

"Allo," he said to me.

Then he saw Genevra behind me and his face took on a glow. He swore he'd fallen in love with her the first moment they'd met, and he'd been heartbroken when she chose Oliver over him. It was obvious from the look on his face that her visit meant a lot to him.

He pointed to the visitor's chair beside his bed. "Sit here, Genevra. You shouldn't be on your feet."

She gave a wan smile and sat down. Rafe and I stood at the foot of the bed.

"How are you feeling?" I asked.

"Lucky," he said. "I feel very lucky. I have no idea how you managed to find us in the middle of that storm."

"It was a team effort," I said. "And Newton's rescue beacon watches were the key. I have to say those things have saved my bacon a few times."

Christophe looked sheepish. "I forgot all about those. You must have been following Newton's beacon. Luckily, I was holding on to him or you might have missed me completely."

"I don't think so. There were two signals we followed," I said.

Rafe nodded his agreement. "I can vouch for that."

Christophe seemed puzzled, then the light dawned in his eyes. "Newton and I both knew we were in trouble. At one point he started struggling with me. I thought it was just a case of the usual drowning person's panic, but I think he must have been trying to make sure that if he didn't make it, you'd still be able to find me. He was probably trying to push the button that turned on my beacon."

I nodded. "Could be. You can ask him when he wakes up. But I have a question. How did Newton get to the *Golden Kelp* in the first place? Do you know?"

"He took the Zodiac that Stewie had attached to the *Tranquility* and putted it over to the *Golden Kelp*. But he crashed into the docking area and slashed one of the pontoons. The boat must have sunk while we were with Lukin because it was long gone when he and I surfaced. I towed him as far away as I could from the *Golden Kelp* and toward where I thought the *Tranquility* would be. I would have made it the whole way if the storm hadn't come up when it did."

"You did great," I said. "We'd have lost Newton for sure if it hadn't been for you."

Christophe didn't say anything, but he looked around the infirmary. "Where is he anyway?"

"Cayman Islands Hospital. As far as I know, he's still unconscious."

Christophe looked sad. "I hope he makes it. He's a very fine man. I admire him greatly."

"Me too," I said finally letting go of the last of my anger toward Newton. Right now, I only knew I never wanted to lose my father. I'd already spent too much of my life without him.

Chapter 46
Liam

RAFE and I stopped at Doc's office to say goodbye and to thank her for all her hard work. She and Stewie were sitting at the small table in her office, sharing a turkey club sandwich complete with french fries and cola.

I laughed when I saw the food in front of them. I would never think twice about seeing Stewie eating fries and drinking soda, but Doc was almost as strict about her food as Rafe was about his.

She blushed when she saw me eyeing her meal, then she defiantly took a gulp of her cola. "I need the energy," she said.

I smiled. "I agree. You probably do need it. You worked unbelievably hard today. You even deserve ice cream for dessert."

"Already taken care of," Stewie said. "We had dessert first."

We all laughed. I thanked Doc again for all her work and then told her Rafe and I were going to stop by the hospital to see Liam and my father on our way home.

"Don't stay long. They need their rest, and so do you." She smiled kindly.

"Yes, Doctor." I kissed her cheek and then we left.

At the hospital we stopped in to see Newton first. He was still unconscious. Maddy and Dane were getting ready to leave when we came in.

"Any change?" I asked.

Maddy shook her head sadly. "No change, but fingers crossed."

Then she and Dane departed.

I sat by Newton's bed and held his hand. I could still feel the chill of the stormy ocean when I touched him, even though he was under warming blankets and had a warm IV running into his arm.

He was pale and tired looking. His hair was a mess, with a couple of locks falling onto his forehead. It was one of the few times I'd ever seen him looking less than perfectly groomed, and it made him look sweet and vulnerable.

"Come back, Daddy. I need you," I whispered in his ear. He sighed in his sleep, and I wondered if that meant he'd heard me.

We stayed a few more minutes, until a nurse came in to take his vitals. I kissed his cheek, and we took our leave.

It was time to check in on Liam.

Liam was awake, but his hands were heavily bandaged. Every finger was in a splint. He had burns and bruises everywhere. His broken leg was in a cast and one arm was in a sling to support his dislocated shoulder.

His face lit up when we walked in.

"How are you feeling?" I asked.

"Like I was in a plane crash and then nearly froze to death before I caught on fire. Like I dragged myself for miles through the woods until a bunch of whacko bad guys caught me and beat me and then lived through a raging storm at sea. So," he grinned, "other than all that, I'm doing fine."

I'd always loved Liam's resilience and his wry sense of humor, so this recitation of his recent past made me smile. It also made my blood run cold at the thought of all this poor man had been through.

I smiled, hoping he'd realize my next words came from a place of caring. "Sounds to me like it might be time to give up this facet of your career and stick to what you know best. Technology. Publishing. Real estate. Environmental remediation. You've got a lot to choose from, and none of it should be life threatening."

He nodded. "I agree. As soon as I can, I'll tell Newton I'm out of the game. I want to focus on Lawton Media."

"You mean Quokka Media, don't you?" I asked. Quokka Media is the company I'd worked for part time. It was the publisher of *Ecosphere* where I'd had a monthly photo column for years.

He shook his head. "Quokka will be part of it for sure, but I've been working on an expansion idea for months. Hence, Lawton Media. Bigger. Better. Multi-channel."

I remembered the contract Del Dunlap had waved in my face—the same contract Newton and I had looked over just a few days ago. Now that I thought about it, both had said Lawton Media, not Quokka Media.

"How does Del Dunlap fit into this new venture?" I asked.

He flushed. "You know about Delaney?"

"We've met," I said dryly.

"Oh, that's good then. Do you like her?" He seemed eager to hear my answer.

"Why does it matter? She's your partner, not mine." This was getting weird.

He hesitated for a moment. "She'll be managing editor of Quokka Media, while I focus on launching the other divisions. I was hoping to lure you back to *Ecosphere* if you like her."

I didn't want to tell him exactly how much I didn't like her, but he had to know. "You know I'm under contract to Will Graham at *Your World* now. I couldn't come back even if I wanted to. Which I don't."

He looked crestfallen. "Your columns are always so popular. You made *Ecosphere* what it was. I was wrong to take Gary's side after what he did. I should have known better. I couldn't be sorrier."

Gary Grayson had been the publisher of *Ecosphere* when I worked there. I'd quit after he pulled a stunt that could have killed Rafe and me. I was happy where I was at *Your World*. There was no going back.

I sighed. "I appreciate the apology and I forgive you, but even though it wouldn't have made a difference, you should have talked to me yourself if you wanted me back. Del tried to trick me into breaking my contract with *Your World* by claiming I was still under contract to Quokka. She threatened to sue me and Will both for breach of contract."

I brushed back a tear when I realized that had only been a few days ago. "Newton was looking into the situation before this mess with Lukin and the conflict diamonds started, and he would have quickly figured out she was making a bogus claim, but you know me well enough that you should have known I wouldn't appreciate her strong-arm tactics. I'm afraid she's as bad as Gary. So, no. Sorry, but I won't be part of your new company."

"Would it help if I swore that I told her she wasn't supposed to contact you until I gave her the okay? And you know I never would have given her the go ahead to threaten you."

"Water under the bridge. I'm happy at *Your World*, so it's a moot point. And besides, she's Peter Robert's niece, and he's one of the bad guys."

I looked at my watch. "I'm sorry. We have to go now. Rosalina's been watching Penny for us, and she must be about ready for a break. We'll stop in again tomorrow."

I patted his good shoulder in a take care gesture, then Rafe and I walked out of the room and went back to Newton's penthouse to pick up our dog and go home.

Chapter 47
Rafe and Fin Dive

As soon as we exited the hospital, Rafe took my hand. "It's been a tough few days, and even seeing Liam was draining for you. Do you want to stop someplace for a drink or an early dinner before we pick up Penny? I'm sure Rosalina won't mind a bit."

I looked at his sweet face and smiled. "You already know what I want to do."

He laughed. "Yes, I do. Where do you want to go?"

"I don't want to take too much time before we pick Penny up. Maybe we can just do the shore dive at Sunset House? It's on the way home and it's a great dive. We can rent some gear there so we don't have to stop back at RIO first to get our stuff."

"Perfect," he said. Then he laughed. "I knew that's what you'd say. Austin is already on his way over there with our gear."

I grinned at him, delighted with our synchronicity. Every day he proved over and over that he was my perfect husband.

We checked in at the dive shop at Sunset House and geared up on the ironshore near My Bar. Once we were ready, we stepped off the wall and just like that, we were on one of the most scenic dive sites in the Caymans.

The ocean is always my happy place, and as soon as I was under the water I felt the stress wash right out of me. Sure, the back of my mind still worried about my injured friends—and Newton—but my attention was all on enjoying the dive.

The late day sunlight slanted through water as clear as gin, highlighting the colors of the varied corals that surrounded us. As we swam, we hovered over one of the coral grooves that led out to the main dive site, which is flat, smooth, and open. Along the way, we saw two southern stingrays buried in the sand, a green turtle, seven parrotfish, a seahorse, and a hefty grouper. Pairs of French angelfish swam sedately above the coral, and a blue tang nibbled on a nearby orange tube sponge.

The journey to and from the site is enjoyable, but the main site is spectacular. We stopped to admire the mermaid statue—Amphitrite—which grows more inspiring each time I see it. Several almost invisible sand tilefish darted around near her feet, their color blending perfectly with their environment. After a few minutes, we continued on to visit the wreck of the *Nicholson*.

The *Nicholson* is a haven for all sorts of sea life. There's the lazy nurse shark who is almost always sleeping in a niche under the hull and the green moray eel whose wide mouth seems to smile at you as he works his jaws to help his breathing. The sharp teeth in those jaws belie the seeming friendliness.

A huge conch was making slow progress across the open sand, headed toward a crop of garden eels swaying in the mild current. We continued past the wreck toward a slight rise in the coral. The coral shelf drops off after a few feet, and there's a healthy robust wall on the other side, complete with slipper lobsters and tiny Pederson shrimp.

The drop off to the hidden wall is a long swim from the entry point, so we had to turn around almost as soon as we reached it to head back to shore. Once again, we followed the grooves and spurs in the coral, which led us directly back to the ladder.

Sunset Reef is an easy shore dive that never disappoints, and as I climbed from the ladder onto the ironshore, I was grateful to Rafe for suggesting the dive. It was exactly what I'd needed to regain my perspective and bring order to the thoughts that had been roiling about in my brain.

Chapter 48
Rosalina's Dilemma

WE RINSED our gear in the big freshwater tank and strolled hand in hand back to the parking lot. It was only a short jaunt back to Newton's penthouse. We parked in the garage and rode up in the private elevator.

Rosalina was reading a book in one of Newton's comfy leather lounge chairs with Penny curled up on her lap. Penny leaped down when she heard us open the door, and Rosalina stood up and straightened her skirt.

"I'm sorry. I should stay in my own room," she said, wringing her hands.

"Nonsense," I replied. "You're family. No reason you shouldn't be out here relaxing, especially while you're watching Penny for us."

She smiled sadly, then she looked uncomfortable. "Thank you. Mr. Rafe, I wonder if you could give me a ride downtown later? I have a lot to carry, and …"

He held up a hand. "It's just Rafe. No Mr. required. And of course I'll give you a ride. Where are you going?"

She blinked, and I'd have sworn I saw tears in her eyes. "I am not sure. I am waiting for a call back on one of two apartments. The landlord promised to let me know this evening. I should have the exact address in a few minutes."

"You're leaving? But why?" I was upset to hear that Rosalina wasn't happy living as a guest at Newton's place.

She cleared her throat and sniffed twice. "Newton's housekeeper called today. She said her daughter is doing much better, and she'll be back tomorrow. Of course he doesn't need two housekeepers. I'll get out of her way so she can have her room back."

"Rosalina, Newton doesn't think of you as his housekeeper. You're a guest. And you're staying in a guest room, not the housekeeper's room. Newton will be very upset if he wakes up and finds you've gone. Please stay."

She shook her head sadly. "I can't stay here if I'm not earning my keep, and I can't steal someone else's job right out from under them. Newton will understand."

Rafe and I looked at each other, our eyes meeting over her head. He nodded slightly, and I knew we were on the same page. I nodded back and tossed my head slightly so he'd know to take the lead in what came next.

"Rosalina, this is perfect," he said enthusiastically. "You're the answer to our biggest problem. Fin and I have been talking about getting some live-in help. We both travel so much, and even when we're home, we work long hours. We have Chico and Henrietta to worry about as well as Penny. And we take care of Liam's garden next door when he's away, so we need someone to help with that. For now, you can have the guest room at our place, but we've talked about adding an ADU—an accessory dwelling unit—to the back yard. That would give you even more privacy. Please say you'll come take care of us. We need you."

I stood up and took her hands. "Rafe is right. You're the only person we'd trust. Please say you'll do it."

Rosalina brushed a few tears from her eyes. "If you're sure…"

We helped carry some of Rosalina's things down to the parking area and loaded them in Rafe's old junker car. On the ride out to Rum Point, I arranged for a moving company to meet her at Newton's the next morning to pick up the rest of her stuff. I also called an architect to meet with us in a few days to talk about adding the ADU we'd discussed.

And just like that, we had a new housekeeper.

Chapter 49
Dane Drops In

WE'D JUST GOTTEN Rosalina settled in the guest room when the doorbell rang. Dane's deep voice carried through the door. "Fin, are you home? I need to talk to you."

Like most dachshunds, Penny felt it was her duty to bark like a nut when someone came to the door, even though we all knew that she knew it was Dane waiting outside. We'd heard his voice, and in addition, as a member of the hound family, it was extremely probable that Penny had already caught his scent long before he'd reached our door.

Penny automatically rushed over to get pats and give out kisses when I opened the door, and Dane bent over to oblige. When our pup was satisfied, he stood. "I'm sorry about what happened to Newton. Has there been any change?'

"Thanks," I said, shaking my head. "He's still out. But Christophe is doing well. So are Liam and Chaun."

"Well at least there's that. No word from Oliver?"

"No. He seems determined to stay with Lukin and Lily," I said. "I don't understand it at all."

"Me either," he said. "But there's something else I wanted to talk to you about."

He came in and sat on the couch. "Peter Roberts has kept the Coast

Guard deployed. They haven't reported any further sign of the *Golden Kelp*."

"I'm not surprised. He's one of the bad guys," I said.

Just then Rosalina came in with a pitcher of lemonade, three frosted glasses, and a plate with sliced lemons. She placed it on the coffee table in front of Dane and poured us each a glass.

As soon as she left the room, Dane started talking again. "He has two operatives working in the distribution center, and they haven't reported any suspicious activity. Maybe smuggling the conflict diamonds was a trial run that failed. According to his operatives, there's no sign of anything illegal going on now..."

I broke in. "Didn't you hear me? I just said Peter Roberts is definitely one of the bad guys. Bert, one of the Kraken team, is his brother. I just saw Bert on the *Golden Kelp*. He's there along with Brock Moran and Garth Jones, the lead weasels in the scheme to steal Rosalina's Island. And I even think Garth is related to Davy Jones."

Now it was Dane's turn to gape. "Are you sure? Those are some pretty wild ideas. Roberts told us his crew had cleaned up the island and that he'd accounted for the whole crew."

"Did you see the bodies?" Rafe asked.

Dane shook his head. "Garth and Moran were listed as missing presumed dead after you shot them in the water. And nobody named Bert appeared on the list at all."

"And another thing. Del Dunlap has insinuated herself into Liam's businesses," I said. "She's Peter's niece, right? We need to stop that from going any further, but with Newton unconscious I'm not sure what to do. And anyway, what can the gang hope to gain from that?"

Rafe spoke up. "They can keep a close eye on both Newton and you through Liam. They could use his media empire to manipulate information fed to the public. They'd have access to his environmental remediation records, which may help their case to gain control of Rosalina's Island. Remember, they wanted that island as a communication hub because of its secluded location. And let's not forget the money. Liam's loaded. Newton's even richer. You're a trust fund baby. Even Rosalina will be wealthy as soon as her case makes it through court. They could put their sticky fingers into everybody's business and you'd never know until it's too late. We have to find a way to put a stop to it before it goes too far."

Comprehension dawned on Dane's face.

I nodded. "I'm on the board of directors of Fleming Environmental Investments, and I'm in charge when Newton's away. I haven't spent much time on it for the last few years because things run like clockwork between Gus and Oliver…"

My mouth dropped open. "Oliver. That's why they want Oliver with them."

I grabbed my phone to call Gus at home. Theresa answered their house phone.

"Hey, Girlfriend. Been a while since we chatted…"

I broke in. "It has been. And I'm sorry. I promise we'll get together for some girl talk soon, but right now I have an emergency. Is Gus around?"

"He's still at the office," she said. "Some kind of computer glitch."

Out of the corner of my eye I saw Rafe knock on the guest room door, and I assumed he was letting Rosalina know we were leaving. I nodded when he turned my way.

My attention was still on the phone call with Theresa. "Okay, thanks. I've gotta get somewhere right away, but tomorrow we'll talk. I promise."

Rafe and Dane were already standing in the foyer ready to leave. We raced out the door and jumped into our cars. Rafe and I were in his old junky-looking car, and Dane had his unmarked police vehicle. We all started our engines. Dane flicked on his flashers and we took off like a bullet behind him, squealing around the corner.

Chapter 50
Fleming Environmental Investments

RAFE DROPPED me off in front of the office and then he and Dane took off to park the cars. It was after hours, so the front door of the Fleming Environmental office was locked. With shaking hands, I rummaged through my canvas tote bag looking for my ever-elusive key card.

When I finally felt the card floating loose at the bottom of my bag, I pulled it out and swiped it against the lock. There should have been a buzzing noise as the lock clicked open.

Nothing happened.

I swiped again. Still nothing.

I turned the card over in my hand, peering at it in the dim light of the nearby street lamp. I slapped my forehead at my stupidity.

I was using an old diver certification card—not my Fleming Environmental employee ID card. No wonder the lock didn't work.

I started fishing through my purse again, but between the wallet, keys, lip balm, loose coins, tissues, and other assorted stuff, it was impossible to find anything. Finally, I upended the bag on the front step. My Fleming Environmental keycard landed right on the top of the pile.

I bent to pick everything up, but the strap of my bag caught in the door handle and tore off. Frustrated, I tossed the now useless bag in the nearby bin.

I crammed everything except the precious key card into the many pockets of my cargo shorts, distributing most things at random to avoid overstuffing any one pocket. I might need to be able to move freely inside, and I didn't want to get hung up because my wallet was digging into my thigh. Plus, I didn't want Seb's team to see my pockets bulging. That might give them the idea that they needed to frisk me.

Once all my possessions were evenly distributed, I grabbed the employee key card and held it to the lock. The strident buzzer was like music to my ears.

"Gus. Gus. Where are you?" I bellowed as I ran across the opulent lobby.

The conference room door down the hall opened and Gus poked his head out. "We have a problem," he said.

"I know. I'm here to help," I said. "We need to shut off Oliver's access…"

My brother stepped out from behind Gus. He was holding a gun trained on Gus.

Seb Lukin stood beside Oliver.

Lily made three.

Gus's face was grey.

"Are you okay, Gus? They haven't hurt you, have they?" I was worried about his heart condition. If Doc said he wasn't well enough to dive, then he certainly wasn't well enough to stand up to hard cases like Lily and Seb.

Not to mention Oliver, the young man he'd worked so closely with for the last few years.

"I see," I said. "Welcome home, Oliver. I don't know what you're hoping to accomplish, but you must know that your password has pretty low withdrawal and transfer caps."

Oliver nodded pleasantly. "I do know that. But I also know that yours doesn't. Come on in. We've been waiting for you to arrive."

I took a step backward. "I'm not going to help you steal from my father."

Seb looked surprised. "Not even to save Gus?" His eyes glinted. "Or Rafe?"

I heard a tussle from the hallway outside the conference room, and then Bert and Peter Roberts frog marched Rafe into the room. They pushed him to his knees.

His hands were fastened together at his waist, and each of the men had a hold on one of his arms. A trickle of blood leaked from his nose, and the collar of his shirt was torn.

"Here's the deal," said Lily in her deceptively sweet, musical voice. She sounded like an angel, but she was so, so very evil.

"We're not greedy. Just transfer two billion US dollars to the account number I give you, and we'll let everyone go."

"Nope," I said. "I told you I won't steal from my father, and I meant it."

Seb reached in his pocket and pulled out a folding knife. It zipped open with a zing. The overhead lights made it glisten and shine. Even the man's knife looked evil.

And sharp.

In fact, it looked very, very sharp.

I inhaled deeply to steel my nerves. "No," I said again, although my heart was hammering against my ribs.

Seb held the knife to Rafe's cheekbone. "Still no?" he said. "Your stubbornness could ruin a very promising acting career.

Rafe leaned away from the knife so he could speak. "Don't worry about me. I'll be fine. You can't give in to evil. Giving in just lets it grow stronger."

I was worried. Not so much about Rafe's face. For sure I loved the way he looked, and I knew his appearance was essential to a career he enjoyed and was exceptionally good at. I didn't want any harm to come to him, but I loved him for who he was inside, not the way he looked on the outside.

But my real worry was knowing that they'd never let any of us go even if I gave in. They'd do whatever they could to hurt me, and all the people Newton and I love.

I worried about my husband, of course.

I worried about my friend Gus, and how Theresa and their daughter Angel would cope if Seb's team hurt him.

Poor injured Liam, who would most likely be next on their list once they'd finished with me.

Maddy, my mother, who stood to lose both her children tonight if I didn't make every choice correctly over the next few minutes.

I took a deep breath. I needed to remain calm and alert if I were going to save the people I care about.

I straightened my posture and looked Seb right in his beady little eyes. "You harm one hair on Rafe's head and you can give up the idea that I'll help you in any way. Drop the tough guy act, and let's make a deal. My brother may be holding a gun, but I'm holding all the cards."

I pushed past Oliver and Gus, walking within inches of Seb and his big shiny knife. I brushed shoulders with the murderous Lily. I crossed to the back wall of the conference room and sat in the middle seat of the long side of the conference table—the power seat in any meeting.

"Rafe, sit here on my right. Gus, you're on my left. The rest of you, pick a seat. That side only." I pointed across the table at the glass wall.

Seb and Lily looked at each other as though they couldn't believe my stupidity. I'd set up the room so my enemies were between me and the only exit.

"Oh, and please set Rafe's hands free before you sit."

Rafe bravely stopped beside Lukin, who had a half smile on his face, like he couldn't believe my nerve.

Neither could I.

Luckily neither my hands nor my voice was shaking, so I wasn't giving off any fear signals.

At least, none I was aware of.

Seb stared directly into my eyes as he raised the knife and plunged it toward Rafe's mid-section. I kept my eyes on Seb's face, not wanting to see what he did to my husband.

I heard Rafe squeak.

Then a second later he slid into the seat on my right, hands free and completely unharmed.

I worked hard to keep my elation from showing on my face, but my heart was hammering hard enough to jump right out of my chest.

"Lily, would you mind getting some water for us. Unopened bottles only please." I smiled sweetly at her.

"I'm not your…" she started yelling, her hatred and anger at me obvious.

Seb put his hand on her shoulder. "They're our guests. Get them some water. Please."

I could feel the corners of my lips twitch in a small smile of triumph, but I stifled it quickly. I had to be cool.

Lily slid three bottles of water—Ice Water brand—across the table, one for each of us. All the bottles had blue labels, meaning they were most likely legit. No illicit "ice"—as the gang called the diamonds—inside.

I knew Newton had brought the case that had contained the exploding bottles here after that day of filming. He'd wanted to hold on to them in case of a lawsuit.

There'd be no conflict diamonds inside the blue label bottles, but maybe, just maybe, one of them might have an exploding cover. I slowly picked mine up and turned the cap.

There was a snap. The bottle turned icy.

But there was no explosion.

At the very least, I'd been hoping for an extremely loud noise that might startle Lukin into making a mistake.

I put the bottle down on the coaster in front of me and slid my hands under the table so the bad guys across from me couldn't see them shaking.

Rafe turned his cap. Mist, but no explosion. His bottle turned icy cold.

It worked perfectly, dang it.

Gus turned the cover on his bottle. There was a fizzing noise. No change in his bottle at all. It didn't even turn cold. It was a dud.

Okay. Disappointing, sure.

But not a problem.

I still had other parts to my plan. And alternatives to those plans too. I would not allow the monster that was Seb Lukin to best me.

I took a deep breath to prepare myself for what was to come. I'd have to think fast. Move fast. Turn on a dime.

But although I usually only think like that underwater, even on land I knew I could do it. I had too much to lose.

Just before I placed my folded hands on the table in front of me, I pushed the record button on the dive watch Newton had given me when we'd made an earlier trek to the *Golden Kelp*. If I didn't make it out of this meeting alive, at least there'd be a record of what went on.

I took a sip of water from the bottle in front of me and smiled at Seb. "What exactly is it that you want?" I said pleasantly.

"He already told you. Money!" snapped Lily.

Seb put up his hand to silence her.

"Thank you." I nodded pleasantly. "This is about more than money. What is it you're really after? Why do you hate Newton so much? I need to understand what you're thinking if we're going to reach a satisfactory deal. Although two billion dollars is a substantial sum, I don't believe it would keep you happy for long. There's something else at the bottom of this. Tell me."

I saw pain break across Seb's face. "Newton murdered my sister. Helena."

That was a shocker. "I don't believe that. Newton would never commit murder."

Seb smiled, the saddest loneliest smile I'd ever seen. If he was acting, he deserved an Oscar.

"No, you're right. Newton didn't pull the trigger himself. But he set the events in motion that led to her death. He deserves to feel the same kind of pain I felt."

"Tell me the story," I said. "All the details. Otherwise, I won't believe you're telling the truth."

He waved his hand in the air, a light gesture that said my words didn't matter.

Then he stared at me for a long moment. "Another time, perhaps. For now, I'll be satisfied with the money."

I stared back, my expression carefully neutral, but my mind working at lightning speed. "I need my own computer to process the transaction. It's the only one that has the right software for the transaction site."

He snapped his fingers. Lily stood and left the room. A minute later, she returned, carrying the rarely used computer that sat on the desk in my seldom used office here at the headquarters of Fleming Environmental.

Her face was hard and cold with anger as she walked around the table to place it in front of me. It was obvious she was furious that Seb was making her do my bidding.

Good. I'd add some fuel to that fire.

"Lily, Hon, I'd hate to have the computer run out of power during the transfer transaction, so would you mind plugging it in please?" I said. I made my voice as condescending and patronizing as I could. I gestured to the outlet near the floor behind the chair where Gus was sitting on my left. "I strained my back rescuing Christophe and Newton earlier, and I'm not sure I could stand up again if I crouch down to reach it."

She snorted with contempt. Then at a gesture from Seb, she knelt behind Gus to plug in the computer.

I shifted my weight forward as though I were trying to give her space to accomplish her task while my right hand sifted through all the objects I'd stuffed in the big pocket on the right hip of my cargo shorts.

I found it just as Lily started to rise. I sprang to my feet and quickly wrapped my left arm around her throat and jerked her toward me. At the same time, I pulled the gun from my pocket and pressed it against her temple.

"Let's go," I said to Rafe. "Easy does it. Gus, slide out behind me and follow Rafe. Wait for me outside."

As soon as I sensed Gus had passed behind me, I pulled Lily along with me. I positioned us between Rafe and Gus in the front of the large conference room.

I looked directly at Seb. "You and your team, hands up and head to the back corner please."

His face was white, and I realized he really did love his daughter Lily. He made a sweeping gesture and all the members of his team put their hands in the air, then they stood up and walked slowly toward the far end of the conference room.

"There's a coat closet there. Everybody inside."

Seb's team formed a circle around him as he walked toward the door.

"Inside," I said again when they hesitated at the door.

He nodded.

Garth leaned forward and opened one of the double doors for him. They all filed in.

"Now shut the door." I would have liked to take an extra second to lock them in the closet, but I was afraid they'd shoot through the door if they knew one of us was on the other side. I pulled Lily along with me as first Gus, then Rafe, then Lily and I left the conference room.

As soon as we were safely out of the room, I pushed Lily back through the open door. She bumped into the table, knocking over a chair and spilling the projector to the floor.

There was a loud bang, and a crash. Lily screamed and fell on top of the projector. As I'd feared, someone had taken a blind shot through the door.

"Go, go, go," I said, pushing Rafe and Gus ahead of me. I shoved them outside through the front door, then took a second to set the alarm and the electronic locks. They function on a timer, like a bank vault.

The alarm would summon the police as soon as they detected motion while the alarm was set. Once locked, the doors would only open with both a keycard and a password. I was certain that Oliver had both, but I counted on the confusion of Lily's injury to give us at least a few minutes.

I pushed Rafe and Gus ahead of me to the parking lot around the corner. A police car screeched to a halt directly in front of me. Dane's lead detectives, Roland and Morey, jumped out just as Dane reached us from where he'd been waiting in his car.

He threw his arms around me. "You cut it pretty close, young lady. I was just about to go in there all by myself."

I smiled at him. "I told you there'd be no problem. Everybody's in the conference room. Oh, and you need an ambulance. Lily's been shot." I held my hands up in a gesture of denial. "It wasn't me. I swear."

Three more cop cars pulled up and a swarm of police raced toward the door. I went over and waved my key card over the sensor and punched in the code that overrode the timed lock.

The doors clicked open. The police ran inside.

I could hear the siren shattering the night as the ambulance headed our way. The plan had worked. The bad guys would soon be headed to jail.

"Let's go home," I said to Rafe. "Can we drop you off, Gus?"

He nodded. "Thanks. I don't think I could drive after all that, so I'd appreciate the lift."

The three of us walked across the lot to Rafe's junker car and gratefully opened the doors.

Chapter 51
Final Dive

Rafe and I slept late the next morning. The heavenly smell of waffles and bacon wafting from the kitchen was the only reason we finally decided to get up.

Rosalina was in the kitchen overseeing the breakfast preparations and sneaking tiny bits of bacon to Penny when she thought we weren't looking. By unspoken agreement, Rafe and I decided to overlook this transgression just for today.

After breakfast and a couple of cups of Rosalina's excellent coffee, we were sitting at the table on the patio discussing our plans for the day. Rafe's schedule called for him to leave soon for filming in Bulgaria, so we wanted to spend as much time together as we possibly could before he had to depart.

"We need a dive first thing," he said taking a final sip from his stainless-steel RIO mug. "I'll load up the car while you call the hospital to check on Newton."

"No need to call," said a cheerful voice from the gate which had just opened on silent hinges. "I'm right here."

He strode across the yard, giving a wide berth to the pool, and gave me a hug and a kiss on the cheek.

"Good job you two. You saved Christophe and me and rounded up some very bad guys. You managed to close out an investigation that's been a thorn in my side for a very long time. Impressive."

"I'll tell you what's impressive. How did you manage to secure your released from the hospital so quickly?" I asked him.

"I woke up late last night. Dane was there keeping watch over me in case you'd missed corralling any of the bad guys. I called Doc as soon as he told me what went down. She called in a few favors to get me sprung, and here I am.

I shook my head. "You need to take it easy."

He laughed. "That's what Doc said."

"How is Lily?" I asked. I hadn't been the person who shot her, and I think she's a despicable person, but that didn't mean I wanted her dead or injured.

"She'll pull through. Garth is in big trouble with his boss though. Seb warned him not to shoot through the door but he did it anyway."

"And what's happening with Oliver?"

His face fell. "I'm not sure yet. As far as we know, he didn't actually do anything wrong. He just wanted to stay with his birth father and twin sister on the yacht since he hadn't seen them in a while. Or ever, in the case of his father."

"You're his father," I said stubbornly.

"Yes, I am. But you know better than anyone that you can love multiple fathers. And I'm grateful every day that you do." He smiled at me.

I pursed my lips, not convinced that Oliver should get off scot-free. "You know he tried to transfer a big chunk of your money to Lukin's account."

"Did he?" Newton asked. "Or did he deliberately use an insecure computer and mistype his login and password? Who can say for sure?"

"I overheard you guys planning to dive today. Would you mind giving me a lift to town? I had to take a cab to come here since I left my car at RIO yesterday."

"Sure thing, Dad," I said.

I dropped Newton off at his car, then I parked in the shade of a palm tree that bordered the far end of the lot instead of in the reserved space right outside RIO's main entrance. I didn't like using it because I didn't like strangers being able to keep track of my comings and goings.

Rafe and I held hands as we walked past Ray's Place. We laughed when we saw Taz dancing up a storm on his perch while Candy glared at him.

Candy didn't want Taz to outdo her, so she croaked out, "Hey! Isn't that Rafe Cummings."

Rafe and I looked at each other in dismay, realizing that Candy's latest catch phrase might be the end of our precious anonymity on the RIO grounds.

We stopped at the dive shop to pick up our gear. Stewie and Austin were both working on tank inspections, so they were happy to take a break when we came in.

"I replaced all the empty tanks on *Tranquility* with full ones this morning, so you should be good to go." Austin looked wistful. "Where are you headed?" he asked.

I could have invited Austin to join us, and Stewie would cheerfully have given him the time off. But I knew Rafe would be leaving soon, and he'd be gone for a few weeks. Selfishly, I wanted to spend all the time I could alone with him.

Earlier, we'd decided we wanted to make this dive a long one, so we opted for a relatively shallow site—Black Rock Reef off the East End. The depths at this site range from twenty feet to just over fifty feet. Although there is frequently some current, it's usually mild and easily managed.

We tied up at the mooring ball and headed for the deeper areas to the east for the start of our dive. The reef has undercuts in multiple places at this site, creating overhangs and ledges that many sea crea-tures—and scuba divers—find enticing.

Our search was rewarded almost immediately when we happened upon a nurse shark napping under one of the deepest ledges. We observed her for a few moments, but we left her alone well before she grew visibly annoyed. We drifted across the sandy bottom, spotting a convoy of conch wending their way along the so-called "conch road." The 'road' is a groove in the sand that many conchs use to make their way across the open bottom.

The reef here is very scenic. It's covered with pink, purple, and white anemones, several large elephant ear sponges, and barrel sponges nearly as tall as I am. A large grouper was taking a break near an immense elkhorn coral.

We saw a hawksbill turtle cruising by, and a southern stingray burying himself in the sand. Three French grunts, a handful of yellow-tail snappers, a slender filefish, and two black durgon all made an appearance as we cruised among the coral fingers.

As our bottom time grew tight, we ascended to the shallow mini wall. We were rewarded by the sight of a hammerhead cruising back toward deeper waters after a visit to the warm shallows near shore.

The mini wall is home to several varieties of shrimp, three slipper lobsters, all of whom were waving their antenna at us, and several blennies. We saw four hogfish and three parrotfish, as well as a variety of smaller but vibrantly colorful reef fish.

Rafe and I turned to each other at exactly the same moment to signal it was time to turn back. I grinned at him, pleased that our air consumption synched up so perfectly. We rose a few feet so we were at exactly the recommended fifteen feet for our safety stops, then we hovered in place watching the busy sea creatures below us.

After our three minutes were up, we climbed aboard the *Tranquility* and stowed our tanks and gear.

I went below to grab us a couple of towels while Rafe poured pineapple juice into our mugs. We sat in the sun, enjoying being together.

We were almost ready to head home when Rafe's phone buzzed with an incoming text message. He frowned when he read it.

"The costume fittings have been moved up a few days. I need to head to Bulgaria tomorrow. I'll be gone for a month."

I was disappointed that we'd have to skip the days of relaxation we'd planned, but I was happy that we'd managed to ensure that the bad guys were in custody and our friends were all on the mend before he had to leave.

I smiled ruefully. "Someday we'll get to spend as much time as we want together," I said. "No schedule changes, no dive trips, no movie sets, and most especially— no bad guys."

He laughed. "Maybe you'd get sick of me if we spent that much time together."

"Never," I said with a laugh. "I adore being with you."

He winked. "Let's head home then. You can show me exactly how much you adore being with me."

"You're on," I said.

Also by Sharon Ward

In Deep

Sunken Death

Dark Tide

Killer Storm

Hidden Depths

Sea Stars

Rip Current

Sea Monsters

Ice Water

Or see the entire series Fin Fleming series by following the link or use the QR code on the next page.

If you enjoyed Ice Water, you can continue reading about the adventures of Fin and the gang by following the links above.

Also, nothing (except actually buying the book) helps an author more than a positive review, so please give Ice Water (and me!) a boost by leaving a review. Here's the link:

Ice Water or use the QR code

And if you'd like to subscribe to my totally random and very rarely published
newsletter, you can sign up here. or use the QR code

Link to SharonWard.com

Links to my Books

Shop my online store

Shop the Series Page on Amazon

Acknowledgments

As usual, there are a million people who helped me pull this together,, and there's a good chance I'll forget someone. If it's you, please forgive me. You probably already know I'm kind of a ditz.

Special thanks to Kris at Dive Alaska for pointing me to the info I needed for Rafe's dive. Since my rule is to never have anything bad happen in a real place, I changed a lot of the details, but I hope I didn't change things too much.

Kate, Mary Beth, Stephanie, and Andrea, my writing and drinking group. Thanks for all the encouragement. And the G&Ts

Michele Dorsey. Thanks for being with me on this path.

The entire Tropical Authors group, a continuing source of inspiration and a fine example of writers supporting each other. Special thanks to Nick and Chris for always cheerfully fixing it when I flub the newsletter.

Additional special thanks to David Berens for the astonishingly beautiful covers.

And Hallie Ephron, a continuing example of class, charm and great writing. Best writing teacher ever. Thank you for everything.

And always:

Erin, Scott, Cam, Taylor, and Milan Lambrinos.

Erin, Pat, Colin, and Anthony Rogers.

Josh, Jenn, Parker, and Isaac Ward.

Ed, Bob, and Dave Hoitt. Good brothers all. With great wives Teri and Trish, plus Patti who is greatly missed

Molly for the snout pokes. She never gives up, even when I do.

And Jack, who continues to be the best husband in the universe.

About the Author

Sharon Ward is the author of the Fin Fleming Scuba Diving Mystery Series, which includes *In Deep, Sunken Death, Dark Tide, Killer Storm, Hidden Depths, Sea Stars and Rip Current,* as well as this book, *Sea Monsters.* The ninth book in the series, *Ice Water* is coming in early 2025.

Sharon was a marketing executive at prominent software companies Oracle and Microsoft before becoming a writer. She was a PADI certified divemaster who has hundreds of dives under her weight belt. Sharon is a member of Sisters in Crime, MWA, ITW, Grub Street, the Authors Guild, and the Cape Cod Writers Center. She lives in Massachusetts with her husband Jack and their miniature long-haired dachshund Molly, who is the actual head of the Ward household.

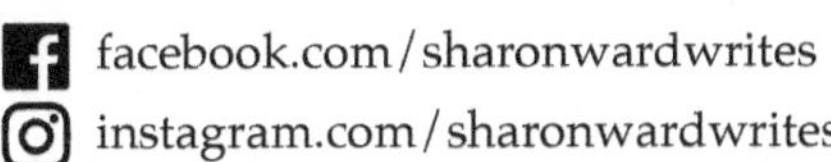

facebook.com/sharonwardwrites
instagram.com/sharonwardwrites